DEFINITIONS

CLARE COOMBES

*Dedicated to the memory of Frances Doran, for
her love of books and through this, the
words that helped define me as a writer.*

"You count the hours you could have spent with
your mother, it's a lifetime in itself."

Mitch Albom, *For One More Day*

ACKNOWLEDGEMENTS

This book started as random chapters and I want to thank my MA group at Liverpool John Moores University for helping me transform them into something with a plot. Special thanks go to those who improved it further, including Matthew McKeown for his editing skills and the 'red pen of judgement', without which this book would have had 'more parties than Gatsby' and other annoying factors. It is an immeasurably better book because of his work and that of my Writing Circle; Hilary Alexander, Nicola Copeland, Angela Pearsall, Shirley Razbully and Sarah Tarbit, thanks to their amazing skills and encouragement. I would also like to thank Anne Doran for getting me into my first writing group and for all her advice, grammatically and beyond.

To Mike Morris and everyone at Writing on the Wall, for everything you do for new writers and everything you have done for me.

I am lucky to be in the company of great writers and great people, which of course brings me onto my family. Their support has been brilliant, and I am very lucky, even if they did want my first novel to be about them. Thankfully you are not like any of the families I have created here. To all my friends who listened to my ramblings about this book and my quest to have it published and to Jonathan Hussey for the link to James Lumsden-Cook of Bennion Kearny who gave me that chance. Through this, my talented sister also provided her business and networking skills, and I am always grateful.

Last but not at all least, to my husband, for providing me with the faith, patience and strength which made this all possible, and for always living up to your position as my favourite person.

20.00 Friday 29th August 2014

The pounding in her head subsided and she gradually became aware of her surroundings.

The metallic taste of blood rolled around her mouth. She found herself unable to open it as a thick, tight band of tape sealed her lips shut and pinched at her face.

Her hands were tied in knots of rope.

She tilted her head to the side. Another burst of agony hit as bits of plaster scratched at her throat and pulled at her tongue. Each breath was too rapid, too irregular. She could do nothing to slow the panicked air racing in and out of her body.

He sat next to her, eyes on the road, silent and calm. Each jolt of the car caused her aching bones to shudder violently but he drove on without caring. Her arm throbbed dully from where he'd gripped it and the pain in her mouth seeped through her cheeks and pooled unbearably at the peak of her jaw. Her mind was blank.

'Keep still, you stupid bitch.' He shoved her back against the seat, keeping one arm on the steering wheel. The car jerked momentarily and through the grogginess, she strained to concentrate. She looked outside for help, turning her head lightly and carefully but saw only a series of distorted flashes. The occasional person-shaped shadow showed up under a street light or against the warmth of a house or pub, but the Audi's tinted windows kept her hidden from view. No one would notice. No one would help.

The car's engine made a low droning sound.

As they slowed down, she realised they would have to stop at a red light, and made a lunge for the door, hitting the handle desperately, using what little power she had in her blood-starved hands. A punch to the ribs put a stop to that. Hot tears ran down her face.

'You do that again and I'll kill you,' he hissed. His eyes returned to the road as the car began picking up speed again. He placed a hand over hers and the rope. 'I'll smash this car into the nearest wall. You know I don't give a shit what happens to me.'

She knew. They continued in silence. Her head banged against the window as the car took another sudden lurch.

She kept repeating an internal mantra: He won't do anything; he won't do anything.

He drove until they ran out of road, almost hitting a bollard before pulling between a gap in some iron posts. It was a practised manoeuvre, made possible by a collision, which had left one post damaged. The space this created was wide enough to allow a car to slip through.

They'd been here before; had walked up and down the pavement, under the twinkling lights of the street lamps, and watched the clouds jump and stretch themselves across the sky.

He reached across and ripped the tape from her mouth. It fought to cling to her skin at the sides and sent a fresh rush of pain along her jawline. The engine was still running. Gina tried to suppress a coughing fit as she sucked in deep breaths through her mouth. It was important to be able to speak. She wasn't ready to give in, despite feeling like the black waters of the River Mersey were waiting to take her down. The sky was moving slowly away from daylight, leaving a pink rim over the waterfront in a final act of defiance against the onrushing night.

'Did you really think you'd get away with it?' he said, turning to look at her, eyes burning.

The car shuddered to a stop. He turned off the lights.

CHAPTER ONE

Auld Lang Syne ~ for old time's sake

~ Sometimes people leave your life only to come back better than ever, but you should watch yourself with them.

January 2014

I'd dolled myself up a bit for shopping. My blue knee-length dress had little ripples that moved when I did, a high-necked white collar and a thick black belt, which gave the illusion of a small waist. Teamed with tights and high heels, I was striding around town like I owned the place.

'Gina!'

A boy calling your name in the middle of Liverpool One can be both exciting and embarrassing. I turned around, prepared for a red face either way. At least I'd piled the St Tropez on the night before.

There he was in front of me, smiling and kicking his Vans against the ground.

I took the opportunity to assess how the years had treated him, as though I didn't already know from sneaky peaks on Facebook, and quickly came to the conclusion that in reality Daniel Ryan was even better than his pictures suggested with his sandy hair, gold stubble, chiselled features and clichéd deep chocolate brown eyes. His white t-shirt revealed strong, toned arms that were a little too big for the rest of him. Normally, I'd think he was a bit too Popeye-looking and move on, but there was something a little bit sexy about those arms. The very sight of them had me fantasising about how they would feel wrapped around me tightly so that I couldn't get away and then…

Jesus, I was going to have to rein myself in before I licked one of his biceps. I was already close enough to see the hairs on his nicely tanned skin.

'Long time no see.' He smiled brightly at me, all straight and clinic white teeth. 'How are you doing?'

'Yeah, I'm fine.' My mouth wouldn't move to say more. Why did I become tongue-tied in situations like this?

'How's the family?' he asked, settling into a laid-back pose as though he was happy to question me all day.

'All fine, yeah.'

'Heard Jen was pregnant? You still see her?'

'Yeah I still see her. She's fine.'

'You two still dead close and that then?'

I pressed my lips together and nodded, realising that my vocabulary had been stripped down to the words 'yeah' and 'fine'. My new bright red lipstick spreading from my mouth must have looked like The Joker's.

'Heard about your Charley,' he said, not looking me in the eye.

'She's doing fine now,' I said quickly.

'Are you working at the moment?'

'Yeah, in a marketing consultants, not very exciting.' I stopped myself before I could prattle on about how I actually quite liked it and it was a good position, considering I never went to Uni. 'What about you?'

'I own my own business.' His chest puffed out. 'Couldn't be doing with office work, like.'

'Oh very nice, doing what?'

'Plastering mainly but also doing up houses in general, with me dad…' He trailed off and then stared straight at me, a glint in his eye. 'Do you want to go for a drink?'

What would he want with me now? It had been eight years since our close encounter of the shit kind.

4

'Only if you've time, like,' he added.

'Yeah I've time.' I smiled.

* * * * *

Daniel offered to get the round in.

'What should we celebrate?' he asked, cocking that lovely face to one side.

'I don't know. New Year?' It was still January after all.

'Auld Lang Syne?'

'What does that even mean?' I laughed.

'For old time's sake,' he explained. I was impressed. No one knew what that meant.

The place he took me to sold cocktails and cupcakes, same as every other bar in the area, but acted as though they were the first to think of it. The smell of fruit, icing and alcohol hit me as soon as we walked in and having declared internally that this was officially a date, I was desperate to nip to the loo, touch up my make-up, and text Jennifer to let her know who I was with. It was too early to check us in on Facebook so I had to let her know somehow.

Guess who I'm having a drink with! xx

As usual, the reply came within seconds. *Fit barman from other night? Xx*

No, he was defo gay...drinks with Daniel Ryan.' ;-) xx

Oh Gina ☹xx

Ignoring her, I applied generous amounts of bronzer, touched up my eyebrows, and gave myself the once over. I'd lost my virginity to this boy. It was in a hazy memory of cider and condoms and a free house while his parents were away and a party raged ceaselessly downstairs. He was the new boy back then; the fit and mysterious one who everyone wanted.

I sat back down to some crazy-looking purple drinks and matching cakes and Daniel's smile. We talked generally, catching up on surface-level stuff such as people we knew and

places we went nowadays to drink, skirting over the 'good' old times.

'What was it like when your mum died?' he asked, a good few drinks in. I wasn't even aware that the conversation was taking a death turn. Normally I'm the one who has to bring it up and see how long it takes before the subject gets changed.

'The worst thing is the fish,' I blurted out. God, give it a couple of cocktails and my mind was anyone's.

He raised his eyebrows slightly but smiled. 'Is that, like, a metaphor?'

'I suppose,' I continued, 'but the worst thing about loss is actually what you get. I know people are always saying that they get a new outlook on life and stuff when someone dies but I think you're more likely to get low self-esteem or catch every cold going. Me, I got fish.'

He laughed and put his hand over mine. I'd never told anyone about the fish I had in place of nerves, except for Charley and Anthony of course, but it doesn't count telling your sister and someone who's known you since childhood. He smiled at me in a way which seemed to say 'carry on, you're not a nutter', and so I did.

'I still remember how they started. It was like a ball in my belly the same night mum died. It was like someone was playing tennis with my internal organs. Time passed but they didn't go away. They got cockier and started biting me. They set up unprovoked attacks, travelling all around my body, inflicting damage where I'd least expect it. Sometimes they even get into my head now, so I feel proper fog-brained and can't get my thoughts straight. They're mostly in my stomach though, kicking me when I'm down and making my insides feel all twisted. That's why I think people say that grief can be, like, literally gut-wrenching.'

When I finished he was staring at the floor. I'd said too much. He thought I was mad. Then I heard a deep choked, sobbing noise as he lifted his head back up.

'My mum's in the Royal – been there a few weeks.' He took a sip of his drink and wiped his eyes.

6

'Is it-'

'Cancer.'

'What type?' It's always better to ask the straightforward question.

'Breast?' He said it like a question. 'I feel constantly sick y'know. I came here today for a break, a walk around. I'm so glad I saw you.'

He put his head in his hands. I put my hand on his arm.

He moved closer. 'I was shit to you when we were going out wasn't I?'

'We were a lot younger and it was different then...' I trailed off. We both leaned forward.

He tasted amazing despite the cocktail and muffin breath. It felt a bit wrong considering what we'd just been talking about, but it also felt madly right. Regardless, I'm not into what our Charley calls 'shameful club-necking', kissing all over the place in bars and clubs. I wasn't one of those girls. I pulled back.

'Should we go somewhere else?' I asked, meaning for a drink.

He gave me a lingering look and picked up his coat.

I avoided the eyes of the bored bar staff as we left. Daniel put his arm around me, pulling me close. I relaxed into it, even though it made us walk like we were in a three-legged race. Then he pushed me into an alleyway.

Before I could ask what he was doing, his kisses were covering me, soft and warm, and I forgot about the bins, the banana skins, the smell of wee all around us, and my morals.

He pulled away for a moment, his eyes locking into mine and then ran a finger along my lower lip. A slight smile twitched at the corners of his mouth before he leaned back in towards me. The shock of his tongue on the tip of my mouth as it ran achingly slowly across it sent rushes of pleasure up and down me, before it moved into dizzying circles inside me. The first ones had been a test, a warm-up. The kisses became more pressing, urgent. Those muscled arms, wrapped tight around

7

me as the kiss moved, turned into nibbles and then bites. It was agonising pleasure, dangerous and delicious.

'Stop,' I whispered but instead he went for me, pulling at the skin on my neck with his teeth, tongue and lips. My brain stopped. I shut my eyes, couldn't move even if I wanted to. He bit down hard on the skin on my neck and then starting sucking and kissing alternatively. I wanted to scream but I murmured 'yes'. I let him carry on, even though I knew that raw circles of red would stay marked long after his lips had left. It had been years since I had let someone do this. I had never enjoyed it before.

The fish fled.

CHAPTER TWO

The TV was off and the windows were closed. Muffled shouts from drunken revellers making their way home after a Friday night out reached inside the tiny flat; the hailing of taxis and fragments of inane chatter, feeling their way through the old brick walls and shaky windows. She'd called them an hour ago.

When the long-awaited knock finally came, it made her insides jump. She forced herself up and opened the door. What was she meant to say? They stood there like two awkward old friends who didn't want to visit and who she didn't want to let in either. These flats weren't a place they usually got *invited* to.

'Miss Ellison?' The man made the two words sound friendly. He was tall, with tight black curls and a slightly chubby, ruddy, but kind-looking face. His frame took up most of the doorway.

'Charley,' she answered and then cursed herself for not keeping distant and getting to the point by nodding or giving the full, 'Charlotte Ellison actually'.

A woman edged around him and placed herself in front. She was half his height and width yet seemed more formidable. Her hat settled neatly onto pinned-back blonde hair that formed in crescent shapes on either side of her ears, out of the way of her piercing blue eyes. She was an advert for the ideal uniformed policewoman. Charley didn't know her, but she knew her type and again her stomach jumped with nerves (or fish as Gina would have called them). The thought of her sister forced Charley to steady herself.

'I'm Officer Thomson and this is Officer Field,' the blonde crescent woman said. 'May we come in?'

'Oh yeah, of course.' Charley stepped back into the room that functioned as a hall, living room and kitchen. 'Do you want a drink or anything?' Her voice went up too high at the end.

They declined and made to sit down, trying to find a suitable space.

Charley caught a glimpse of herself in the mirror and took some courage from her appearance. The copper colour of her hair took the edge off her paleness, as Gina had said it would, and in jeans and cheap Converse impersonations, she looked tidy and clean.

'You'll see how much difference nice hair can make,' Gina had said as she frog-marched her into a local salon a few months back. 'You'll get snapped up in no time.'

Charley didn't see how a change of hair style and a pair of waxed eyebrows could get her a job and it was still a bit weird doing sisterly things after such a long time, but it was good; it was progress. She'd also missed it, even though they'd never really had it much before, and more besides, it worked. She had her first proper job in years.

There was not much that could be done about the flat. It was passable, a 'snail's shell', like most places she lived in, with its fold-up furniture and possessions that could be packed up at short notice. The smell of damp was helped out by one of those plug-in fragrance things, bought by Gina.

'How can you not notice the smell?' Gina had said, spreading her arms out and almost touching the walls on two sides of the living area. 'And the size of it! I'd be so claustrophobic, I couldn't cope.'

Charley shrugged and joked that she was used to small spaces. Gina blushed and fumbled with the plug adding a hint of lemon and lavender to the room.

It still lingered as Officer Field perched himself on the edge of the red couch, his dark uniform contrasting starkly with the bright fabric. His legs settled awkwardly around piles of magazines. Charley took a proper look at him and realised that he couldn't have been much older than her. She wasn't sure if this made her feel better or worse. The police in this area weren't familiar (how times had changed). He caught her looking at him and smiled.

10

Officer Thomson sat in the rocking chair. She wasn't smiling. 'This must have been expensive?' She ran her fingers along the arm of the chair.

Charley shrugged. Ignoring Officer Thomson's sly looks, she moved a stack of magazines and books and forced herself to sit down.

'You said on the phone your sister might be in trouble?' Officer Field opened a notebook. 'You mentioned an ex-boyfriend?'

'Daniel Ryan. Gina's just split up with him.'

'You also mentioned that you haven't been able to get in touch with either of them?'

'I've been trying both their phones and went round to their houses.' All bloody three of them. She'd banged on that horrible red door for fifteen minutes.

'What makes you think she's in danger?'

'The text she sent wasn't...right.' Charley realised how stupid this sounded. She thought of the words again. *Getting away from it all for a few days. Phone and Facebook going off. G x'* It *was* Gina's way of speaking but then it *wasn't.* It was difficult to explain.

'When did you last speak to your sister apart from this text?'

The room was suddenly too hot. Charley could feel her face starting to burn up.

'A week ago at a party.' She felt the lie leave her mouth quickly and bit her lip. Officer Thomson closed the notebook, placing it down on the table.

'Do you normally have regular contact with your sister?' she asked.

'Yeah.' Apart from the last twenty-seven hours, they'd had nearly a year of regular contact. A year of being sisters again, despite Daniel.

'What was she like when you last saw her?' Officer Field said.

Charley had almost forgotten he was there. Officer Thomson looked annoyed that he'd dared to speak.

'She was all over the place to be honest,' she said. 'Something wasn't right.'

'Was she still with her boyfriend at the time?' Officer Thomson asked.

'Yeah.'

'And they split up soon after?'

'Not long after.'

'Why would that text make you think something was wrong?'

'Because it doesn't make sense,' Charley said. 'The text isn't like her. All her friends got the same text, even our dad. She wouldn't do that.'

'I need to understand why, if you haven't seen her for over a week, you're suddenly so concerned now?'

'I know something is wrong,' she said, raising her voice without meaning to.

'Have you tried other family and friends who might know where she is?' Officer Thomson pressed on.

'Yeah.'

The phone call with her father had not been productive.

'Dad?'

'Gina?'

'No, Charley.'

'Charley…it's three in the morning and I'm up early tomorrow for Kathryn's art exhibition. You never remember the time difference.'

'Dad, I'm worried about Gina.'

'That makes a change, normally it's her calling about you. Why, what's she done?'

'She's gone missing.'

'What?'

'I think Daniel has something to do with it.'

'But she texted me a couple of hours ago, woke me up actually, said she was going away for a few days. Hardly something she needed to text me about so late when she knows I'm busy with Kathryn's art-'

'Alright Dad, let me know if she gets in touch.'

'Charley…are you…you know what again?'

'No.' She ended the call then. Any slightly odd behaviour and her dad was off on one. It never made him come back from Hong Kong though.

'Miss Ellison?' Officer Thomson broke in, derailing Charley's train of thought.

'No one has heard from her apart from that text.'

'Do you know if any clothing, money or personal belongings have been taken?' This was said in a pointed way.

'I don't know,' Charley replied, not rising to the bait. 'Some of her stuff is at our old family home and I think she was staying there.'

'You *think* she was staying there?'

'Yeah,' Charley said more definitely, 'she was staying there. I couldn't really tell if she'd taken anything because her stuff was still in boxes. Her car wasn't there.'

'Obviously she has her phone too,' Officer Thomson sighed.

'Oh but I have this!' Charley took out the scrap piece of paper and handed it over. Maybe these two could make sense of it. 'I'm trying to find any others she might have done.'

Auld Lang Syne ~ for old time's sake

~ Sometimes people leave your life only to come back better than ever, but you should watch yourself with them.

13

'Does that mean anything, Miss Ellison?' Officer Thomson gave it a quick glance.

'Well no, but she does this thing with words you see, definitions and that, where they make sense to different parts of her life and I was thinking…' Charley trailed off.

Growing up, it was Charley who always had her head in a book and spent hours scribbling her own stories. Gina had started the definitions as a deal-breaker.

'I'm going to choose some words out of your stories and make up my own meanings for them,' she said sitting down and picking up one of Charley's notebooks, 'then you're coming to play rounders with me and the others outside.'

There was two years between them but Gina had been a 'cool kid' since birth; an attribute their mum seemed to see as more important than having a higher-than-average reading age. Gina hated reading but she liked her sister, at least at that point.

'See, we're both ready to go out and play now.' Gina would call out, and Charley would often catch their Mum at the window when the game was underway. She would have her blonde hair fixed around her face in soft curls and a full face of make-up, a lot like Gina now, but styled in whatever happened to be the fashion of the time. She'd check up on them playing with a smile through the glass, a smile that Charley always felt was directed more towards her sister.

'Let's have a look,' Officer Field moved forward, knocking the table with his knee and grimacing slightly. Charley handed him the piece of paper.

Officer Thomson spoke again. 'It's not our responsibility to investigate lost contact cases. If you and your sister have fallen out or you're upset that she hasn't been in touch with you since splitting up with her boyfriend, we suggest you wait a few days for her to get in contact with you or another family member or friend.'

'He was violent,' Charley said. 'They split up because of it. We stopped speaking over him.'

Officer Thomson opened the notebook again, slowly. 'Was a police report ever made?'

'No.'

'Do you have evidence of this?

'No.'

'Were other friends or family witness to this?'

'They could have been. You could ask them.' Charley swallowed but the lump in her throat didn't disappear.

Officer Thomson didn't say anything. Her gaze lingered hard, as though she was trying to perform a telepathic interrogation. Charley sat up straight and looked her in the eye. 'So what can you do? Can you get patrols out looking for her? I have a photo of her.'

It was a recent photo that Gina would like. She was wearing her favourite red lipstick with feathered blonde hair framing her smiling face. The fake tan she always liberally applied wasn't Oompa Loompa orange for once. She had on skinny jeans (she must have been having a skinny day) and a plain blue vest top. Her face was long but she had a good jaw line and bones that jutted out in the right place; a small, snubbed nose and a set of grey-blue eyes. The long face used to make her look a bit horsey, though in a posh, sophisticated way. It had been childhood ammunition for arguments, until the time came when it was easier to ignore each other. Unlike Charley, who despite everything had always had a 'posh' tint to her voice, when Gina opened her mouth, what came out was completely 'Scouse', with the usual Liverpool hock over words like 'chicken'.

Officer Field took the photo and studied it. 'You don't look alike,' he concluded.

'Miss Ellison, it has only been a few hours since your sister sent that text,' Officer Thomson said. 'If she doesn't turn up to work on Monday and you still haven't had any word from anyone then maybe you could contact us again?' She raised her eyebrows by way of announcing they had finished.

'She isn't working at the moment,' Charley said quietly.

Officer Field gave her another smile, one full of pity this time. He placed the definition on the table.

'But what about Daniel being missing too?' Charley asked as they both prepared to leave.

'There's nothing to suggest he *is* missing,' Officer Thomson said as they headed out. She said this in a way which implied there was nothing to suggest that anyone was missing, especially Gina who had no job, no ties, no places to be. She could vanish, even at the same time as an ex-boyfriend and no one would think to question it.

CHAPTER THREE

WHITE WALLS: 22.30 Friday 29th August 2014

She had a pillow and a bucket.

Her arms and legs were free now, at least. She gently rubbed her red raw wrists. The harsh taste in her mouth made her consider the glass of iced water and the packet of aspirin next to the blanket.

With fuzzy vision and a banging headache, Gina tried to get up, but the throbbing in her temple had her sitting quickly back down. Her legs were rubbery. A smell of disinfectant and chemicals mixed with something stronger, more unpleasant, rose without apology from a puddle of sick on the floor.

In the car, he had pulled a cloth from his pocket, stuffed it over her mouth and held it. The cloth was soaked in something that weighed on her senses, made her eyes shut slowly. The last thing she heard was the car shifting into reverse before everything went black.

'Charley will know something is wrong.' Her last words to him.

'You think she'll even check up on you?' he'd asked, head cocked to one side, a winning smile on his face. 'Remember what you did to her?'

She'd thought of little else in the moments when she could think.

A naked bulb lit up the room. Everything was painted white from the ceiling to the four walls, one of which had shelves filled with bottles and packages. There were no windows and only one door, which was closed.

She had no idea what time it was or even where she could be. Then she heard footsteps.

Gina braced herself, trying to make her body seem as small as possible, to somehow melt into the patchy brown blanket so rough against her skin. The door swung open.

He came into the room, heavy boots thudding against the floor with his slow steps. There was a faint smell of alcohol coming off him.

She stayed silent. He moved towards her. Trembling in shorts and a white t-shirt, she scrambled up, her upper body becoming part of the room, sinking into the walls until she didn't exist. It was then she noticed her shoes were gone.

He smiled. 'Couldn't leave you with them, right little weapons they could be. Shame about your phone too.' He took it out of his pocket. It was a shattered mess.

'What do you think I'm going to do?' he asked, holding his arms out.

'Someone... will... wonder... where I am,' she said, the words sticking in her throat.

'Like your sister?'

Her stomach tightened.

'But…eventually, someone will wonder where I am,' she tried again.

He smiled again, as though they were having a friendly chat. 'Everyone knows you need some space, you might even lose your head a bit, do something stupid. Let down by your sister *again,* leaving your fiancé when you were supposed to be getting married Sunday. Who knows what you might do?'

CHAPTER FOUR

DETAILS: 22.45 Friday 29th August 2014

The car spun around the corner so fast that it almost hit the large hedge which framed the front of the house. Charley parked in a skewed way, a mirror of how Gina often left her car when she bothered to take it up the path at all. The neighbours would be annoyed, but they were always annoyed.

There wouldn't be any point asking any of them for help. The new ones didn't know who Gina was. The old ones probably assumed that the white Audi, which had been parked on the road before Gina went missing and had vanished with her, belonged to some drug dealer who had bought the house and not taken down the 'For Sale' sign.

Their dad finally wanted to sell it. His wife Kathryn probably wanted a holiday home or something, but Gina was adamant they would get their share when it was sold. 'You could move to a new flat then,' Gina had suggested in a way that said, *'you will'*.

The quiet road and the hedges all around the front garden had always scared them as kids. They made up stories about monsters and, later, men hiding in them. She got inside and slammed the door, locking it quickly and taking out her phone. She began dialling in a panic.

'Anthony, are you in?' There was a light on in the house across the road.

'Yeah but-'

'Have you heard anything?'

'No.' He sighed.

'Nothing at all?'

'She's obviously got back with him and is too embarrassed to admit it. Anyway, you'd be the last person she'd get in touch with-'

She ended the call and cut him off, not wanting to hear it. Throwing her bag onto the kitchen cabinet, she headed to the garage which connected to the kitchen via a small side door. On the dusty old shelves was a bottle of red wine. She took the bottle and ran back into the kitchen, locking the door again behind her. Taking a glass from the cupboard, she poured a drink, paused and then threw it down the sink. She moved into the living room where Gina's boxes were, the ones she'd quickly searched through earlier and brought in from the hall, looking for a note or something, anything, before she'd gone back to the flat and called the police. A couple of them were squashed up like someone had jumped all over them.

The first box looked like old work stuff, notebooks of scrawled business reports and charts, phone numbers and email addresses annotated with doodles of fish. The chipped 'I love spreadsheets' mug made Charley smile at what a geek her sister was when she wasn't getting spray tans and painting her nails. The job was probably as boring as Gina had described, but Charley had still been surprised when she'd left it.

The work notebooks didn't contain anything helpful. Other boxes were filled with piles of clothes and there were also some old photos of their mum. The pictures were taken before the cancer started to show itself straining out of her body. It began with an extra thickness in her neck, ankles and stomach and then the ageing of her face, all of which eventually came together to take the light out of her eyes. Charley put them to one side, refusing to get lost in them - to feel that heavy ache of guilt.

She thought about the last time she had seen Gina. There was a shadow around her eyes that even her heavily applied make-up couldn't cover. The weight had fallen off her in places and the ASOS dress she was wearing looked like it had been handed to the wrong model. Daniel Ryan had successfully driven a wedge between them with what he'd done, and started to destroy Gina in the process.

Heading upstairs, Charley found more abandoned possessions strewn across the unmade bed, as well as an open box on the floor. She went through a variety of sticky cosmetics with the tops not back on properly, and then came across another notebook. It had glittery fish on the front, purple and pink, smiling and frowning. All of the pages had been torn out but some of them seemed to have made it into the box next to the bed.

Spread out on the floor, there were three bits of paper. She added the 'A' of Auld Lang Syne from her pocket. Each one had only scraps of sentences, the odd name. There had to be clues - details of some kind. Charley knew where she needed to go first.

In the car, she went over what Gina's definition B had said in her mind.

* * * * *

As Gina would say, 'her nerves were gone' by the time she approached the large detached house. It was whitewashed at the front, with black railings and an old-fashioned door with a bell and those horrible football-shaped plants instead of hanging baskets. It was a mix of modern and classic, trying too hard to be both. The place definitely screamed wealth though, and Charley didn't want to question where that came from. Matthew was only a casual labourer at the company Daniel ran and as far as she knew, Melissa had never worked.

When the door opened, Melissa gave her a startled look. There was a busy smell of washing, biscuits and babies coming from inside the house.

'What the fuck are you doing here?' She stood sideways with the door closed against her body so that Charley could only see half of her face in the light of the hallway. Her wild blonde hair provided some cover, but the black and purple on her cheek was still visible. 'It's nearly midnight, you mad cow. I've got kids asleep in here.'

'Is Matthew in? I'm trying to find Gina.'

'Really?' Melissa went to shut the door but then stopped. 'Listen, I like your Gina but her and Matthew didn't exactly get on, so she'd hardly come here would she?'

21

'I might have to go to the police if she doesn't get in touch or turn up soon. Maybe Matthew knows where she is.'

'What's that got to do with him?'

'I know he's threatened Gina in the past.'

'He would never do anything to Gina, you stupid bitch. The pair of them never saw eye to eye that's all,' Melissa snapped.

'I know he hits you.'

'I fell on the baby's toys actually,' she said, straightening her body position and towering over Charley, 'and it's none of your business anyway.'

'Yeah alright then, and the rest of the time. Your 'fella' is the type to kick off at the slightest thing, isn't he? Even at a funeral-'

'Did your shit-stirring sister tell you that?' she snapped. 'Because Daniel can be a sly bastard, you know. Don't be fooled.'

'No, she didn't tell me anything,' Charley said and decided to take a gamble, 'I read it in her diary.'

Melissa looked disgusted. 'Why are you reading your sister's diary?'

'Because she's missing!'

Melissa stared at her. 'Don't tell anyone about what you've read about me. If you do, I'll deny it all. It'll be your sister's stupid fucking diary over my word,' she said. 'And I'll tell you something else you cheeky cow, Matthew is working with Dan this weekend. They're doing up a house down south. Your sister has probably gone away to get some peace from the cranks in her family like you, and I don't blame her.'

The door shut in Charley's face.

CHAPTER FIVE

Breakdown ~ spiritually or physically ill or exhausted

~ Families at funerals often do this.

~ Daniel and Matthew ☹ - try to sort out or leave well alone? Matthew = mad, kicks off at slightest thing - needs help? Melissa scared.

January 2014

At the funeral, I stood at the back.

The family passed down the church aisle. Daniel was one of four who carried the coffin on his shoulders, their arms wrapped around each other for steadiness. More than anything, I wanted to rush over and support him - even walk alongside him.

I recognised Bob, Daniel's Dad, with his gentle face creased into grief, his big-boned body somehow shrunken. He walked unsteadily, supported by another woman from the family, possibly an aunty on Daniel's mum's side judging by the harsh look in her eyes and the leather-tan skin.

The church was packed with varying degrees of grief but I knew how alone Daniel would feel. A woman standing in one of the pews, wearing a bright orange wig, wiped her eyes dramatically and then peered around the coffin to see the faces of those carrying it. I had to look away. I knew her type.

After losing Mum, I'd gained inside knowledge of how these things work. Indirect mourners, and by that I mean ones not really involved in the family, who kind of knew the person, love to watch you. See how you cope. They take mental notes, like grief journalists scribbling away in their heads, giving marks for how upset you look. And you'd better look upset.

I followed the coffin with my eyes, willing Daniel to get through each step until it was placed in front of the priest at the altar, and then I tried to focus my mind on staying calm. I was surprised how much it bothered me. I was welling up and my head was pounding. I hadn't even met Daniel's mum.

Usually the ceremony, the coffin, the actual reality of it all, is never real to me on the day. It'll be some random time when I'm on my own making tea or running a bath that I'll be blindsided by grief and then feel the fish start to make their bite marks inside my stomach, pulling at all the strings of my nerves.

My legs were like jelly, wobbling with worry. The cold seemed to travel in echoes across the church, stirring the fish inside me. One of them bit into my heart angrily and took away a chunk. It had been a long time since they had been strong enough to grip like that but then grief is a feeding frenzy for them.

I wondered if Daniel was taking dream-like steps too, or considering whether he should shed a tear right now to satisfy people. I moved cold fingers across my forehead; listened as the priest talked.

'A caring mother, a loving grandmother, aunty, friend…' His words were little taps inside my stomach, pulling strings of grief that were already well overplayed. I was glad Charley hadn't come. She'd offered, of course, but I couldn't risk something to set her off again. She wasn't ready for anything like this.

The church was decorated with beautiful orange flowers - his mum's favourite colour – and the faces of most of the girls in attendance were shaded to match. It was a striking display of unintentional tribute.

The deceased wanted to put the fun into 'funeral' and Orange Wig Woman was only one example. On the seats to the left of me were a group adorned with orange feather boas. They cackled at the anecdotes read out by Daniel's uncle about his mum's 'wild' girls' weekends to Benidorm.

Daniel's cousin Karen, dressed in a vintage pale orange dress, placed a bottle of spray tan solemnly on the coffin. I couldn't quite catch Daniel's face as his head was dipped down.

* * * * *

Karen caught me in the gardens, hovering, unsure of my role as the new, little-known-about girlfriend who had been on the scene about a week.

'Our Danny's told me all about you,' she drawled. Her accent was so thickly Scouse it sounded put on. She was tall with flowing blonde locks and pouting lips lathered with gloss. Her shoes were like daggers in the ground on the sodden bit of grass. I hadn't banked on meeting a Tropical Fish at a funeral.

I pulled the orange scarf up closer around my neck, for all the good it did. I caught Karen's smirk.

I had to admit that the 'look' she'd put together for 'grieving niece' was fantastic. Even being near someone like her always puts me back in my plain goldfish bowl, reminding me that I'm swimming around in circles failing to look as good as someone like her.

At school she'd called me and my friends 'mingers', although she always said it to our faces.

'You know our Dan's in a bad way,' she looked at me, assessing my suitability for dishing out sympathy. 'Your mum died after we left school didn't she?'

The abrupt way she said it made me feel as though I should apologise.

With a jab of the heels, she turned back to the pool of friends that had come to support her, each rocking the glam-grief look. They earned their tropical status with smoky yet brightly coloured eyes, luscious lips, blush-tastic cheeks, fabulously high heels and tiny waists. I tried not to look at them directly because Tropical Fish are something else, especially en masse. My insecurity fish started nibbling away at my belly.

Still I went to the social club where orange and white bunting stretched across the room and photos of Daniel's family were pinned up on a notice board. His mum laughing and joking

25

with family and friends, always tanned, mostly with a drink in her hand.

'She was a good laugh, was Tina.' I heard one of the Feather Boas say to the others while they picked over the images of nights out and holidays. I noticed more of these than family ones. Daniel didn't seem to want to look at any of them.

Everyone was excited by the free bar; there was a lot of shrieking. After what seemed like a really short amount of time the music got louder and the DJ got mouthy. At one point he seemed on the verge of playing the Conga or Madonna's 'Celebrate'.

People kept coming over to Daniel, kissing him on the cheeks and leaving smeary red lips down his face, or shaking his hand in a hard manly style until he told me if one more person did that his fingers would fall off. The only ones he didn't mind seeing were his niece Olivia and nephew Thomas. Olivia had that wide-eyed, worldly look that told me her mental age was older than her actual age of seven.

'Where's your dad?' I asked her, looking around for Daniel's brother, Matthew.

'At the bar, getting pissed as usual.' Olivia sighed and played with the orange flower she had pulled out of her plaited hair. Then she forgot me and went back to playing tick around the table with the four-year-old Thomas.

'Do you want to go over and see him?' I eventually said to Daniel, nodding towards Matthew who looked like he was doing Jäger shots.

'We're not really on good terms at the moment.' Daniel took a swig of his beer, closing up the conversation. He had chatted with Matthew's wife politely enough. She stayed with the kids, occasionally giving worried glances in the direction of her husband, who was getting rowdier with each drink. He didn't look over at all.

'Want a drink, Dan?' One of the cousins shouted over from the bar into our dark corner. Daniel waved back in a way that wasn't really a yes or no.

26

'I'll go over.' I stood up and adjusted the scarf. When I got there, the bar area seemed to have transformed into a mini-Irish sanctuary.

'I hope you don't mind all this, what's yer name, Gina?' One of Daniel's cousins, I think his name was Rory, grouped me into an awkward family hug at the bar. 'She wanted a celebration like, so that's what we're giving 'er.'

'What's that on your neck there, Gina?' Another shout.

'Daniel likes to mark his birds,' Matthew called across and they all burst out laughing. I tried to hide my mortification with a smile. Matthew was nothing compared to Daniel, even in the physical sense. They had the same sandy hair but that was where the similarities ended. Matthew was all long and thin, from his face shape, his nose through to his gangly arms. I had a long face but knew that my cheekbones saved me. There was nothing that stood out about him. He was the type of person you could easily forget.

'What would you like to drink, me love?' Another one of them shuffled next to me, all whiskey whispers and sympathy at my red face.

'Erm, a lime and soda please.'

This request was met with silence.

'A steamboat without the Southern Comfort,' I explained, trying to smile. I needed a break from all the wine and beer everyone had been leaving at Daniel's table along with the hugs and kisses. Against our better wills, both of us were getting bladdered.

'She wants a slowboat, Bernie. Did you hear that?' he laughed and threw his arm around me.

'Put some Southern Comfort in it sweetheart,' Bernie called to the harassed barmaid.

'Pricks, the lot of them,' Daniel said quietly as I sat down. 'They're like bloody gypsies, me mum's family.'

'Did Matthew say anything about coming back over?' Melissa asked desperately as she jigged a bored Thomas around the table. I shook my head.

'I don't know why she bothers with him,' Daniel said. 'He's a fucking drunk like the rest of them.' The hard, cold and low tone shocked me.

'Alright lovebirds!' Matthew took a wobbly seat on one of the stools. 'Thought I'd come and have a drink with yer latest bird, our kid.'

'I'm going for a smoke.' Daniel stood up suddenly, unsettling the empty glasses we had littered around the table. 'Come on, Gina.'

Matthew held his arms open in a 'not my fault' shrug. 'You seem too good for my bruv – what yer bothering with him for? Bit of a tool but thinks he's proper boss getting me da's business. The joke's on him really with all the work he has to do ha! Never has a bird get serious with him either – you'll be bored soon, love.'

'Fuck off, you prick!' Daniel called back over his shoulder.

The sound of glass breaking was the only warning and then Matthew had Daniel pinned against the wall by the throat with surprising strength.

'Watch who yer talkin' to,' Matthew said through gritted teeth. His face contorted into rage. And then his expression changed, softened into a smirky, smile and he let Daniel go and started laughing. Instead of fighting back like I thought he would, Daniel stormed out as Matthew chuckled to himself walking past me. He caught my eye, stopped for a moment as my blood ran cold from his stare and then carried on. Melissa was fixed to her seat, face frozen.

* * * * *

Daniel was leaning against the wall outside, staring at the sky. I tried not to breathe in. Smoking didn't suit him. Whenever he took a drag, his skin seemed to dry up and become paler.

'You ok?'

28

'Sorry about him.' He breathed the words out in between the smoke.

'He's drunk,' I offered.

'My whole family are fucking drunks.' He threw the ciggy on the floor and stamped it out.

I didn't know what to say.

'Sorry.' He grabbed my hand and made it sticky with drink. 'You don't deserve all this. You should be with someone better than me.'

'Move in with me,' I said, kissing him. 'Get all your stuff together and move in.' I didn't know where that came from but it felt right.

He put his arms around me and kissed me. I could taste the smoke but that didn't put me off, and I let his hand slide down my body and finish between my legs.

'I need you.' He breathed into my neck as his hand worked its way up my dress. His other hand clenched into a fist of my hair and pulled at it.

It was then I noticed he was crying.

CHAPTER SIX

Stay Close: 3.00 Saturday 30th August 2014

Wire dug into Charley's wrist, rubbing red lines against her skin as she tried to break free. Her face hurt and her cheeks pinched.

Gina was tied up opposite. 'Charley!' she kept calling, her voice growing fainter.

Charley woke up from the dream to a room full of shadows. She felt along her face, rubbed at her eyes, but there were no tears. Her hands were free of wire and painful lines. There was a tapping sound at the window.

The curtains were closed but there was a silhouette of a person working away at the panels - an easy way to get into old houses. Charley knew this well. Whoever was trying to get in would assume she was asleep.

Edging towards the window, she picked up the nearest thing to a weapon, an old and broken umbrella, the spindles sticking out. She thought about the screwdriver under the pillow of her bed back at the flat. Pulling back the curtain, it was a thick branch that faced her, with twigs like fingers, nudging the glass.

Sitting back down on the bed, she picked up the phone, checked the time, ignored it, searched through her contacts list and pressed call.

'Hello,' the voice answered sleepily.

'Jennifer?'

'Gina?' A baby started crying in the background.

'No, it's Charley.'

'Charley? Why are you ringing at this time of the night? Has something happened to Gina?'

'I haven't heard from her since that text we all got,' Charley replied. 'I wanted to see if you'd been in touch with her since.'

'You rang me at this hour to ask if I'd heard from her since last night? You're lucky I was up with our baby.'

'I'm really worried about her.'

'Not being funny or nothing, but why would she tell you her every move?'

'No, *you* know what Daniel is like, Jen,' Charley answered, hoping that would kick Gina's best friend into action.

'I know he's a bit of a mad head but he's no different from other lads really,' she sighed. 'I haven't spoken to her since the hospital, after the party and she hasn't even seen our baby Jake since then...I was surprised to even get a text. Can we talk about this at a normal hour please?'

Jennifer's outburst at the party. Charley remembered Daniel's rage, Gina's shock and Anthony's horrified expression. None of it had made any sense.

'That's what I mean. Didn't it seem a bit odd to you?'

'Charley, nothing Gina does anymore can shock me.' Jennifer took a deep breath. 'She'll have got back with him and wants everyone to think she's made up about it.'

Charley pictured Jennifer down the phone, purple-red hair, slightly overweight - and not because of recently giving birth, although she would blame that - perma-tanned in her little new-build that smelt like fresh paint mixed with baby sick.

'Did you know about what happened in Paris with the French man?'

Silence on the other end of the phone. Charley wished she could see her face.

'Gina told you about that?'

'Yeah. I couldn't believe it.'

'Mark would have done the same and so would any fella defending his girl,' she said. 'I'm not a major fan of what Daniel did but you can hardly blame him.'

'But there was no need for him to do what he did, was there?' Charley played along.

'The man was a perv and anyway he would have been fine. As Gina said, there were people around. You know what police are like about Brits abroad, especially Scousers. They would have locked Daniel up and thrown away the key.'

'But Gina wouldn't have left anyone would she – a man who looked like he needed to go to hospital?'

'I know, but I told her I would have done the same for Mark.'

'Who the fuck are you on the phone to at this hour?' The angry voice of the 'lovely' Mark.

'It's Gina's sister!' Jennifer shouted back. It sounded like she had at least got some balls to stand up to him since the baby was born.

'Put the fucking phone down. It's the middle of the night and I've told you we're having nothing to do with Gina, that wanker she's going out with, or any of her family.'

'He has a right to be angry,' Jennifer's voice got more certain as she knew it was something her boyfriend would approve of her saying. 'Mark's been struggling for work since-'

'Since what?'

'Well it's obvious Gina tells you even less than she does us these days.' She sighed and Charley could hear more ranting from Mark. 'I'll have to go. I can't help you Charley.' The call was finished.

Desperate to stay awake, Charley went downstairs, searched the cupboards for coffee, and then scooped a ridiculous amount into a cup. There was no milk. She didn't mind.

Stay close to your sister. The words threw themselves into her head suddenly.

One of her Mum's only demands in the last days of her life. There would have been others, but she'd lost the letter from her mum years ago, unopened and thrown somewhere in an angry moment not long after she had died. Whenever she thought of this, her insides would ache with regret and longing, at the knowledge that she would never read the words her mum wanted her to have. One of the things it would have been easy for anyone else to do. The gaping hole in her head, the one filled with darkness and bad thoughts was trying to break open again.

Charley sat down and tried to gather strength to stop her mind wandering the wrong way. She went around the house and checked every lock. The security light came on in the garden twice. She told herself it was a cat but she didn't dare leave until morning, when people were about and it was clear enough to see properly. Then her phone rang.

CHAPTER SEVEN

Checks ~ examine (something) in order to determine its accuracy, quality, or condition, or to detect the presence of something

~ On the background of people you get into relationships with to detect if anything wrong in their past - but would that be fair?

~ With your friends - told Jen about flirting, French man and the fight - she thinks normal, Mark would have done same. But why avoid the police if you've done nothing wrong? Should have rang ambulance myself.

February 2014

'There!' Daniel said as we arrived in the eye line of the Eiffel Tower.

He let go of my hand. I clasped it with the other one to soothe the pain from where he'd held me too tightly in his excitement. My eyes followed his free fingers. The great spike came into view, strikingly set against the grey sky.

'Well?' he demanded. His cheeks were ruddy with excitement.

'Beautiful.' That one word took all my energy. Some things are better on a postcard. I moved around to the front of him. His head kind of drops off at the back, as though someone has flattened it with a shovel and then let the hair grow back. I've learned that his side profile is not his best, apart from his arms.

Maybe the tip of that Tower could pierce something in my brain to spark the same happiness as him. I was too nervous. Even my clothes were wrong; black skinny jeans and an oversized knitted jumper with a big pink heart across the front, like I was constantly trying to remind my boyfriend to love me.

'Come on, we still have some walking to do, but at least it's a straight run,' Daniel said, grabbing hold of my hand again.

I wanted to walk faster, but my shoes pinched. They were gorgeous, little ballet pumps, pink and white with detailed lacing across the front, but I was regretting the decision after zig-zagging across the city. We'd passed a C&A before (they seem to pop up everywhere in Europe) with rows of boots, Ugg after Ugg after Ugg. My feet pleaded for them with a toe-curling pinch.

As a teenager, I'd drag Mum through C&A on many a weekend, before they closed it down and it retreated back to Europe, and the city redefined itself around Liverpool One. Sometimes we'd go to the Hole in the Wall cafe for chocolate calorie cake afterwards.

'Wish they'd spruce Liverpool up a bit,' Mum often said as we walked down the alleyway past the crumbling walls. They did in the end but she wasn't around for it. Liverpool was now a beautiful ring of contradictions, old and new, scruffy past and chic modern. But at least you were unlikely to get lost, even as a tourist. The Radio City Tower was easier to spot than the Eiffel.

I kept up the pace, not daring to mess with Daniel's list. There literally was one, printed out and in his pocket. I wasn't allowed to look at it but still knew what was coming. There was one thing I did know about though.

That was why I was nervous. Every time I pictured that box, barely concealed in Daniel's pocket, I was back on the bathroom floor at the hotel, cold tiles on my face, trying to calm down. I kept telling myself it was a bit soon, yes, but we'd grown so close over the last six weeks, like we'd always been together. I was even considering letting him meet Charley.

'It's only a bit further – Gina, you have to hurry up. We're already late enough as it is, the place'll be heaving,' Daniel urged.

I shifted my scarf up higher around my neck. The latest love bite was fading but the redness still showed. I was going to put a stop to them as soon as. People must have thought we were into kinky vampire style sex-games. It wasn't doing my career any good either; in my team it was the lead topic of banter.

I upped my pace. Being whisked off to Paris might be romantic, but it was bloody tiring.

We finally arrived under a series of chains disguised as a building, and an ugly one at that. Even standing there made me think that a branch of metal could loop down from the middle and coil around my body, lifting me up into it, gone forever. I didn't want to feed the monster of Paris. I'd never seen a 'building' so arrogant yet so ugly in my whole life.

Glittering mini Eiffel towers in a range of colours covered the floor, along with little wooden insects crawling across the filthy ground. Without thinking, I picked a sparkly tower out. The man selling them was beside himself.

'I give you good price.'

'I'll take it,' I said at the same time, feeling sorry for him in his sweaty t-shirt and unshaven face. He snatched the note out of my hand before I could say barter. The toys reminded me of cheap sweets; bursting with the right colours, but when they hit the inside of your mouth, the realisation comes that something isn't quite right. Three diamantes fell off the thing as I walked away.

'What the hell are you doing?'

'Getting a souvenir,' I answered.

'You buy a cheap piece of crap when we're under the real thing?!'

The next person got theirs for a fifth of the price.

'Should we join the queue to go up?' Daniel asked. A gang of school kids ran past us. 'We need to be quick - there are coach loads of them pulling up.'

The Tower seemed like a monster in motion now. Its spiralling legs stood around me defiantly. I tried to look up but felt like I was going to fall over.

'Oh, I don't know.' The idea of going up in the lift terrified me.

'We could take the stairs,' Daniel suggested, seeing my face. There were stairs? How would that work? I quickly found out. People were moving like spiders up and down the legs. I felt sick for them.

'Gina, get over it. Come on, it's safe - please!' His voice was strained.

'Well maybe the lift then, I don't know…how safe are those stairs?' I ummed and ahhhed, the fish tapped at my belly with their fins and bit me at random. 'Daniel, I don't think I can go up there,' I decided finally.

'Come on, please.' He tried to pull me towards the lift.

'No, I definitely can't.' I was frozen rigid to the ground, couldn't do anything about it.

'Gina, please!'

'I can't. What's the big deal about going up there anyway?'

'I wanted to ask you to marry me!' he blurted out almost in tears. 'We were meant to get here hours ago when it was quiet. I forgot you were scared of heights. I'm a fucking idiot!'

For a moment I thought he was going to throw away the ring he'd taken out of his pocket. The people around us would probably melt it down and produce another mini Eiffel Tower.

'Yes! Yes, I'll marry you!' I screamed putting my hand over his and trying to secure the ring onto my finger. Now it was out in the open I did feel excited, happy - everything I was supposed to.

38

Daniel's mouth was drawn into a hard line which only broke with the hug I gave him. When I pulled back he was smiling.

No one burst into applause. In fact, I think some of them were sizing up how easy it would be to rob us. The ring stuck halfway.

'Why don't you put it on properly? It does fit doesn't it?'

'Yes, I want to admire it.' I pulled it off. I tried again. I pushed it further onto my finger even though it hurt and cut-off the blood supply. It seemed a bit of a weird choice when I looked at it properly, spirals looped wiry white gold, and a clotted patch of diamonds in the middle. It must have been expensive, though.

'What are you doing?' he asked as I took out my phone.

'Letting Charley know,' I replied. 'She'll be made up.'

He took the phone off me and put it in his pocket.

'What are you doing?'

'*We* need to celebrate first.' He nodded towards the only restaurant I could see around. The official Tower one actually. Well, the bottom of the Tower one, for cowards like me.

'The restaurant will be really expensive.'

'Don't worry about it. Oh for fuck's sake.' Daniel was patting his jean pockets.

'What?'

'I've left my wallet in the hotel. What do you have on you?'

I pulled out some change, a few notes, not enough.

'Why did you buy that fucking blue flashy thing?'

I didn't dare say the ten euros would have bought us an ice-cube in a place like that.

It started to lash down so we walked quickly towards a tent/café/restaurant thing. The wind was battering against the edges and the canvas kept lifting and letting the cold in. It smelt of dodgy cleaning products and poverty, but we were too hungry after our journey to care.

39

A woman in a hairnet sweated over onions, hotdogs and burgers. The only other customer was sat on one of the bench table things with a box of toys, a pocket of change, which he jangled from time to time, and a bottle of whiskey that he slipped into the flat coke. He gave me a sloppy, sleazy smile as I headed up to order.

'Yes?' The woman barked at me in French accented English.

'Erm, two hot dogs, please.'

I brought them back over, slithers of onion dripping onto the floor. Daniel greeted me with a big smile, as though I'd found caviar and champagne.

'I was thinking of something,' he said, one strong arm around me. 'If I had one more hour with my mum, I would tell her all about you.'

'That's so nice.' I choked up a bit. 'I'd love my mum to have met you.' This part was true, but what I didn't tell him was how this idea of seeing her again had changed over time. If Mum came back now, truthfully, I'm not sure how I'd handle it after spending eight years getting my body and mind prepared to live in a different way, even if it was for that one hour which everyone always wants in those quotes you see posted on Facebook.

'Going to the loo.' I planted a prolonged kiss on Daniel, partly for the benefit of the increasingly sleazy man who watched me walk all the way to the toilets.

It was worse than I thought. The hair I had spent so long blow-drying had taken off a bit, so instead of a great sweeping statement at the top, I had a Hitler comb-over. The rest of my long, blonde tresses had mashed together in the rain, forming very badly done dreadlocks. It was almost making a political statement.

The make-up had melted off my face, although the blusher on my cheeks had clung on – which left me with an over-enthusiastic look. There was no sign of any lipstick or mascara, despite the fact I'd been very heavy on both.

I was sure an invisible force, probably my mum, followed me around with wipes made of air particles that take everything clean off. Fresh-faced, but not really. More like a person living through constant trauma. The fake tan had stayed in place though. It was goldfish coloured but it was something.

Lathering soap across my hand, I jammed the ring onto my finger with a final push. I headed back out to Daniel. Unfortunately, I had to pass by the sleazy man again, who, for some reason, had gained the confidence to give me a full on stare as I headed back to my seat. And I mean full on, from my legs to my face, pausing at all the key parts.

'What the fuck is he doing staring at you like that?' Daniel threw his arms up, upsetting the coke so much that it almost looked fizzy. My hotdog took a final suicidal leap off the paper tablecloth.

'Back off, mate,' he said, turning to face sleazy man. The muscles bulged in his arms. The man held his hands up and smiled as though to shrug off any chance of a fight. He said something in French and then looked at me, laughing.

'It's ok. I think he's drunk, leave it.' I went to place a hand on Daniel's arm but he wasn't next to me.

The sound was like a smack in the air. The man fell back and hit a bench, with a sickening crack. He didn't move.

'Shit,' Daniel whispered next to me. His face turned an ashen colour. The woman at the hotdog stand started screaming.

'We have to go,' Daniel pulled at my arm.

'But…is he ok?'

'Fucking come on, we have to go,' he pleaded. My feet stayed glued to the spot.

'Come on, please,' he yanked at me harder. 'Gina, I can't get questioned by the police, I really can't!'

I couldn't stop staring at the man, lying on the floor, completely still. And then I saw his head move to the side and his arm raise slightly. The woman was crouched over him, on her phone. She turned and looked at us. I ran, ashamed of

41

myself. We caught our breath by a bar. Daniel leaned against the wall, his face dripping with sweat.

'What did you mean about the police?' I asked.

'What?' he panted.

'You said that you couldn't get questioned by them, why?'

'It was to get you to move! Foreign police are lunatics anyway. They'd have locked me up on the old Brits Abroad vendetta.'

'You shouldn't have punched him,' I said.

'He was being disrespectful about you! I've done nothing wrong.'

'You understand French now?'

'I understand the universal language of dickhead.'

'Daniel, there was no need.'

'I know,' he said quietly. 'I'm sorry.'

We stood in silence. I could feel his eyes on me. The clotted diamonds on my finger sparkled in the sunlight. Inside I felt dull.

CHAPTER EIGHT

HELP: 4.00 Saturday 30th August 2014

'Charlotte Ellison?' The voice was deep, formal, sure of itself. 'It's Officer Field.'

'Who?' Charley asked, sitting up and putting the lamp back on, eyes adjusting to the sudden light.

'I was around at your house yesterday evening.'

Her brain scrambled into action. 'Have you found Gina?'

There was a pause. 'No…and I'm sorry for calling at this time, but I wanted to speak to you as soon as I could.'

The security light beamed on in the back garden again, shining through a gap in the curtains and fighting against the dim lamp. Her heart raced.

'Have you started to look for her? I could come down to the police station now if you need more information-'

'It's not an official investigation,' he said quickly and then paused as though weighing something up. 'The thing is, because of the situation and your, well, your past record, the police are not going to be looking into it formally. They don't think there's anything in it. It looks like a family dispute to them. They'd need more evidence to back up your claims.' His words cut deep into the headache that was forming across her temple.

'So why are you calling me then?'

'Because I don't think it's fair when people won't listen to someone because of their past.'

A familiar panic started to choke her.

'I want you to know I can help,' he continued. 'I'll give you my direct number so you can call if you find anything else out we can use.'

'I can give you details of her car, where her office was when she worked for Daniel, the name of his company…' she rattled off the list she'd wanted to give the police the night before.

He repeated back some of the information. He was taking notes. The tightness around her chest subsided as though everything she'd wanted to say had been a weight crushing into her.

'I know it might be difficult for you to talk about, but was there anything else about the party when you last saw her?' he asked when she'd finished.

'There was something about an accident.'

'There was an accident at this party?'

'No, something that had happened earlier,' Charley said.

'What did Gina say?'

'Nothing. She wasn't acting like herself and then she made us all leave.'

'This was the last time you saw her?'

Charley swallowed the lump in her throat. 'Yeah.'

'Didn't you try and get in touch with her after the party?'

'She didn't reply to any texts or ring me back,' Charley found herself saying, 'but she'd been like that since things got serious with Daniel.' Parts of that were true at least.

'What about the definition you showed me? If any more of those come up, I'd be happy to take a look at them for you and see if there is anything I can work out,' he said.

'I did find a few more,' she said and hesitated, wondering if any of the information made any sense yet, or if it was worth mentioning before she had the chance to talk to more people. 'There was something about Paris, so maybe the accident happened there. Gina seems scared of Daniel's brother too. His name's Matthew. I could give you his address. ' She didn't want to mention calling around at the house; Melissa could turn this around by complaining about her.

'But Gina never said that Daniel was abusive?'

'No.'

There was silence down for the phone for a few seconds.

'I'll look into a few things,' he said finally. 'At the moment there isn't really anything concrete to go on but ring me on this number if you get anything else or you find any other notes she's made that are a bit more definite.'

'I will do, thanks,' Charley said.

'But you have to keep this between us or I won't be able to help you at all.'

'I will, don't worry and thank you again.' She wasn't sure what else to say. She'd certainly never experienced anything like this with the police before.

'If something has happened to your sister, and I'm not saying it has, I wouldn't want you to put yourself in danger because of narrow minded-' he tailed off. 'Anyway, ring me.' There was something about the tone of his voice which made her trust what he was saying.

A slice of moonlight had replaced the blaring security light. 'Ok,' she answered.

'I promise I'll help where I can, Miss Ellison.'

She wanted to ask how he had got her mobile number but then his voice was gone. She was alone again.

CHAPTER NINE

Denial ~ refusal to admit the truth or reality

~ My case - not facing up to who people really are

~ Do people just deny that they'll do something again? Daniel - Paris, Charley - old ways

~ Is Anthony right? Did humiliate Daniel though - right to be angry and with me for letting it happen

February 2014

'I can't believe you still see her.'

'People can change Daniel,' I replied through gritted teeth as I fixed my hair in the mirror.

'After what she put you through? I'm telling you, people don't change like that. You're in denial.'

'Kind of contradicts what you said about Paris.'

A dark look appeared on his face.

'She's looking forward to meeting you,' I added in a lighter voice, trying to prevent the mood which usually followed that look, 'and everyone else will be there too.'

'Why does *everyone else* include that Anthony?'

'I've told you about a million times that Anthony is like a brother to us.' I could feel the red rising under my foundation, threatening to out-do my blusher. 'I put up with Matthew.'

He closed up clam-like at that, his mouth set into a hard line. My stomach jittered.

'Well, do you want to meet them or not?' My voice shook slightly. This wasn't going as I'd hoped. When it was me and Daniel, just the two of us, the world was a proper amazing place and I'd never been happier. But when other people came into the equation, flirty Frenchmen or family members, our little bubble of happy got smaller and sometimes burst completely.

'We're going to be late.' Daniel rattled his car keys and opened the front door by way of an answer. The beautiful crisp new shirt I'd ironed earlier was tucked into his belted jeans. I was still prone to melting at the sight of him, arm stretched out against the door, exposing well-worked muscles.

We had one other person scheduled to join the group who wasn't one of my family or friends, which I thought would make it easier but as we pulled into the driveway, Daniel sighed.

Bob climbed in and shut the door a little too loudly. That slightly, unwashed, neglected old man smell made its way through the car.

'Nice for us all to be getting together isn't it?' he said cheerfully, putting on his belt with a snap. Daniel didn't answer.

The restaurant was a good choice at least, very trendy. A waiter, youthful and studenty, with freckles dashed across his face and a northern Irish lilt to his voice, showed us to a table by the window. Shame that the view was of the Childwall Fiveways roundabout, which spun car after harassed car around concrete and an island of unkempt grass and dead flowers. I ordered a glass of white wine - a large one - as we waited for the others.

'Why not a bottle and we'll share it?' Bob suggested. Daniel ordered a diet coke and put his head inside the menu.

Panpipe eighties music battled the awkward silence.

'There they are,' Bob announced, waving across the room and revealing little sweat stains under the arms of his shirt. They looked old and worn in; his shirt was full of creases now he'd taken his jacket off. I felt a pang of guilt. We needed to keep

48

an eye on him more but Daniel always said he was perfectly capable and in fact got angry whenever I brought up his dad so I'd stopped mentioning it.

Charley was in a green skater dress with a slash neck - slashed a bit too low, if you know what I mean - but I was glad to see her looking more confident and in something I'd picked. I was trying to get her to dress a bit more adventurously than jeans and a hoodie.

Anthony was close behind her. His shirt with button down collar made him look smart and manly. Jen came in with them, only two months pregnant but looking double the size and double the time. It seemed like longer seeing as she'd announced it on Facebook the minute she conceived. She was dressed in a cutwork hi lo dress and strappy shoes, all black. Her bigger-than-usual-but-always-been-big-boobs got a glance from Daniel. He hadn't let me wear my similar Sequin Bodycon Dress. He said it made me look like a snake out on the pull.

Jo couldn't make it as she was at a family meal. Obviously, we were also minus my Dad, who'd moved to Hong Kong years ago, when him and Mum got divorced. He only came back for really important things, like when Mum was dying, before leaving us again as soon as he could. Mum had no sisters or brothers and my Nan and Granddad had died before I was even born. Dad's side were a no-go area as he'd cut them off years ago. With such an incomplete family, it was no wonder we'd adopted our neighbour, Anthony, as a 'brother', and I'd nearly fucked that up before Daniel came along.

Jen pushed in front of Charley and Anthony and gave out hugs even though she knew I didn't like them.

'Oh Daniel, lovely to see ya.' She smelt like a MAC make-up pick and mix. 'And you too Bob.'

'Good to see you too Jen,' Daniel said. She beamed and sat down.

'Nice to finally meet you, Charley.' Daniel gave my sister a kiss on the cheek, while I breathed a sigh of relief and then turned to Anthony. They shook hands.

'Ohh let's take a look at the menu then.' Jen was doing her best to dissolve the tension. 'The fishcakes look fab. I'm getting three courses since Mark isn't here to call me a fat pig.' She laughed but it was true. He'd been calling her variations of the phrase long before she got pregnant.

'Good choice, but it's the classic meatballs for me!' Daniel added. 'I'll pay for this,' he murmured. I squeezed his hand under the table.

I never ate out much with my last boyfriend, Jonathan, mainly due to his tightarsedness and my skintness resulting from his tightarsedness, and never with family. I got saddled with debt due to the simple things with him; the household (sorry, flathold) cleaning, shops and even trips to the cinema. He didn't pay for things he didn't want to do, the lovely fucker. I looked at Daniel with gratitude; here was a man who knew how to treat someone, especially when I was trying to pay off my credit cards.

'How are the wedding plans going then, Gina?' Jen asked. 'Have you set a date?'

'We will do soon - thinking of this summer actually,' Daniel said, taking my hand under the table again. A fish nipped at a nerve in my head and unleashed a sudden headache. What was that about? I didn't think we were planning for that soon.

Before I could reply the starters arrived. Charley had ordered goats cheese on toasted crostini which the waiter put down as though he'd travelled a great distance to fetch... despite the kitchen being about three steps away. Irishy student boy arrived at the same time and placed a bowl of soup, a red gludgy thing, on the table in front of Daniel. 'I didn't order this.'

'I thought you pointed at that when the waiter came over - the Gazpacho,' Anthony said. Daniel threw him a look.

'I did. I thought it was a posh name for meatballs.'

'No, mate,' Anthony shook his head, smirking, 'the meatballs were the description above.'

'I'll eat it anyway. It's only tomato soup.' Daniel shrugged and I watched as his spoon went from bowl to mouth, my stomach twisting. 'Why is it cold?'

I clenched the napkin under the table. The fish danced away any appetite I had.

'It's meant to be cold lad,' Anthony answered. He was definitely taking the piss. *Mate* and *lad,* two words Anthony never used. He thought they were scally scouse, for the ruffians of the city who liked to use them as punctuation marks.

'I'll go and sort it out. The waiter knew I wanted meatballs,' Daniel launched his napkin onto the table, scraping his chair as he got up and muttered, 'the little prick.'

I wasn't sure if he meant Anthony or the waiter but luckily only me and Jen heard. Her mouth dropped open like an O, and then she carefully popped her pink lipstick lips back together.

One slip, I thought, *he has to deal with Anthony's patronising bullshit and he's only had one slip of anger.*

Daniel came back with the waiter, who removed the soup promptly.

'I'm going to leave the starter.' Daniel said stiffly.

Anthony hid behind a bottle of beer but I could see his shoulders shaking with laughter.

'Where are you thinking of getting married?' Charley scraped her starter around her plate. She was making an effort, although going out for a meal was quite new for her. The dress hung awkwardly off her shoulders.

'Maybe abroad somewhere?' Daniel cut in. That was the first I'd heard of it.

'Oh, great,' Charley said, trying to smile.

'Guaranteed some nice weather if you go away for it.' Bob had been quiet so far. I noticed a new bottle of wine by his glass. He was already glass-eyed.

'I'm going the loo,' I said, needing a break. I'd got as far as the corner, out of sight of the others, when I felt a hand on my shoulder.

'Isn't it a bit soon?' Anthony said, his eyes darting from the ring to my face and back again.

'What?'

'You've only been going out with Daniel about six weeks,' he said, 'and in that time I've seen you about twice and never with him.'

'You and I hadn't been seeing much of each other before I started going out with him, had we?'

He at least had the decency to look a bit ashamed at this but his face told me he wasn't giving up yet. 'I just can't believe that on your first holiday with him, you got engaged!'

Your charms don't work on me anymore, I felt like telling him. *I have a ring now that makes you almost invisible as a boy and back to a brother figure. A one night lapse means nothing.*

'There was something else I wanted to tell you about him,' Anthony paused. 'His family, they're properly mental. Matthew Ryan and even his dad - yes that man at the table getting leathered at a quiet meal. They're all known for trouble, kicking off, getting into fights. The brother-in-law Ken is notorious…'

'What are you on about?'

'I'm worried about you.' He put his hand back on my shoulder in a way that made me furious.

'You're a snob. We can't all go to Oxford. And since when has what someone's family done mean that they're the same?'

He couldn't answer that. The evidence was on the table. I headed to the toilet and stood by the sink for a minute before heading back out.

* * * * *

'Your mum really liked this place, God love her.' Bob was saying to Daniel.

'How are you coping, Bob?' Jen asked. Her bright pink fingernails reached across the table to pat his hand.

'Not too bad, up and down, you know.' Bob sighed, rubbing her hand in a way that made me flinch.

After what felt like about a year, the mains arrived at the table. It was all amazing, proper beautiful food. There was belly pork with caramelised peppers and onions for Charley, roast chicken fillet wrapped in sweet cured bacon for me and sea bass fillets for Jen, pan seared in olive oil with salsa verde and lemon mayonnaise dips. Bob had fish and chips and Anthony had some complicated seafood dish. I was expecting him to name the ingredients in Latin or something.

Daniel tore into his steak with peppercorn sauce when it arrived, as though he was taking revenge on the chef for the soup incident.

'How's work, Daniel?' Charley asked.

'Great ta – going really well.' Daniel didn't pause from eating his steak. A speckle of sauce hit my dress. 'Think we need a new office manager though.' He nudged and winked in my direction.

'Are you leaving your job?' Charley's fork stopped halfway between her mouth and plate. She thought my job was the best thing ever: stable, well paid, something she looked up to.

'I wouldn't know what to do in that role, Daniel, I've told you!' I said, passing it off as a joke. He had started bringing up the fact that Sheila, good old reliable mumsy Sheila, would be retiring soon, and they'd need a new admin. He dressed it up for me as 'Office Manager'. Anthony cast me a few looks but didn't say anything else.

We finished and watched the desserts roll past us to other tables. Luxury chocolate cake with coffee cream filling, crème fraiche sorbet, shortbread biscuits, fresh strawberries and liqueur-infused cream. None of it was worth prolonging the awkwardness. Daniel signalled for the waiter and got out his wallet as the bill was brought over.

'I'm not leaving a tip though,' he announced loudly, and the heat of the restaurant hit my cheeks.

'Well I have some change-' Jen started rooting in her bag.

'No, leave it.' Daniel closed his hand over the receipt dish. 'He screwed me over with that meatball thing.'

As Daniel went to the toilet, Anthony piled some coins into the dish.

* * * * *

'That was ok wasn't it?' I asked as Bob got out of the car and shuffled up to his front door. He turned and gave us a quick wave which was our signal to speed backwards down the drive.

'Don't you ever fucking do that to me again.' Daniel's voice was low, angry.

'What do you mean?'

'You let that Anthony make me look fucking stupid.' He took one hand off the wheel, and raised it up.

'He didn't-'

'Shut the fuck up.' He smacked his hand back down on the wheel. My stomach was jittering ten to the dozen, with more and more fish waking up.

CHAPTER TEN

OLD FRIENDS: 7.00 Saturday 30th August 2014

Charley scrambled off the bed, the duvet tumbling to the floor. Despite all the coffee inside her, she'd still managed to sleep.

Officer Field's offer of help, strange as it was, rang around her head. She was only going back to him when she had something more concrete; at the moment he was her only hope and she couldn't waste his time. It was like a miracle that someone like him was giving her any attention at all. She wondered what the deal was with that.

Forcing herself into the shower, she scrubbed quickly, ducking around to avoid getting her hair wet.

The clothes situation was awkward. She didn't want to go back to the flat so she looked in Gina's wardrobe. The skinny jeans she found were too big but she hid them beneath an oversized jumper with a big heart in the middle. It was weird trying to be Gina. After using the last of the milky jasmine shower gel she even smelt like her.

Gina would have been pleased to see her like this. One of her new favourite games was dressing Charley up. A particularly disastrous attempt was the time she'd been introduced to Daniel.

There was something about him, even his quick, uninterested kiss on her cheek that first night, which made her skin crawl, and she'd met plenty of people who had the ability to do that. His dad wasn't much better - drinking the table dry, something Gina would have commented on if it was anyone else.

Gina's weakness was being flattered by men. It was obvious that Daniel had the strength to overcome her, physically and mentally. Charley had watched as he'd gripped Gina's hand under the table in a way that must have hurt. He'd controlled the conversation too. Meanwhile, all Anthony did was play the arrogant, jealous arsehole. He might not have helped then but he would have to step up now.

* * * * *

It was light enough to take a good look around before she ran across the road and knocked at the door. There was little chance he would answer the phone to her again.

He answered, bleary eyed and wearing a pair of grey tracksuit bottoms and nothing else. His top half was toned and tanned. This was a new development. Anthony had always looked after himself but he wasn't the type to do weights and try to crease the six-pack.

'Charley, what the hell-'

She pushed past him.

'I need to ask you some things about Gina,' she said. He followed her into the kitchen, perching on the breakfast barstool.

'I want to ask you something first,' he said. His voice was more alert now and he was staring her down. 'Are you-'

'No, one hundred percent no, and I swear on Gina's life,' she answered before he could finish the question that dug needles into her nerves. 'I can't believe you would think that.'

'What do you need to ask about Gina at seven in the morning on a Saturday?' He yawned. 'I told you on the phone, she'll have gone away with him.'

'I found something,' Charley said, taking the pieces of paper out of her pocket. They looked scruffy against the shiny black surface of the worktop.

'She still does these?' Anthony picked up 'A' and then put it back down again.

'Did she give you any?' Charley asked.

Anthony shook his head. He wasn't conventionally good looking but there was a weird confidence that seemed to glow out of him. His hair was a light, strawberry blonde, with green eyes and a subtle cockiness that got girls going. It was easy to

56

see why Gina had always loved him a little bit. He was such a 'player' though.

Charley pointed at the last definition. 'What did you say to Gina about Daniel?'

'When was that? I've said plenty of things about him.'

'It's from February, so it was when we all first met him and you took the piss out of him over the soup.'

A smile spread over his face, then he read it again.

'She mentions you here too,' Anthony pointed out. 'Old ways?' He gave Charley a sharp look.

'Yeah, well, that's Daniel filling her head with shit,' she replied. 'What did you say at the meal?'

'I warned her about his family, that's all.'

'If you think the family's bad, don't you think something could have happened to her?'

'No,' he said, looking away, 'I think she got back with him.'

'But she does write something about the family and a fight earlier on.'

'There's a lot of fighting in that family.'

'Do you know anything about Paris?'

'Only that she got engaged there.'

'Did something happen between you and Gina when she was with Daniel? Something to make him mad enough to want to punish her?'

'This is more like the old you isn't it?' he smiled. 'Finding it impossible to sit still and let things happen if you don't agree with them.'

'It isn't that! I think she's in danger. Try and ring her again, go on. You feel bad don't you?'

'I think we've both got track records of letting Gina down.' He pushed his arms down on the table. His biceps looked even bigger.

'Charley,' he started, 'listen to me. I think Gina will turn up after the weekend with that ring back on her finger and that nutcase by her side. She chose him, ok?'

He walked out of the kitchen then and left her sitting there, not sure what to do. She heard him going upstairs, footsteps in one of the rooms overheard, before he came back down again carrying a small plastic bag.

'When she comes back you can give her this stuff.'

Charley looked inside the bag. There was a toothbrush stuffed down the side and face wipes along with a pile of gym clothes.

'She stayed here?'

'I don't want to talk about it.'

'But why did she stay here?'

'Charley, she isn't going to get in touch with me. I can't help you, please, go.' He walked out of the kitchen, leaving Charley clutching Gina's stuff. She let herself out.

As she got back inside the house, she poured the bag out onto the floor and searched through the clothes. In the pocket of the tracksuit bottoms were two more definitions.

CHAPTER ELEVEN

Exercise ~ activity requiring physical effort

~ Getting fit to fit in with friends I don't even want - but then Karen and co understand Daniel - my own friends don't

~ Still think it's weird to be that close to your cousin though - should exercise some restraint in what he tells her

March 2014

'Come on, love, why aren't yer ready?'

I'd opened the door to three Tropical Fish fronted by Karen. She was wearing a purple fluffy tracksuit, with hair that tumbled over her shoulders and a full face of make-up. Lydia nodded while Jemma beamed at me. They wore variations of Karen's tracksuit and matching war paint.

'Ready for what?'

'We're going to the gym,' Karen announced. 'Hen party prep hun. We can't be on that beach like pure whales can we?' She lifted her top and patted her non-existent stomach fat.

'The beach?'

She gave me a *look*. 'You need to make the most of a hen, hun. It's a proper good excuse for a girly holiday. I know your bridesmaids have been a bit useless but I'm on the case babe. Got a little Facebook group set up and everything."

I tried to ask where exactly the hen party would be, but Karen bundled me into her brand new white BMW like some kind of fitness-themed kidnap and screeched off. Lydia threw a bag into the back seat which caught me in the face.

'New gym stuff,' Karen explained, zooming around a corner so that my head hit the window. Lydia smirked in the mirror. 'Daniel gave me his credit card to get you kitted out.'

Inside the bag was a bright blue version of Karen's fluffy purple tracksuit, a stretchy white vest top, some black trainers and a sports bra. Jemma offered me some clear lip-gloss which I took and applied solemnly.

We arrived at the gym and made our way to the changing rooms. Karen talked loudly about cellulite, as though it was a life choice, as I considered my new exercise gear.

The clothes were too tight of course. I was always telling Daniel that a size eight was a bit too small for me. I suppose this was meant as an incentive. We walked out of the changing room and into the hall which smelt like chalky sweat. Soon it was filled by music and shouting.

'Come on, girls, don't give in!' The whole class was punctuated by shouts like this, mainly from Karen.

* * * * *

'Well done girls. All give yourselves a round of applause!' There was an actual round of applause. And cheering. I couldn't cope.

'Don't worry, you'll get better.' Lydia walked past me, taking her step and weights back to the equipment room. She hadn't even broken a sweat. I took a good look at her. She was cat-like with her deliberately thick eyebrows. You could tell that she didn't wake up good looking, not at all; this was meticulous make-up art. In the morning, her face would be a blank canvas which she would work on carefully, matching it with bouncy, long, black hair that would have been set in rollers all night. After endlessly brushing a palette of colours and blushes, she'd then perk her boobs into a bra which pushed them up and out. Today, she had perfected the Hugh Hefner's girlfriend-goes-to-the gym look. Her waist actually looked corseted, even in the tracksuit. It was so pulled in and impossibly tiny. Lydia had the honey coloured skin I wanted. Her figure was enviable, like she'd been cut out of a magazine as a body template.

60

'I haven't been to the gym for ages.' My voice bounced around the room like my body had. Wibble, wobble, jelly on a plate.

A large woman threw her pink weights back into the basket in front of us and trundled off. Lydia crinkled her nose up in disgust.

'They knock me,' she said.

'Who?'

'Fat people, they knock me sick.' She glanced at my arms. They always gain weight first. I end up looking like Hulk Hogan after a spell of non-exercise. I crossed them as I waited for the others outside the changing rooms. To make matters worse, Anthony was headed towards me, holding a gym bag and wearing a t-shirt that had definitely become tighter since I last saw it on him.

'What are you doing here?' The bastard actually grinned.

Before I could answer, Lydia stepped in front of me. 'Good to see you, lad. Hitting the gym? Didn't know you went here?'

'Didn't know *you* did,' he said, peering around to look at me.

* * * * *

'See much of Anthony?' Lydia tilted her head as Karen drove back.

'Not really.'

'Is he going to Glasto?' she asked, playing with her nails.

'Not sure. Ask him.'

'Going with me mates aren't I?' she snapped.

'Hoes before Bros,' Jemma said gravely.

'Why are we driving in the opposite direction to mine?' The houses that were flying past weren't on the right route.

'Love, you're not going home yet. We need to sort those eyebrows out. Jemma is a master at it.' Karen drove until she swung the car into a space outside her salon. She called

61

herself the manager but most of the time she bullied the customers and painted her own nails while they waited.

'I'm an MUA,' Jemma explained.

'A what?' I asked warily.

'A Make-Up Artist,' Karen whispered as if I've broken some kind of sacred girl code.

I was hurried into Jemma's area and told to lie down on the bed.

Jemma worked on my eyebrows like a surgeon performing a life-changing operation. When she handed me a mirror in what seemed like hours later, I went into shock.

'I'm on a mission to give everyone brows like that babe.' Jemma admired her work.

They were 'Scouse brows', thick and straight. They looked like KitKat chunkies.

'Fab!' Karen said decidedly, when we came out into the main salon. 'Next step is that you need to come shopping with us. I can see what our Danny meant.'

'About what?' I was sure she only called him Danny to annoy me. He didn't let me call him that.

'That you wanted to be in proper shape for the wedding, full-on styled and that.'

Before I could answer, she whisked me back into the car and then drove at the highest speed possible, practically throwing me out onto my driveway.

'I'll see you both at the party later mwah,' she said, blowing me a kiss. I thought only American high school cliques on TV and in films did things like that. And what party? Daniel always made plans for us these days, giving me minimal time to prepare.

I decided to walk to the shop under the pretence of buying a bottle of water for my next gym expedition.

He answered after one ring.

'Hi, it's me.'

'Oh, hi,' Anthony replied.

'Bad time for me to call?' I didn't want to see him face to face or risk Daniel seeing me going over there.

'Does Daniel know you're on the phone to me?'

'He's in the room as a matter of fact.'

'Then why does it sound like you're walking down a busy road?'

'You made a show of him at that meal.'

'It's not my fault he hasn't got a shred of a sense of humour. That meal was, like, two weeks ago as well. Good session at the gym?'

'No, actually, and don't try and change the subject. You don't even know Daniel,' I protested.

'I don't know *you* anymore.'

'What do you mean by that?'

'It's like you're not even allowed to breathe without asking him.'

'You know nothing about our relationship.'

'Getting engaged, getting a mortgage, possibly even going to work for him, all in about five minutes.'

'Why do you give a shit anyway?' And then that night was between us again, unspoken, the near kiss, the near miss.

'Gina, I-'

'You, what?'

'It doesn't matter. I'll see you soon.'

I ended the call, resisting the urge to put two fingers up at Anthony's house when I went past and then did the customary deleting of his number from the outgoing list.

* * * * *

The hall stunk of paint and sweaty feet as I took my trainers off. Daniel was always trying to improve the house, even though he had no intention of us ever buying it off my dad and living here.

'Good session?' He was stretched out on the orange sofa with his iPad, six-pack on show.

'Hard,' I threw myself down in the mastermind-style armchair across the other side of the room.

'Well that's why I've been saying you should get into the gym.'

'Did you tell Karen I was fat?' I said.

'I told Karen *you* think you're fat.' He forced himself up from the couch. 'Here, have a look at these.' Selections of beautiful houses were on his iPad and in my face. A few resembled mansions, some with old-fashioned charm and others with drug-dealer-done-well-but-a-few-years-from jail stamped all over them.

'I like this one.' He pressed on a gorgeous cottage, painted white with thick green spirally plants growing around the front door. As he scrolled through the country kitchen, living room with original fireplace and football pitch of a backyard, I looked at the address.

'That's in Alderley Edge,' I said. Now I'm not one of those scousers who can't leave the country, I mean city, but this was a bit too far for me. 'How can we afford a mortgage like that?' When in doubt use debt, but I did think of all my credit cards and the chunky loans I'd had over the years. My credit score was shocking.

'I have the money,' he said, 'and there's loads of reasons we should move there. Our Karen lives there for a start.'

'Then we'd have to see her every day,' I muttered.

'She's like a sister. You could at least make an effort to get on with her,' Daniel said. 'She's always been there for me.'

'Alright, but I find it hard to get on with her myself that's all.'

He didn't answer but instead leaned over me slowly, looking right into my eyes. I couldn't face another torrent of abuse or an argument. He opened his mouth to speak, his lips curled up and his brow creased. I braced myself.

'What the fuck's happened to your eyebrows?' he said.

CHAPTER TWELVE

NO ONE: 8.00 Saturday 30th August 2014

It was pitch black.

Something scratched at her skin, and in a panic she fell on her side and was exposed to a cold, hard surface.

The fogginess started to clear; any sense of dreaming faded, and for a moment, the fear was paralysing. It took every inch of strength to start moving again in a slow crawl, hand patting every inch of flooring until it came to a wall. Pressing against it, she eased herself up and continued around the room, trembling with each step. It was as though he was still in there, waiting in the corners for her to reach him in the darkness. Sometimes she thought his breath was against the back of her neck, his fingers brushing against her bare arms. Eventually her hand felt its way around a light and the room snapped into view.

It blasted with whiteness. The scratchy brown blanket was heaped in the middle like a body was still under it. But it was only the folds of the material.

The surroundings seemed to get smaller the more she looked at them. It was cold but a heat ripped through her body. She found herself screaming.

With a strength she couldn't account for, Gina battered the door until her wrists went limp. She shouted for everyone she knew, even him. But no one came.

CHAPTER THIRTEEN

Fridge ~ a unit consisting of a separate refrigerator and freezer

~ My fridge-freezer insides are my own fault

March 2014

'I've bought you a present.'

That's how it started. Fifteen minutes later, the conversation had turned.

'Why would I want to live with a frigid bitch?'

The black bed sheets crackled under my skin. Daniel had painted all the walls plum, which I'd liked at first, but the room had gradually become smaller, darker and more and more sinister every time I was in it. It was like being in a giant bruise which was closing in, matching the one creeping up my thigh from where Daniel had pressed too hard.

'You could at least try.' The words came out of the side of his mouth, an angry angle of letters from his lips. 'I'm trying to sort things out here, add a bit of excitement back in and you lie there.'

I'd been trying to ignore this.

I'd read *Fifty Shades of Grey* three times, all of them, and kept passages marked for emergencies. Getting drunk was another option. So was having a bath.

But the last time, the bath idea hadn't worked. His lips swept over my face as I lay on the bathroom floor on a towel, my hair slightly damp, the bubbles still on the surface tipping over the edge of the bath. The water and heat helped but by the time we'd got to the bedroom, I was tight again, all wound up like a coil of disappointment.

'Thought you'd have got better at it by now,' he muttered, climbing off me. His comments about the first time we'd done it were always the worst part.

Since I'd put a stop to the love bites and public foreplay, Daniel had become more demanding in the bedroom itself.

This present, a bag of 'toys', was spilled across the room. A scarily large pink vibrator rolled across the wooden floor, landing near some kind of leather gag. My throat got tight looking at it. A nurse's outfit was lounging by the door. I've never got the nurse's thing. How can sick be sexy?

There were other outfits too, worst of all a French Maid's one. I could hardly explain why I wasn't rushing to put it on again.

As my ex, Jonathan, was more interested in rolling a joint than rolling my knickers off for most of our relationship, I'd taken the initiative. I went to Ann Summers and bought a maid's outfit, got a tight-fitting bra and dispensed with knickers. It was a surprise for his birthday.

Turns out Jonathan decided what we really needed was all our friends around for his birthday. That was a surprise to me, particularly when they all walked in to find me lying in the new gear on the shitty beige rug we had in the flat, with a bottle of chocolate body paint in one hand and a duster in the other. It was true, we did have a better time in a group than together, but I wasn't planning an orgy. It took me a long time to get over that night.

'I'm sorry.' Daniel leaned across and pressed his face close to mine. 'We don't have to use any of this stuff if you're not comfortable. I worry.'

'Worry about what?'

'That you don't fancy me anymore, that you've gone off me already 'cos you seem a bit cold-'

I stopped him with a kiss. But what I got in return were his hands going for every inch of me. I had a banging headache and a splintering pattern of fish up my spine.

He pushed me down onto the bed. His weight was on me and trapping all the breath I had in my body. His fingers dug into

70

my arm, pressing against my bones. He wasn't stopping. I clawed at him. It hurt with each thrust.

Finally, it was over.

'Daniel, what the fuck!'

'I thought you were playing games with me.' He laid back, hands above his head, his post-sex pose.

Everything ached.

He leapt off the bed and headed for the shower.

CHAPTER FOURTEEN

ACCUSATIONS: 9.15 Saturday 30th August 2014

'I'm here to see Karen.' The box thing at the entrance to the house was designed like a McDonald's drive-through.

'Nails?' The tinny voice asked.

'Erm…yeah?'

The huge gates started to open and Charley squeezed in when the gap was big enough. The driveway was ridiculous, lined with about a million carefully circular cut trees and with gravel like cat litter. As she walked, Charley had the chance to think about the F definition. It didn't tell her much but it was different from the others. Gina had scribbled something on the back, two words 'rats' and 'tails'. Charley had no idea what it meant.

Eventually she reached the door and pulled at the knob, calling the owner one at the same time.

Karen threw it open wearing a Charlie-Chaplin style hat, a metallic blue studded jumper and black leggings. Her blond hair was twisted into pin curls under the hat.

'What do you want?' Her lips puckered into a pout. 'I thought this was me nine thirty with Jemma?'

'I'm looking for Gina.'

If Daniel told Karen everything then she would know something. And if Jennifer, her best friend, couldn't provide answers, then maybe Gina's best enemy would.

'Why would I know where she is, love?' she asked, drawing out every word. Charley wanted to pop a pin into the Botox and watch her mouth sink into her gums.

'I thought you might know where Daniel is.'

'He'll be working or something.' Her hand was pressed against the door, gradually closing it.

73

'Have you spoken to him then?' Charley resisted the urge to put her foot in the door.

'Not being funny or nothing, but what does that have to do with your sister?'

'I thought they might have got back together and gone away for the weekend-'

Karen's laugh was like a cackle. 'He wouldn't get back with her, not a chance in hell.'

'You don't know that.'

'You need to chill out, doll. You and Gina aren't even speaking are you?'

Charley's insides clenched up at this.

Karen added a lip-curling leer. 'I mean, 'cos you never approved of our Danny did you?'

Charley wasn't sure how much she knew about that night or if this was a game. 'I'm trying to find Gina. She's not answering her phone and I need to speak to her,' she said before adding, 'about family stuff.'

'I'm up to me eyes hearing about your family stuff.'

Charley gritted her teeth. Karen came from the rough estate section of where they had grown up. Her parents were still in the type of roads where the pavements were painted red like a 'welcome to hell warning'. Her family had plenty of issues themselves.

'I tried to be friends with her but she treated our Danny like shit,' Karen said playing with her nails.

'Where is he really this weekend?'

'Probably working, like I said. You want to be asking your sister some questions!'

'I would if I could find her!'

'Like why she chose that meff Anthony over our Danny.'

'There's nothing going on between Gina and Anthony.'

'All right then, love, whatever you say, but when you do find the little cow, ask her why she was sneaking Anthony into your old house when our Danny was dropping her stuff off.'

'We've grown up with Anthony-' Charley began, although she didn't know about that.

'Fuck off now, yer doing my head in.'

A girl with fake red hair was walking up the driveway.

'Jemma, hurry up and get in, this crank was leaving!' Karen shouted, giving Charley the once over like it was the first time she'd noticed her properly. 'Pity you weren't coming for a hair appointment love. Yer look like yer sister with those rat's tails.'

The girl was right next to them now. Charley recognised her from various parties. She raised her weirdly thick eyebrows and looked like she was going to say something, until Karen pulled her in and slammed the door in Charley's face.

* * * * *

When Charley got out of the gates, she called Anthony. No answer. It was probably all lies anyway. Daniel accused Gina of being with Anthony at least once a week. She ran to the car and locked the door. She took the definitions out of her bag and looked at F again. Karen had helped her piece something together without realising it.

When Charley got back to the family home and searched through the boxes, she found the next set of definitions, hidden in the 'rats' tails' of Gina's hair extensions.

CHAPTER FIFTEEN

Guilty ~ responsible for a specified wrongdoing

~ Everyone has something to feel guilty about or something to hide - including me

~ Who started the fight, Bob or Ken?

~ Daniel would never cheat on me like that - would he?

~ What did his mum do to make her guilty like Bob?

~ Daniel only told Karen the truth - I should feel guilty over that last night with Mum.

March 2014

'Well this is quite a spread.'

I looked down at the juicy melon and pineapple, sausage rolls, pork pies, samosas, bhajis and sandwiches bursting with egg cress or ham.

It was better than watching Daniel's aunties parading around the garden and pouncing on any of Karen's footballer boyfriend's teammates. Aunty Eileen was currently cornering one of them using her boobs.

'Doll, sort yourself out. Who's said 'spread' since the Coronation abar sixty years ago?' Karen picked up a carrot and crunched it next to my ear. She was ignoring the lecherous women, probably glad that her mum wasn't one of them for a change.

I was stuck with her. She hadn't invited any of my friends to this party. Daniel had already been claimed by his mates and they were Jäger-shotting. The whooping and roaring of too many boys over one bottle was already getting to my ears.

I turned back to the table. Dessert consisted of cupcakes made by Lydia, because apparently she was the best in the business at 'Sweet Nothings', as she called her little venture. It seemed like everyone who had a business page on Facebook thought they were an entrepreneur these days, and everyone was making bloody cupcakes.

Moving away from the 'spread', I saw Lydia walking down the stairs sniffing in a lady-like way. As she moved, her long legs poked out of the slits in her black sequinned dress. Raising her eyebrows by way of saying hello, she headed over to the rest of the Tropical Fish who were Maxi-dressed in a corner of the party.

At least my phone was making me feel wanted. I had another text from Jennifer, 'we never see you anymore', followed by several sad faces and some harsher ones from Jo - 'binned us off then?' followed by angry monkey faces.

A sharp nudge distracted me. 'Your Dan has some lovely looking mates aye.' One of the aunties, I think it was Vera, had broken off from the group to fill up on some food. Her platinum blonde hair clashed with her orange face.

'They're José's friends,' I replied.

'Footballers?' she said with a new brightness as she looked out into the garden. 'It's all fresh meat.' I couldn't tell if she meant the chicken drumstick in her hand, or one of the players posing with his thumbs in his jeans and trying to avoid the older women who had started to circle him like piranhas. 'Oh there's our Tanya, didn't think she was showing her face today.'

Karen stiffened next to me and I turned to see what she was looking at. A large man (in the stocky way, not fat) with a bald head which bounced sunlight, stormed across the garden as though the grass had personally offended him. He was followed by a small, slight woman with a perma-tan and a perma-smile. I recognised her as Daniel's Aunty, Karen's mum. But I hadn't seen the man before. The amorous aunties lost interest in their prey and headed over to welcome the new guests.

'Oh fuck,' Karen muttered as they headed straight for us. Across the garden, Daniel put down his drink and headed over. Karen had an even faker smile than usual on her face.

'Alright, darling,' the man said, his angry features softening for a moment. Karen's mum tottered around and kissed her on the cheek.

'Dad!' Her voice broke slightly. 'Didn't think parties were your thing like?'

'You know I love a good few bevies, and I haven't seen you for a bit have I?' He looked around.

'Listen, Dad, he isn't here yet but you can't cause any trouble.' Karen was unusually subdued. She even sounded less Scouse.

'I was good at the funeral and I'll be good today,' he replied before turning to me, and who is this lovely lady?'

'Gina, Daniel's fiancé.'

'I'm Ken, Karen's dad. He's a good one is our Dan, not like his dad,' he said and then thankfully turned away from me, not even bothering to introduce his wife who teetered nervously on her heels nearby. 'Now, where's the drinks?'

They walked off, pausing to greet Daniel before carrying on into the kitchen.

'Why the fuck is he here?' Daniel hissed at Karen when he reached us.

'He won't cause any trouble,' she said, unconvincingly.

'Me dad will be here any minute.'

'What's going on?' I finally asked. Neither of them answered me because at that moment we were distracted by someone else entering the party.

'Your guest list is shocking, cuz,' Daniel said, taking a large swig of beer as Anthony walked towards us.

He was wearing a smart t-shirt that folded around his body in all the right places. I pulled the loose cardigan across my stomach as I felt my jeans dig into the over-flesh around my stomach. I was a lot more toned when I was single, too.

'Lydia wanted me to invite him.' Karen snapped back into party mode as she waved at Anthony and gave me a pointed glance.

'What's this party for anyway?'

'Erm, it's like a thing for you two, your engagement, the happy couple, D and G!' Karen raised a glass half-heartedly.

'Congratulations.' A sarcastic addition came from Lydia, who sauntered over to Anthony and gave him a huge hug.

'Want to come and do some shots with us?' Daniel said, grabbing my hand and already pulling me towards his pile of friends, including Matthew. Anthony and Lydia were deep in conversation.

* * * * *

After a few 'bombs' with the boys, I went to get a glass of water from the kitchen to wash away the sickly sweet taste of Red Bull and Jäger. Anthony was pouring himself a drink.

'Why are you here?' The dizziness of the shots gave me courage.

'Karen invited me.'

'Come to see Lydia have you?'

'Leave it, Gina.'

'Why? You're going out with a gangster's moll.'

'We're not going out.'

'Shagging, sleeping with, whatever.' The words were like knives even though I was saying them myself.

'I came to keep an eye on you actually. I can't ignore Lydia if she talks to me, can I?'

80

'I'm fine.'

'You didn't sound fine on the phone last week.'

'I wanted you to apologise for being rude to my fiancé.'

'I'm surprised he isn't here now, watching you talk to me.' His eyes glowed with anger.

'What are you two up to?' We both jumped at the sound of a voice at the door. It was Matthew. 'What's this then? Bored of me bro already then? Can't blame yer.' But he stared at Anthony with a hard look that I'd seen in Daniel. It meant trouble. 'She's engaged yanno mate.'

'Leave it, Matty.' Bob was in the doorway. He stepped down into the kitchen and blocked the path between Matthew and Anthony.

'You know Anthony, Bob. He's my neighbour and an old family friend,' I said. 'Karen invited him because he's been meeting her friend Lydia.'

'Ah I remember. Nice to see you again, lad. My memory isn't what it used to be.' His demeanour changed slightly and he held out a gristly-skinned hand.

'Yeah but look at her, dad, flirting away and they're not even married yet,' Matthew protested, trying to edge around Bob.

'Go and enjoy the party, son.' Bob shoved him towards the door.

'Didn't think you'd give a shit about something like this. Should have known not to bother telling yer.' I heard Matthew say as he left. Bob smiled at us apologetically and followed him.

'Don't give me a hard time, Ant. It's my life and I'm happy.' I ran out of the kitchen before he could say anything else.

Matthew was outside the door. 'I don't like people who cheat.' His hands were shaking slightly around the can of lager. 'Remember that.'

A commotion from the middle of the garden distracted him. Fairy lights tumbled down and wrapped themselves around Ken and Bob, who were throwing punches at each other.

Bob drew himself up in an almost professional move, shaking off the lights as he hit Ken square in the face so that he fell back. I expected Ken to be knocked out cold. The power in Bob was something I hadn't expected, like the rage in his face. But Ken got back up.

'No one messes with my family.' Ken moved back towards him, his nose exploding with blood. Several of Daniel's friends were on him now and trying to hold the two men back. The footballers and José watched from the sidelines, a couple of them backing away towards the edge of the garden where there was a quick escape to the driveway.

Daniel said something to Bob, who was then led off towards the front of the house, with John, Daniel's work friend pulling out his car keys as they walked.

Ken headed towards us, blood like speckles of tomato sauce on his face and shirt. 'Sorry, Karen love, we're leaving.'

She scuttled after them.

'Crazy family, yes?' José was beside me. He was a good-looking typical footballer, all dark and muscled but with a much smaller frame than it looks like he has on the telly. He was quiet too, preferring to stay in the background.

'Karen always say, don't wind up my dad, don't wind up Bob or…' he pretended to slit his throat.' I tried to fake laugh at this but José wasn't smiling. He walked away and I went to find Daniel. He was leaning against the wall at the side of the house, away from the party, on his own.

'You ok?'

'My dad feels guilty enough. He doesn't need this shit.' He blew out a puff of smoke.

'Guilty about what?'

'You never told her about Dad?' Matthew was standing in the shadows too. 'So you didn't know he cheated on Mum for years, even when she was ill? And that your fiancé seems to think it's ok.'

'Fuck off, Matty, you know I don't.' Daniel's fists were clenched.

'As if you'd fucking dare.' Matthew looked down at Daniel's fists and laughed before walking away.

'I don't agree with what he did at all, Gina. You know I would never cheat on you, but I only have one parent left, you know what that's like?' He took another drag. 'I've always stuck up for him and Matty's always stuck up for Mum.'

'Stuck up for your mum over what?'

'Let's talk about that another time.'

I sat down next to him. My dad was no angel either. He hadn't cheated on Mum but he'd lied to her and left us in loads of debt. I wasn't in the mood for a 'who's got the worst dad' competition, though. I needed a drink and Daniel did too. I went to get some as he lit up another ciggy.

Cigarettes and hairspray permeated the air. There was a lot of sniffing. I realised one of Karen's balconies was above me.

'Have a bit here so they don't know we have anything extra,' Lydia said. I heard Karen snorting.

'I still don't like her,' Lydia said.

'She's a bad meff, like, but our Danny thinks he's proper in love,' Karen replied.

'Anthony needs to give his head a wobble over her.'

'What do you mean?'

'He bangs on about her like she's proper amazing.'

'Anthony is a muppet though. Is anything going on between youse?

'Me 'ead's cabbaged with him to be honest,' Lydia sighed.

'I think he's only bothering with Gina cos she pure guilts him and makes him feel dead sorry for her.'

'Abar what?' Lydia said.

'Don't tell anyone I told you this ever, swear down,' Karen replied, 'Danny said that she had something to do with her Mum dying.'

'Oh my God, really, what did she do - assisted suicide?' Lydia was tripping over her question in excitement. 'Couldn't she go to jail for that, like?'

'Well, did you know about her sister…' They were enjoying the conversation. I wobbled on my heels, leaned against the door and felt sick beyond my stomach.

'What does Daniel think?' I heard Lydia say. 'Did he say it was assisted suicide?'

'He told me she feels guilty about the night her mum died. But why would you feel guilty if you didn't do anything wrong?'

CHAPTER SIXTEEN

TIME: 9.45am Saturday 30th August 2014

The hours passed slowly.

Gina thought about everything, over and over, letting her mind tick back through her life to see what she could have done to deserve this. Of course she knew.

She'd known for over eight years that one day something would happen and Karma would punish her. She'd let herself slide down the cold wall next to the door, at first nursing her sore wrists and knuckles from the stupid attempt to escape and then letting them fall loosely into her lap.

There was silence all around her. Even his footsteps would have been welcome, a chance to escape from her bad thoughts.

In the hours spent with no way out of this room, she'd found that the body couldn't sustain long-term panic. Instead it came over her in waves. At times it took her breath, hammered at her heart and battered her stomach. But in the slower sections of these waves, when the body calmed down, came the lowest points of her life.

Charley never forgave herself for not going into the hospice that night. Gina never forgave herself for going in.

A positive wave overtook her unexpectedly when she thought about Charley, because she'd remembered something; the scraps of thoughts she'd written down and in some weird kind of shame, had hidden in places with clues only Charley would understand. She might find them. There might be something she could use.

Her breath started to quicken again in a mad kind of elation at some hope of getting out. Gina might have written the clues out so that only she would understand them, but a fraction of herself was in her sister. She would get it. And despite the waves that continued, the horror of what she'd done to Charley, she knew her sister would realise something was wrong. This thought relaxed her until the surroundings became unfocussed and the bright light diminished and she was back in her dreams again.

Despite everything, she didn't want to die.

CHAPTER SEVENTEEN

A Hug ~ a tight clasp or embrace

~ an ornament that looks like a piece of shit >>shit-hug

~ the type that kills, a love you to death. >>death-hug

~never forgive myself

November 2006

'That ornament looks like a piece of shit.'

Mum laughed but it hurt her. I could tell. The ornament, a get-well gift from a friend, sat on the hospital bedside table, a brown goblin-type thing that someone had stuck the word 'hug' under and framed in a small cardboard gift box. As though you could stick hug on anything to hand and sell it. A shit-hug. The ward would have provided other marketing inspirations that day, of dried-up vomit on the sheets of the next bed, blood-phlegm in a paper bucket opposite us or malignant tumours hidden in the bodies of the patients.

The smokers-with-the-drips came back inside, slippered feet lugging their failing bodies and trailing medical equipment. They brought the smoke from outside back in with them. I could almost taste it, feel those last desperate 'fuck it' drags on my tongue. All the women smokers looked the same to me; thin or fat, but they were all raspy and craggy in some form. There was one with shoulder length, fudge-coloured hair in a hospital bed-head style. I can't remember her name. She's certainly dead now. None expected to live. Even when surrounded by the dying I was still class-conscious.

The nurses walked the ward, 'angels' with stern faces. They brought the teatime trolleys behind the smokers. We slipped in and out all the time, us relatives of the dying. The nurses rattled the plates and one brought over a mass of Spaghetti Bolognese that looked and smelt as though it had suffered during the cooking. She put it onto the tray which stretched across the bed in front of where Mum lay and cleared away a dirty cup. Another nurse moved to the side of one of the end beds and pulled the blinds closed. The view of the city of Liverpool, that glimpse of Paddy's wigwam, disappeared behind white blinds. This daily routine was like a reverse take on the old game show Bullseye, when they reel the main prize out to the losers and then take it away again. Patients, there's a life out there you could have had, now watch it leave.

'Yer alright, Marie.' The smokers said as they moved back to their beds. Mum nodded. I don't know if she was jealous that they could still walk. Her legs were the size of balloons. So was her stomach.

'You look pregnant.'

Why did I say that?

She smiled and said. 'I wish I was.'

Sometimes I can't even think about it.

I was in hospital ten years before what happened to Mum. I must have been about seven, and I should have learned something from what she said and did, always comforting and reassuring me. Mum had nursed me through a two-week stay, a stint in a wheelchair and a long course of antibiotics that turned my teeth yellow like the smokers.' When it was her turn in a hospital bed, I made accidental insults, like the shit-hug comment or over-polite conversation.

'You got your place in the hospice then?'

'Yes. I've got a place in the hospice.'

* * * * *

I didn't get the bus the night it happened. Dad drove. He was back then, you see. It was really weird what happened. One minute he was a distant dad who we saw reluctantly every so often and received obligatory cards from since he'd left us as kids. But then Aunty Lesley rang him when Mum got really ill and he came back, just like that. She wasn't our real aunty, but with us not having any she was happy to step in. Over the years, she stepped right back out again. It didn't help that her and Uncle Malcolm moved down south. I always think she could have made more of an effort to keep in touch though, especially with what happened to Charley.

Mum and Dad didn't get back together or have any sort of Hollywood ending but I know Mum appreciated the help. And she made him promise to look after us, make up for leaving us with nothing all those years before.

* * * * *

That night, when Dad drove to the hospice, there was no rain, no melodramatic weather. It was cold. He observed every traffic light rule, every roundabout pause, although the roads were quiet. We pulled into the car park and Dad parked between the lines. I ran ahead, across the car park. Everything except me went into slow motion. The wind was cold and whipped against my cheek but there was fire beneath my feet. I heard a few more cars parking up and somebody shouted, 'Gina.' I didn't stop.

I don't know what I expected, but it wasn't what I saw. Mum was drowning. She struggled to breathe. Her head was moving from side to side as she lay in the bed. Her eyes were closed.

Nobody knew what to do. Dad must have come in behind me. I remember him standing there in his Liverpool shirt as I turned around. *You'll never walk alone.* It's been eight years but he still brings up that day with guilt in his more honest phone calls, or on the rare times we see each other face to face, which have been less frequent since the 'Charley Times' ended.

'She insisted I went,' he says, 'I should have spent all day and night with her. But she insisted I went.' It was the match. Mum had told him to go, said we all needed a break and to come back the next morning. But at that moment, when more people came into the room, we all felt that we shouldn't have left. Mum's best friend Anna Harrison moved me forward with a gentle nudge, towards the bed. In the whitewash of faces behind, I saw Dad start to take steps forward too, letting

89

me lead. Anna and her husband Tim stepped back. The room smelled of the lilies crawling out over the vase on the table. I remembered being told that the last thing to go is the hearing.

Anna Harrison is dead too. She spent six months after Mum died feeding us home-cooked food, spaghetti bolognaise, hearty stews. Then she turned yellow and died of liver cancer. It was a wonder anyone ever dared to try and feed us. Or that we wanted to carry on eating.

That night with Mum seems like a series of badly edited film scenes. My memory switches from being inside the hospice to the car park, outside, without warning.

The limousine hadn't been able to fit into the hospice one. The driver was waiting. A few people were leaving the pub, eyes taking us in with drunken confusion. A girl in a miniskirt fell on the pavement. A pink thong. Taxis hailed. Smells of beer and burgers, grilled gammon, chunky chips, cheap two-for-one meals.

Charley arrived in the limousine, picked up from a neighbour's with a young, startled face. Aunty Lesley and Uncle Malcolm always travelled in one for their scaffolding company's annual charity dinner.

Charley, in her pyjamas and a heavy coat, Uncle Malcolm dressed in a full dinner suit. Aunty Lesley wore a glittering dress with matching bag, and a fur coat over her arm. She was shouting at Uncle Malcolm.

'Why did you make me go to that dinner, you shit? We should have been there!'

That fur coat. When I was a child, I thought she had slaughtered a hundred and one Dalmatians for it. She never reassured me, in fact the opposite.

'Where did you get that?' I would ask.

'There was a litter of puppies no one wanted.' She would reply. There was a cruel bastard quality to her and there still is. I was so good when she babysat us.

We sat in the kid's play area for a bit. The three monkeys of grief together. Charley with her hands over her eyes crying;

90

Aunty Lesley with her hands over her mouth in-between being sick, and me, I might as well have had my hands over my ears, not hearing anything properly and understanding little. I asked if we could go in and see Mum. Charley didn't want to. She never forgave herself.

Dad told me that the priest who arrived when we were all gathered in the room had thought Mum was a pensioner. Aunty Lesley hit him with her jewel bag. A piece of glitter went in his eye and the nurses had to come over and help him. And all the time there was a dead body in the bed, surrounded by people dressed for a dinner party, some kids in pyjamas accidentally posing like monkeys, and a priest everyone wanted to kill. At least she'd gone before all that arguing kicked off. I wandered off and thought of what to do next, who to tell about what had happened, what I had done.

There was no Facebook back then and I'd like to think that I wouldn't leave a status. But who knows? Maybe I would have contributed to the countless 'There's a star in heaven shining for new angels' 'RIPs to Mums and Dads, Nans and Granddads'. Bereavement shout-outs.

I would have posted something like that, but not that night. What I wouldn't have done was update everyone on the whole process. One girl, Debbie Matthews, took Facebook through her Granddad's first night in hospital (she checked in at the Royal on every visit). The finale was the uploading of a photo album during the funeral, featuring all the flowers at the grave. Shout-out for my popular dead Granddad.

I was angry with Anthony over something at the time. Those things don't stop. He came home from Oxford the next day though, got a train as soon as he found out despite being a poor student. Gave me a hug. Daniel, later, accused him of using it as an opportunity. Not to his face, only to me.

I did call Jo and Jennifer too. Jennifer texted me a few hours later.

me and me mum have been so upset for you

She never thought about her choice of words, but I was wrong to expect her to. Of course other people still had Mums.

In another memory scene there is me, sitting in an empty room in the hospice, wearing a collection of coats.

I went outside straight after I did what I did and found it was still Saturday night, but in a courtyard in a hospice. It was freezing. There were people sitting on a bench, one of those benches for people who have paid to be remembered. The light from the kid's room reflected off the plating. Matthew Hunter reduced to a gold brass plate on a hospice courtyard bench since 1997. I've been back and sat on the bench.

Two men and a woman stood by that bench. The woman looked exactly the same as one of the hospital smokers. Her face was worn down, with a mouth sunken back and pocket holes for eyes. I couldn't describe colours and things, not now, but she spoke like she was only allowed a limited number of words a day; wheezy, cracked and harsh tones that seemed forced out. It was like being back on the ward. I had to wonder if they manufactured these women like Stepford Wives for council estates.

The craggy woman was in my face.

'Here, love, have a drop of whiskey,' she said then turned to the first man. 'She's still shaking. Give her your coat.' I stood for a moment shivering.

'She's blue. Give her your coat too, Kev. I said now!' she barked to the second man.

'Here, love, have mine, I've got a cardie underneath.' It felt like one of those attempts to get on a Ryanair flight when your baggage is too heavy.

I woke up the next day back at home, with the coats all on the floor by my bed. There must have been some people who left that hospice, tainted by grief but also freezing and furious at giving their coat to me. Even back at home I could smell lilies, as though the stems had crept in through my nostrils in the night and were growing from my stomach, each breath from me a victory for them. The smell of death on a Sunday morning. My hospice hangover.

I'd never taken in the word death before. Once upon a time it had no meaning to me - great aunties and uncles - and then it was personified, became a person I really knew.

Anna Harrison's gentle nudge. That was when I moved forward to Mum and did what I did. I hugged her. Told her nice things that I'd want to hear if I was scared and dying and nobody could do anything about it. I told her she could go.

Either the words or the hug made her colder, stopped her breath, caused her to leave. I claimed the final seconds of life with that hug, stilled her weak but thrashing movements. The scent of bed baths and final cleansings mixed with the lilies in my lungs. Then those last few breaths, against my face. When she finally stopped, I moved with her, placing her head back onto the pillows which had held her up for the eight days of her hospice stay. My arms fell to their sides. A one-way hug. I took everything. A death-hug. I'd done the final thing that made her go.

I stepped back onto the shit-hug which had survived the journey from hospital to hospice, and it shattered across the carpet next to Mum's rosary beads.

Eight years later and the heaviness - that ball and chain from throat to stomach which started with the hug - was with me again.

I saw someone die from cancer sitting in a pub on Coronation Street once, like it was nothing. In reality, it takes time to heave out the last signs of life, a gurgling from the lungs building into a sound like a soul being ripped from a body. It can be helped along with a hug, a Love you to death.

I don't know what the word 'Mum' means anymore. I've lived a third of my life without one. I can't have that word. It isn't mine.

I still blame myself.

CHAPTER EIGHTEEN

BAD PATHS: 10.00 Saturday 30th August 2014

Charley had never been friends with her mum.

Gina had, and somehow, inexplicably, she'd been friends with both of them; the one in the middle, linking up the three, until after their Mum was gone. Then it all changed.

Like Gina, Charley had punished herself for years over that night. She'd gone over and over in her head why she'd kicked up such a fuss when 'aunty' Lesley and 'uncle' Malcolm had picked her up from a friend's house, so much so that they'd been late - too late. In the end, all Charley could do was leave that stupid kids' play area and hide out in the gardens, using the only thing she could think of to numb the pain. She was angry at everything: her mum, death, God, but mainly herself. The problem was, until that moment, her fifteen-year-old self had refused to accept their mum would die. Her stupid teenage head told her she had more time, that this was a moment which would pass and everyone, including the doctors, her dad, Gina and all the other adults who thought they knew everything, were all wrong about her mum dying. Charley thought she would have the chance to continue the awkward, rebellious hate-your-parents years like all her friends. But she was, inevitably, as something deep in her mind kept telling her - wrong. After that night, the bad path Charley was already on took worse turns. If she couldn't be good enough, she would be bad enough.

* * * * *

It was Gina who came to find her in the hospice gardens. Gina who took the cigarette out of her hand and said, 'You need to stop this now.'

Charley grabbed it back and took a long drag. This action set up the pattern of how they lived together for the next couple of years, with their dad spending most of his time away on business. Gina turned a blind eye to a lot of things but the same arguments kept coming up and kept getting worse.

The first time it all came to a head was when they accidentally went on the same night out. Charley was seventeen by then, and although she looked much younger, she knew how to get into places like the awful 'Pulse' bar on a wink to the bouncers and some age enhancing make-up. Gina was nineteen. Of course they were both there for different reasons.

Gina caught her by the toilets. 'What are you doing?'

'Working,' Charley replied.

'Don't try and be funny,' Gina replied. She was all dolled up to the nines as usual, tight-fitting dress and stupidly high heels. For once Charley had dressed like that too. It would have been unnerving for both of them, except Charley wasn't in the position to care.

'Better than what you're doing,' she said. 'Slag.'

Gina looked like she'd been slapped in the face. Only minutes earlier, when Charley was dealing with a 'customer', she'd caught a glance of Gina 'club-necking' with a random boy.

'I've had enough,' Gina said. 'I'm calling the police.'

'Don't you fucking dare!' For once Charley didn't think she was bluffing. It was the look on Gina's face, tired and desperate, not just the usual disappointment.

'I swear, I'll tell them everything. I know what you've been doing, what you've got in your pocket.' She was already stumbling off in her heels.

Charley followed her. 'You wouldn't.'

Gina ignored her. They got outside and she put her hand out for a taxi. As it stopped and Gina opened the door, Charley launched at her and they both crashed down onto the floor.

Later in A&E, with Gina waiting to have her wrist examined and Charley trying to stem a nose bleed, the guilt set in.

'I'm sorry. I'll stop,' she said, turning to Gina. But she didn't. She got better at hiding it. Gina never told the police that time. Maybe it would have been better if she had. Neither of them told their dad.

His last attempt at helping involved moving Gina's stuff into that dick Jonathan's flat and dropping Charley off at university before he moved to Hong Kong. The family home was rented out.

'So, you two will be alright then?' he'd said, running a hand through his thick grey hair. 'You're both past eighteen now so I'm kind of done here aren't I? He tried to pass that off as a joke and smiled.

'Yeah,' Charley replied because it was easier. But she didn't smile back.

* * * * *

The argument over the ring happened much later. Charley came back from university and was about to move in with Callum. She needed money. Unfortunately, Gina found out before she'd had the chance to pack and leave.

Gina flew at her, pulling at Charley's hair and saying over and over. 'You bitch, you selfish bitch!'

'This time I'm not covering for you.' She added before getting up and walking out of the room. It was the last time Charley would see her for a couple of years, apart from outside the pawnshop when Gina forced her to look straight at their mum's ring, gleaming with guilt.

By the time their dad got involved again, Charley had fled to an unknown address.

* * * * *

He answered after only a few rings.

'I might have something,' she said. 'Will you look into the backgrounds of Bob Ryan and Ken Henderson?'

'Why?' Officer Field replied.

'Bob is Daniel's dad and Ken is his uncle,' Charley said. 'Gina wrote something about them being involved in a fight. I also know that Daniel's family is a bit dodgy.'

'So you found more then?' he said and then paused. 'Is there anything else in the definitions that implicates any others?'

97

'Daniel and his brother,' Charley said, 'but nothing too specific.'

'I'll look into it for you. Remember you're not to approach these men yourself.'

'Ok.'

After she got off the phone, she wrote out a list of people to question and then tried to ring Anthony again. There was no answer. That was when something clicked.

She went quickly to their mum's old room. Inside the top drawer, where they still stored an eclectic mix of memories of her, was the shit-hug replica. At the time she hadn't understood why Gina wanted to buy it. They were out shopping and she caught sight of it and insisted on buying the ugly, little thing.

'Didn't someone buy Mum one of those?' Charley remembered saying but Gina had gone all closed off and focused and bought it without answering. So Charley knew what it meant when Gina had scribbled shit-hug on the back of $\mathcal{H}$. The brown 'ornament' was still attached to its box and as Charley pulled the cardboard up from the bottom, the definitions fell out. There were five in total, taking her to $\mathcal{M}$.

* * * * *

A door slammed outside. Still clutching the definitions, Charley went to the window. Anthony, dressed in jeans and a fitted white t-shirt, was hurrying down his path clutching a plastic bag and a bottle of water. With the houses being in such close proximity, she could see his face. He was angry as he threw the bag into the back of the car, got in and raced away. He was normally a really careful driver so she knew he was avoiding her. Not that it mattered - she had enough to do first before going and questioning him again.

She would have to get this right. It wouldn't help Gina if she went down the wrong path by asking the wrong person.

CHAPTER NINETEEN

Irreplaceable - Impossible to replace

~ Coffee- accident? The wall and my hand aren't sure.

~ Jo is a liar anyway and wound him up - wouldn't call a girl the c word.

~ Friends aren't irreplaceable.

March 2014

'I'm really sorry.' Daniel met me in the hall and enveloped me in a hug. His unwashed work smell was all over me. I struggled out of his strong grip.

'I'm on my way out,' I said, pushing past him towards the front door while trying to balance on my heels. He grabbed my hand.

'Gina, for the hundredth time, I didn't say to Karen that you'd done anything wrong.'

'But you must think I did do something wrong if Karen got that impression?'

'I told her you didn't like talking about the night your mum died because you felt guilty,' he replied, looking me straight in the eye. 'I didn't want to go into the details, because I don't know the details Gina. You never talk about it.'

'Do you think I would help my own Mum die?'

'No, I don't,' he said, firmly. 'But I also know that there are things you need to face up to about that night and I don't know why you won't talk to me.'

I carried on past him.

'We can't leave it like this. Where are you going?' He pulled me back towards him.

'Out with Jennifer and Jo.'

'I need to know we're ok first before you go,' he pleaded, with a tight hold still on my arm.

'I need some time on my own. It's fine, honestly,' I lied.

He stared at me for a bit, but then finally he let me go as I heard the grunt of a taxi engine outside.

* * * * *

The bar was busy. The whole place was tinged with blue, and a strobe light bounced out across the dancefloor. It was also packed to the rafters with Tropical Fish. Orange skin, big hair, dangerously lengthened and expertly painted nails, carefully blended brows and bright eye make-up.

Jo and Jennifer were standing near the bar. Jennifer's rapidly growing bump was moulded by a long black dress. Jo had on some hot pants and a t-shirt. Daniel would have said she looked 'slaggish'.

'Here she is finally. Hello stranger,' Jo said pouting her red lips. Blonde and flimsy looking, Jo had one of those rosebud mouths you read about in Jane Austen. She used to love fake tan until she saw how her natural paleness could work. She didn't suit red lipstick though.

Jen scooted around for a hug. 'You got your eyebrows done!' she exclaimed. 'I've wanted a scouse brow for ages!' Her purple-red hair looked very punkish in the lights of the bar. She'd switched from sunbed to bottle tan since getting pregnant and was forever getting 'little top ups' done professionally. Her eyes were painted in a smoky style to stop them sinking into their dark brown sludginess caused by lack of sleep from sitting up worrying where Mark was. With the combination of heavy make-up and liberally sprayed perfume. She smelt like a pick and mix, all melting sweetness.

'It was a bit of an accident but I've got used to them,' I said, as Jo raised her own normal, straight, thin brows at me.

'I was out with me mum the other night,' Jennifer said, 'we went for a few drinks and a curry. Well, she did like, I had one rose with lemo, and I said to her that I wanted me

100

eyebrows done like that. Everyone in the restaurant we were in had them.'

The fish took a few nips at my stomach lining. I always felt like that when people mentioned doing things with their mums so casually. It happened a lot but it didn't seem to get any easier. I couldn't imagine I would ever find a replacement for that type of mother-daughter friendship, even though me and Charley were closer these days.

'I asked our Charley to come out tonight,' I said, 'but I don't think she's up to it yet.' This was in fact a total lie, as the real reason I suspected she said no was because she couldn't stand Jen and Jo. However, mentioning her was all part of my process of 'integrating her back into society'.

They both went quiet for a minute until Jen piped up: "I was always surprised when your Charley turned out how she did. She was always dead posh and that, getting into a private school for her A-Levels and going to Uni and all that."

I couldn't think what to say to that. My sister's attempt at pulling off a double life ended as quickly as it did badly.

'Drinks!' Jo shouted over the music, which had picked up in volume. She ordered a round, and then another and then another. This suited me fine. I could feel my shoulders relax, my body loosen up, the fish get weaker and my brain get mushier.

'Anyway, we both wanted to talk to you about something,' Jo slurred slightly, not a good sign. She was prone to vodka rage and with each passing drink, seemed closer to unleashing it. 'Your hen do.'

'Nothing's been planned yet,' I said, taking another sip of my blue cocktail.

'Karen seems to think differently,' Jo replied, taking out her phone and searching through it. 'Here,' she thrust the screen in my face. *Karen Henderson: Can't wait 4 11/8 to party wit my girls for Ginas hen – wer guna av a ball xxxx*

It was a private group that I hadn't been invited to, so I hadn't seen any of the details.

'Karen told me Daniel was paying for me as a surprise but no one had asked me if it was ok. I thought it was all ideas,' I said, being completely honest. Jo looked sceptical.

'Mark would never think of surprising me like that,' Jen said glumly, 'but I'm not sure I can fly in my third trimester. Did you tell Karen that?'

'I didn't know the plans had gone so far.'

'This is another example of Daniel controlling you,' Jo said.

'What do you mean by that?'

'We never see you,' Jo said.

'We hardly see you,' Jen added more kindly.

'You never see your family anymore either, or Anthony,' Jo continued. 'I know it's nowhere near the same as having a mum, Gina, but in a small way getting along with Charley and having Anthony is always how you've got by, helping each other and that. It's important to keep in touch with people you've grown up with and your family. Daniel is stopping all this and you're letting him.'

I was furious. This was a rehearsed speech.

'Daniel is not stopping anything,' I said, 'He is the best thing in my life.'

My stomach turned thinking of the argument we'd had.

'The best thing in your life has come to collect you,' Jo said sarcastically and pointed towards the doors. There he was in a light blue striped shirt, his hair swept to one side.

'Can't he let you out on your own?' Jennifer sounded stunned. 'How does he know you're here?'

Probably because I checked us in on facey,' Jo said and stormed towards him. She whispered something in his ear when she reached him. His face changed quickly, creased up into anger and he bent down to whisper something back to her. She stumbled back, her face horrified. Daniel continued walking towards us.

'I wanted to say sorry again.' He took my hand gently. 'You can carry on having a night out with your mates, of course, but I had to let you know I was sorry.'

'It's ok,' I said. 'I want to go home anyway.'

Jo was back then, tugging at my arm drunkenly. 'Gina, he called me a cunt.'

'Stop trying to cause trouble, Jo,' Daniel said. 'I asked you to get out of my way and stop f-ing and blinding down my ear.'

'Gina, are you going to believe that?' Jo shouted, sloshing pink cocktail all over us.

I had my two friends on one side and my fiancé on the other. My two friends who never accepted it when I had a boyfriend because their love lives were always so fucked up. Jennifer got treated like crap by Mark which we were all supposed to ignore because it was 'what he's like' while Jo's constant sleeping around had to be treated as funny instead of pathetic.

'You're both jealous. You can't get your fella to marry you and you can't even get a fella.'

They both looked at me like I'd punched them in the face. I regretted the words straightaway, but they gave me a chance to leave, with Daniel.

When we got in I pulled off my coat and went to make some coffee. I hadn't realised Daniel had been drinking too, but his kisses tasted of stale alcohol as I joined him on the sofa. There was a can of lager at his feet.

'Don't you think we should go to bed?' I yawned and stretched a hand across to lightly touch his shoulder. 'I've made you a coffee.' I indicated towards the steaming hot cup on the table.

'Don't tell me what to do.' His eyes were cold slits.

'Daniel, I think we both need to sober up,' I said, reaching for him again, determined to get him past the anger.

The noise took me by surprise; the smash against the wall, the wet splashes on my hands. I looked at the pieces of the cup on the floor, and then my hand started to turn into pink patches.

He looked up from the pieces scattered on the carpet. The colour drained from his face

'I didn't mean it. I didn't aim it at you…' He disappeared out of the room and came back with a wet tea towel. Still swaying slightly but with an obvious effort to be sober, he applied gentle dabs on my hand, guided me to the sink and ran the cold water from the tap, placing my hand under it. I couldn't speak, couldn't move.

'Can you please say something? I know I'm a piece of shit that doesn't deserve you, doesn't even deserve a mum.' He was crying, leaning against my shoulder. I remembered what our Charley was like after mum died, blamed herself but did unforgivable things that I'd now forgiven.

'It's not your fault that your mum died.' I managed to say. I wanted to storm out, scream and shout at him. But I couldn't.

'Isn't it?'

This type of talk, this mad sense of blame, I knew only too well. We stood with arms around each other and then his grip became tighter. The scarf was lifted gently from my neck and thrown to the floor. His tongue found its way to the skin on my neck and teased at the already sore spot. His hands lifted my dress, pulled down my tights and his fingers found their way inside me, quickly, fast, slightly painful. I let myself be lowered to the floor. My hand throbbed but it didn't matter. One of his hands kept mine down, gently, avoiding the burns, while the other pulled at the knickers around my thigh. I knew we should have been talking, sorting this out, that it wasn't normal. But as he took over me, moving expertly in all the right places, and as I gripped at his arms, which I could never fight against even if I wanted to, I could see in his face that I was the reason he was forgetting everything at this moment. And all I could think of was how good it felt. It was fine when it was just the two of us.

CHAPTER TWENTY

FRIENDS AND THREATS: 10.45 SATURDAY 30th August 2014

The view was amazing. In any other circumstance, Charley could have spent the day watching the ships glide up and down the Mersey through this window.

'Sure you don't want a drink?' Jo shouted from the kitchen, which was really an extension of her living room, with a small breakfast bar in-between.

'No, I'm ok.' she called back, trying to stay patient. Jo had insisted on going to get a drink and had spent about five minutes blasting a blender. It had been hard enough getting buzzed in, after repeatedly reassuring Jo that she was alone and no one else was hanging around outside. Jo had never seemed like the paranoid type before, but she'd been jumpy since letting her in. Finally, she came back into the living room.

'I don't have long,' she said, sitting on the edge of the sofa and sipping her fat-free smoothie. 'I was about to head out for a lunchtime jog - bit safer going when the streets are busy.'

Jo's spindly legs didn't look like they could manage more than a mile.

'I wanted to see if you'd heard from Gina again,' Charley asked casually.

'Not since the text last night.' Jo took a gulp of her green drink.

'When was the last time you'd heard from her before then?'

'That party,' Jo said, flicking her thin blonde hair in its ponytail, eyes darting around the room.

A great wave of tiredness came over Charley. She wouldn't have the energy to question everyone like this.

'Jo' she started and then took a deep breath, 'I don't think Gina has gone away to get her head sorted, or that she's back with Daniel.'

'But she texted from her phone, and then put that status on Facebook,' Jo was almost shouting.

'I don't think that was her.'

'What do you mean?'

'Whoever has kidnapped her sent them,' Charley replied trying to stay calm.

'Kidnapped?' Jo looked terrified. 'Why do you think she's been kidnapped?'

'It doesn't seem right. I need you to help me.'

'I can't help you. I don't know anything.' She shook her head. Charley was certain she was lying.

'Do you know Megan's surname?'

'Daniel's ex? *No*, why would I?' Jo said.

'Did Gina ever show you any burn marks?'

'No, why-'

'What about that night in Igloo?'

'What night in Igloo?'

'When Daniel came to meet Gina and you argued with him.'

Jo tilted her head and thought about this for a moment. 'Oh, that was nothing really,' she said quickly. 'I was drunk and mouthing off, and anyway me and Gina made up after that night, even if we didn't see much of her after it.'

'But what did Daniel say besides calling you a cunt?' Charley pressed on.

Jo looked shocked. 'Did Gina tell you about that?'

'Yes,' Charley lied.

'Sorry, I didn't think she told you anything,' Jo said flatly.

There was a bang from a distant corner in the flat. Jo jumped out of her skin, spilling smoothie down her top. A fluffy little fur ball padded into the room. Jo scooped it up and hugged the thing close to her chest. They both looked at Charley with terrified eyes.

'So, what did Daniel say that night?' Charley carried on. She wondered how much Jo and Jennifer knew about her, exactly how much Gina had told them.

'It was silly really. Honestly, it was nothing.'

'Did he mention his family?'

Jo lit a cigarette and looked away again.

'Please, you're one of Gina's best friends,' Charley pleaded.

'He said that someone would make sure I didn't cause trouble for him and Gina. It was the way he said it that scared me... but, I mean, you *know* what they're like, he would have been winding me up.'

'Who do you think he was talking about?' Charley said. 'Who would you think is the one who'd threaten people for Daniel?'

She considered this for a moment. 'Don't go around telling people about this.' Her eyes were wide and frightened. 'I shouldn't have said anything.'

'I won't say it was you. Gina could be in serious danger, Jo. You have to-'

'I think he meant his brother, Matthew.'

* * * * *

The phone rang as she got outside Jo's apartment block. It was Field.

'Did you find something?'

'There's nothing on Bob Ryan,' he answered with a tone of regret.

'But there must be, on Ken at least-'

'All I'll say is that we spend long periods of time tracking certain people to get the right evidence against them. I can't risk messing up any current operations.'

'So someone is watching Ken?'

'I can't tell you that,' he replied. 'Anything else from the definitions?'

She hesitated. There wasn't enough to mention the coffee incident with no back up from Jo - in fact, nothing was definite enough without further investigation. 'No,' she replied.

'I'll be in touch soon. Remember, be careful, and let me do this for you.'

'Ok,' Charley lied and started up the car.

CHAPTER TWENTY-ONE

Jealousy ~ Resentful or bitter in rivalry

~ Matthew mental - so jealous of Daniel - must stay wary of him - keep him out of office if only me there

~ Can't believe I'm in the same position as Megan (work-wise only, hopefully)

~ Who the frig is Natalie??

April 2014

'You alright?' Matthew appeared at the top of the stairs. 'Straight down to business I see.'

He glanced over at the papers piled on my desk, and then at the computer blatantly showing my Facebook Newsfeed.

'Daniel's given me extra hours as he's busy at the mo,' he said when I didn't answer. 'Cash in hand, so don't put it down or anything. I came up to see if he was around. They're plastering a massive house and the owners don't have a clue about cost - proper thick officey types.'

Matthew hardly did any hours, but got paid a hefty amount for 'emergencies'.

'I'll check with Daniel about that,' I said, trying to make out that I knew what I was talking about and ignoring his jibes.

'You can take my word for it,' he snapped. 'I know as much about this business as he does.'

'But you don't run it, do you?' I muttered.

'Me arl fella used to do the same for Ken. Cash in hand for a brother-in-law who was practically a brother,' Matthew said, moving closer to me. 'Before he found out what a cheating twat me dad actually was.'

There was a thudding noise on the stairs. The old wood always made it sound like someone was climbing them in a rage. Matthew took a few steps away from me.

'Hiya!' A voice called out, over-friendly, as though the greeter was expecting a hug at the end of her trip.

It was a Tropical Fish dressed as a barmaid. Her bunched out blonde hair, stood out against her black shirt and matching pants. Her name badge introduced her as Natalie, and she was carrying bottles of beer.

'Who are you?' she drawled, putting down the alcohol stack.

'I'm Daniel's fiancé and the new office manager.' It felt good to try out my new titles.

'Where's Danny?' she asked.

'He's hardly ever in the office.'

'Well he's back here lunchtimes usually, and then they all come down for a bevvy after work don't they?' She gave me a very unsubtle once over. 'Daniel didn't mention he had a girlfriend.'

'I'm his *fiancé*.' I stared her out.

'When the last one worked here, he introduced us properly.' She smirked. 'Tell him we'll catch up when he's next in.'

The fish gave me a real battering as Natalie skipped back down the stairs. Matthew stood with a triumphant smile on his face.

'Did Megan work here before me?'

'I'd check with Daniel about that,' he said, before grabbing a bottle of beer and leaving.

I couldn't concentrate then. I tried calling Daniel several times but it went to voicemail. I sent one text in the end - *who the frig is Natalie and why didn't you tell me your ex used to work for you?*

My breathing was becoming erratic. I had to calm down. Facebook wasn't helping. I couldn't stop stalking my former best friends who were out doing a lot of baby shopping without me.

* * * * *

Jo: Sooo happy my bestie got everything she wanted today and I bought her a fab moses basket and a pamper that she fully deserved. Lovely little girly get together planned tomorrow night too. Can't wait xx

I paid for half of that Moses basket! There was certainly no apology coming from me when they were the ones who asked me to go out only to have a go at me and my fiancé. My fucking lying fiancé. And ok, I did say some horrible things. Jen was gutted that Mark hadn't asked her to marry him - even getting pregnant didn't solve that, and I knew how lonely Jo was.

The packet of anti-anxiety pills was still in my bag. The Doctor had prescribed them because I was having panic attacks again.

'Don't take the pills, leave your job,' Daniel said when I told him. 'That's what's stressing you out.'

A text from Charley flashed up on my mobile. I'd ignored her earlier call.

Have you left your job??xx

She was as bad as my ex-Team Leader Colin. The meeting where I'd announced my resignation hadn't exactly been easy. He'd basically accused Daniel of masterminding my escape from the place.

'Is this your decision?' he said. The man sweated Gregg's pasties and always held meetings in small rooms. It was sweaty, cheesy, oniony hell.

'Why wouldn't it be?' I demanded.

'Well, I hear a lot of calls from Daniel and I don't think-'

'You don't think what?'

'He seems very controlling,' he replied, and spread his hands out as though he'd given me some fantastic insight that was going to change my life.

'They are my private phone calls Colin,' I said coldly.

'In work time,' he replied, matching my iciness. Then his hands came together and he frowned but in a sad way. 'My point is that you're good at your job when you want to be, and I think it would be a shame.'

'I'm not giving up work completely.'

'Oh.' He practically fell out of his seat. 'Is it a salary thing then? Can we match it?'

It was then I realised that Daniel had never actually discussed a salary with me.

'No it's not that – I'm going to help in Daniel's business…' I trailed off. It sounded stupid when I said it aloud.

'Oh. Well then, if you ever want to come back'…he trailed off and pretended to concentrate on the clock above our heads. After a few moments, he coughed and remembered himself.

'I'd put a good word in for you,' he said, and I felt a little better, like there was a safety net.

'It's a month's gardening leave notice as you know, so I guess you're free to go when you want to.' His face went blotchy, like it did when he'd been in a difficult meeting with the Director Mr Simons, or taken a customer complaint. He gave me an awkward hug that was more like a double pat and a chest bump. The fish complained inwardly.

* * * * *

In my new job, I made my own decisions. For instance, lunchtime could be 11 am if I wanted it to be. So fuck Daniel, Megan, Charley, Colin and, in fact, everyone, I was going shopping.

It was only when I was in the depths of Marks and Spencers, looking for a new bra and knickers set, that I realised my mistake; *everyone* was with their mums. Where were all the other half-orphans? Why can't people buy bloody buy bras on their own? Why weren't they all in work? The fish kicked and bit, letting me know that they were my only companions on this trip.

As luck would have it I needed to get measured again.

'Right, love, I'll be two minutes.' The assistant in the green uniform with the tape measure around her neck was the closest thing I'd get to a mum all day. I watched some of the mother-daughter teams around me.

One Mum had short cropped grey hair and was arty-nerdy. She was in her sixties wearing some kind of terrible shimmering purple blouse and black trousers that didn't fit properly. I'm sure her coat classed as an anorak. The daughter was half-Tropical Fish, half-mess, as she blatantly didn't want to end up looking like her mum, but was already clutching at the same colour purple in bras as her Mum's blouse. So, yes in around thirty years' time, she too would look like a retired feminist.

'Mum, I can make my own decisions,' I heard half-Tropical Fish, Half-Mess say as I followed Julie, my green uniformed lingerie Marks and Spencer's Mum, into the changing room.

You ungrateful bitch, I thought, despite myself.

After Julie tells me I'm a C not a B, something that would sometimes cheer me up, I felt a few tears come on in the cellulite mirrors. But there's a time and a lonely place for all this or at least there should be. The realisation that 'my mum really died' can hit you any time, anywhere even when you're half-naked in Marksies' changing rooms.

I went to a café on my own to calm down. The waitress set down the smoothie, all berry and bubbling, and darted away from the table. I could usually make my tears look like hayfever, but I realised they had crept out over my eyelashes and down onto the magazine I was pretending to read.

There was no chance I was going back to that office so I spent some time imagining Mum with me in Liverpool One as I walked around the shops.

Her skin would be clear and normal, no bruises or marks from the needles. It takes ages to paint back my best memory of Mum pre-sickness, but it's worth it. She would wear a pretty pink blouse, a black trouser suit and high-heeled boots. I couldn't quite conjure her smell but the perfume wafting past from the woman walking next to me did the trick.

* * * * *

When I got home, Daniel was reading at the kitchen table.

'No drinks with Natalie tonight?' I said.

'For God's sake, I tried to call you back,' he said getting up from the chair. 'She's a little divvy who stalks me.'

'Stalks you?'

'Yeah, but we only have a few drinks there after work every so often and hardly ever since I've been coming home to you,' he said and then added, 'because I would rather come home to you.'

'I've had a horrible day,' I said. 'Oh and thanks for telling me you also gave Megan the same job as me when you two were going out.'

'She lost her job. I felt sorry for her and she was there a few days, that's all,' he said. 'She did everyone's heads in. Never knew what she was doing.'

'I don't know what I'm doing either! And you should have told me about the Megan thing.'

'Stop stressing - we all have a past. We're together now, I love *you*. And you'll get used to the job.' He hugged me then pulled back as though he was going to make a big announcement. 'And, anyway, forget about work, I've booked us a holiday.'

For some reason my stomach lurched with panic fish.

CHAPTER TWENTY-TWO

SECRETS: 11.15 Saturday 30th August 2014

'I know about Amsterdam.' Charley pressed her foot into the door to stop it closing.

Melissa's curly hair had been pulled back into a strained blonde bun on the top of her head. Her blue eyes peeped out through fake lashes and layers of mascara. The bruise on her cheek had taken on a bluish tinge in the light, and was still visible even under the matted foundation, fake tan and a few strokes of blusher. She was holding a cigarette awkwardly. A couple of fingers didn't bend right. Her eyes narrowed. 'I could get you done for harassment if you carry on.'

'Did Daniel hit Gina too?' The sound of kids playing inside was making Charley feel uncomfortable.

'So, you accusing both brothers now then?' She blew the smoke in Charley's face and then froze as a car swung into the driveway at an alarming speed.

Matthew got out almost as quickly as he'd driven. His sandy hair and clothes were covered with speckles of plaster. There was a horrible, sly grin on his thin lips.

'To what do we owe the pleasure of an Ellison sister?' he said and bowed down, bits of white scattering on the driveway.

'No more work this weekend?' Charley forced herself to ask.

'Did the foreigner down south get called off then?' Melissa cut in quickly.

Matthew's brow creased in confusion. 'There wasn't enough work for the whole weekend,' he said slowly, looking at Melissa.

'Was Daniel working there with you?'

'What's it to you?'

Charley could smell the sweat off him, he was standing so close.

'I'm going to get a wash,' he said, rubbing past Charley. She stepped back and Melissa went to slam the door. Charley practically threw herself in.

'You're proper getting on me nerves now,' Melissa said.

'I'm trying to find my sister.'

Something changed in Melissa's expression then. The smoke escaped from her fingers and drifted into the air. 'I honestly don't know where she is. I'm not lying to you.' She looked at Charley for a moment like she was going to say something else and then the sound of kids shouting and laughing came from the hall. Melissa stumbled off the step as Matthew pushed past her.

'Where you going? There's still bits of plaster on yer!' she called after him as he headed back to the car.

'Got business to sort out - be back soon,' he replied.

'Don't you want a butty?' she shouted.

'I'll get something from the shop on the way.' He got back into the car.

Melissa stormed off the step and leaned into the car window to have a whispered argument. Charley saw her chance. She started steadily down the path and got into the car, taking out her phone and pretending to be engrossed in it until Matthew rumbled past. As his car turned the corner ahead, she started up the engine.

CHAPTER TWENTY-THREE

Kept - a woman maintained by a man

~ Secrets, appearances, a kept woman - Melissa, not me - I would never let things with Daniel get that far

~ I found out a few things in Amsterdam that the whole family would rather be kept secret

~ What did Matthew say to Megan to keep her quiet?

~ I feel so guilty - must keep what I did a secret from Charley ☹

April 2014

'Ready to go?' Melissa smiled sweetly at me. We grabbed our cases and followed the boys through the airport.

'Do you smoke much weed?' I asked her, trying to keep the nervous edge out of my voice.

'I like a spliff or two with Eastenders,' she said, 'No more than that though.'

I didn't want to remind her that Eastenders was on four nights a week and did she mean the omnibus too?

'I used to be far worse y'know,' she whispered, 'used to smoke it on the way to work until they noticed and sacked me.'

'Oh right, but you don't do that now with the two kids…'

'Haven't had another job since. Not needed to. I'm not smoking in the mornings anymore, though.'

I'd been worried about this 'holiday', especially when Daniel told me who we were going with. I went mad at the fact he'd booked Amsterdam after everything I'd told him about Charley. I couldn't believe that Daniel would want a holiday with his brother.

'We don't argue when we're stoned,' Daniel reassured me. 'You'll proper love Amsterdam, so don't worry. You need to remember that marijuana isn't a dangerous drug. That's why it's legal there! And there's so much more to do than get high.'

He talked me around far easier than he should have been able to.

As Melissa and Daniel went through the security screening, I found myself with Matthew. He cleared his throat.

'I'm sorry about being a knob in the office last week,' he said. 'I wasn't meself. Kids keep us awake all night and that. We ok?'

I nodded because it was easier.

'Great, let's go and get smashed,' he shouted, and I worried (or maybe hoped) that the security guards would stop him from getting through.

Melissa turned around and smiled, her freckles showing underneath the sunbed tan. She swept her blonde curly hair, which stood out like a lion's mane, away from her face. She was tall, despite wearing flats because she didn't like towering over Matthew, who was that average height which men can get shitty about. In a pair of beige linen pants and a pink vest top, she showed off a body fighting baby weight but doing well.

The flight was rough. Not in the turbulence way, but in the state of the passengers. Some already looked stoned, lolling in their seats in their tracksuits and caps. It amazes me how committed the Scouse scally is to their 'uniform', which was a variation of the shell suit really, worn rain or shine, even in extreme heat.

118

First course of action when we arrived was to throw our bags into the cheap hotel and find a coffee shop.

'Don't worry babe, we have plenty of time for the culture stuff later.' Daniel gave me a big kiss and threw an arm around me.

On the way, we passed a 'worker' in a window going through her seduction routine.

'I wonder how they end up doing this,' I said watching the girl slink around her small pink quarters.

'Chill the fuck out!' Matthew threw an unwelcome arm around me. It was his catchphrase for the holiday.

The coffee shop reminded me of a cave. To brighten it up the bar area served drinks in coconuts with little umbrellas. We declined those and I sipped at a vodka and cranberry. It was quite refreshing but the ice crushed out the flavour. Nobody gave a shit about the drinks anyway. There was a pool table upside down on the ceiling. At the bar, smart little rolly ups and bags of weed were labelled behind glass but they had a separate area for smoking so the air wasn't wrecked with it.

'We have to go in a little area over them ways to smoke in here.' Matthew purchased a bag and headed over.

'Oh I don't know if I should…' I started quietly. The room looked more full of fumes than people. Daniel touched my arm gently. 'You can get herbal ones you know, or what about a cake?'

'Will it be ok-'

'You'll be fine, darling. I wouldn't let you have it if it was dangerous. You can't get hooked.'

I decided on the herbals.

'Ah, look at yer bird with her herbal rollies.' Matthew laughed like a five-year-old girl, all high and ridiculous. I looked down at my selection, bought from the man at the bar who didn't laugh at me. The jasmine and rosemary ones were the only things I felt I could handle. Daniel didn't laugh at me either.

119

I was fine on them, or at least able to keep up a conversation with Melissa, who didn't seem at all affected by the 'real stuff' she was smoking. She asked me how I found working for Daniel's company, and then more pointedly why I was doing it if I didn't need to.

'I feel like a kept woman if I don't work,' I explained.

'Oh being a mum is a full-time job, believe me,' she said. 'But I love them to the moon and back so it's worth it.'

'Come on, try some of the real stuff!' Matthew rolled with deft fingers, interrupting us. The air smelt terrible, wrong, too heavy.

'Go on, love, it's fine - will proper relax you, like.' As if to prove her point, Melissa leaned back.

I thought of all the bad things that had happened so far in my life. I wanted to blot them out for a bit. The fish batted back and forth in my head. As they nipped my stomach weakly, I decided I would be stronger. Why shouldn't I relax and enjoy myself? Daniel was right.

I took a long drag and really tasted it, that weird choking taste and bitter dryness in the throat, freedom from my own mind and then my head was happy. I sat spaced out, occasionally taking more from Matthew and letting the harsh taste lick my throat. I tried going back to my own milder ones, but it was like smoking one of those fresh herbs you buy from Tesco to make posh dinners.

Everything happily spun for a while until Daniel went to buy more weed and Melissa went to the toilet. It was then I noticed how battered Matthew was.

'Yer a lucky bitch,' he muttered. His eyes were murky. 'But I'm warning yer, try and treat him like that last cunt did and I'll teach you a fucking lesson.'

I tried to talk, to respond, but the words wouldn't roll off my tongue. The fish had gained access to my mouth and were dancing around in it. Daniel came back.

'I want to go.' I stood up, swaying.

'What? Why?'

'What's up, lad? Is she on a para?' Matthew smiled.

'I don't feel well.'

'You're having a whitey that's all. Let's go outside for a minute.' Daniel led me out of the weed chamber.

'Soz abar you, Gina!' Melissa screeched across the room. 'You're fucked, babe.'

I tried to explain a panic attack to Daniel once; the mixture of a cold heat, the tightening of every muscle in my body, that pressure on the chest, the burning pain in the back of my left shoulder. My head starts thudding, my heart races and boom; I'm fired up and it's all got to come out, the energy overflowing.

'Do you want to go back to the hotel?' Daniel held me up against the wall and pressed soothing fingers into my back. I heard the door open and the sounds of the bar spilled into the street.

'Lad, the night is young!' Matthew spoke in a distant fog.

'She's having a panic attack, you tit! We're going back to the hotel,' Daniel said. 'You're ok, Gina. You're fine. I'm here.' I saw him hand Matthew a big wad of cash.

'What's that for?' I managed to croak.

'Don't worry yourself about it,' Daniel replied.

By the time we got to the hotel my head was spinning and I couldn't see anything.

'I'm blind,' I croaked.

'Your head's in the bin,' Daniel said patiently.

'I'm really sorry. I'll look after you from now on.' His face was distorted concern.

All I wanted was for Mum to bring me scrambled egg on toast on brown bread. She always did that when I was ill. Huge dollops of real butter and cheese grated over the soft eggs that would slip down my throat like medicine. Because isn't that what parents do? Tell you off for doing something wrong but then make you scrambled egg. It struck me that I'd never get to know my Mum's mistakes, her own pre-scrambled egg moments, and the time before me when she was a person and not a parent. In my foggy and tired head, I tried to clear some of the fish and picture her, before she was 'Mum'.

Daniel's hand moved through my hair and I started to breathe properly again. He stroked my head until I fell asleep.

* * * * *

When I woke up a few hours later, Daniel was asleep. I checked Facebook to bring myself back to reality. Matthew had uploaded a photo hours earlier.

Me and Danny Boy outside the greenhouse with a big long joint la!!'

It was a horrible picture of Matthew and Daniel with the hoods of their hoodies over their heads with two long spliffs hanging out of their mouths. I went to Anthony's profile next. He'd been tagged in a photo with a girl who was wearing a straw hat and had peace signs badly drawn on her cheek. A cut-off t-shirt revealed her flat stomach, little denim shorts and grey socks to the knee and black wellies completed the festival chic look. It was Lydia.

I had to get out of the room for a minute, and noticed Matthew and Melissa's door was open a crack. There was a loud slapping noise. I looked through the gap and saw Melissa fall on the bed, clutching her face. Matthew stormed off into the bathroom and slammed the door. Melissa sat up and breathed slowly. The shower ran loudly.

'Are you ok?' I asked. She jumped at my voice and then ran to the door.

'What are you doing spying on us?' she hissed.

'Did he -'

'He does everything for me, Gina. He's a great Dad. I don't even have a job. Please don't say anything. His family would…it hardly ever happens.'

The shower water stopped and Melissa shut the door in my face.

CHAPTER TWENTY-FOUR

Following: 11.30 Saturday 30th August 2014

Charley was careful to stay out of sight.

He wouldn't know her car anyway. She hardly drove the battered old thing, but she knew it was right to be careful with Matthew.

He came out of the shop swigging from a bottle of water and didn't look in her direction. She waited until his car pulled out, heart hammering and sweat sticky on her face.

They drove through the side roads of town. She nearly lost him twice - and then she saw him head up to the office of Daniel's business. Even from a distance she could see his permanent smirk as he entered the building, cocky enough not to put any money in the meter.

There was nothing else to do but wait, and watch a street cleaner attempting to get rid of the alcoholic froth of the night before. Keeping an eye on the door, she rolled down the window slightly and the sounds of the brushing and prepping of the roads were joined by a voice asking if anyone could 'spare a few quid'.

The man was skinny with a shaved head and wearing a filthy tracksuit. He harassed passers-by and thanked them for not giving him any money. Charley knew all the tricks. One man, dressed in smart jeans and a t-shirt came back and threw him a pound.

This skinny man was in a good location, far enough away from any of the hostels and close to some of the more expensive hotels, where tourists would flock in and then back out again, thinking they had seen all of Liverpool after visiting the docks, the Beatles Museum and a few bars. This man was a hint towards the darker side of every city - the darker side of people. He caught her staring and flashed a toothless grin. She quickly rolled up the window and blocked out that life, those memories.

Matthew was lighting a cigarette at the door of the building, phone stuck to his ear as he shuffled down the steps and headed to his car. He threw the half-burned cigarette to the floor and pulled open the car door. Charley got ready again. Her hands were shaking.

He wasn't heading back to his home. That was clear almost straightaway as he took the Dock Road. She kept going at a careful distance until she realised where he was heading.

For a moment, Charley wanted to get out of the car and have it out with him, bang her fists against the door, against him, and demand to know where Gina was.

With his phone still pressed to his ear, Matthew circled the same patch of driveway again and again as he kept knocking at the door. The sweat formed on Charley's palms and thighs. Eventually he gave up and got back in the car.

They were back on the Dock Road, but this time Matthew picked up speed and dodged in and out of cars until Charley lost him and had to stop at the side of the road. She took deep breaths to calm down, head in her hands. A tap in the window made her jump.

'Don't follow me, you silly bitch!' Matthew shouted through the window. And then he was gone, back in his car and speeding off before Charley could stop shaking.

CHAPTER TWENTY-FIVE

Lost ~ Unable to find one's way

~ Losing yourself in the same arguments but finding out new things

~ Can people get so lost that they don't act like themselves (violent)?

~ Can't believe I've lost Mum's letter ☹

~ At least Daniel has lost the urge to partake in the selfish white powder at parties

May 2014

'But he slapped her across the face!' I stormed around the living room.

'We've been over this,' Daniel said. 'We can't get involved.'

'What about the kids?'

'He wouldn't touch them. He wouldn't. Believe me, I'd kill him.'

'How do you know he wouldn't?'

'We've been arguing about this since Amsterdam,' Daniel said. 'Didn't she slam the door in your face?'

The rest of the holiday had been awkward. Melissa made sure she was never alone with me and I made sure that I was never alone with Matthew.

'Why though?' I asked. I'd kept on at this, determined to know why Daniel let his brother off, why Matthew thought he could act like that.

Daniel leaned forward on the sofa and put his head in his hands, rubbing his forehead, bits of plaster from the working day falling onto the wooden floor.

'Matthew saw things when he was younger.'

'Like what?' I sat down next to him.

'It only happened when we were really young.'

'What did?'

'What Dad did to Mum,' he said. 'He used to get a bit…violent.'

'He hit her?'

'But only when he was off his head drunk… He never touched me or Matt.' Daniel rubbed his hands on his bare thigh. He always did this when he was nervous, scratched and rubbed odd spots on his body until they were red and sometimes raw. 'He stopped drinking as much when he got a few odd jobs again, and then he started the business.'

I put my hand over his to stop the scratching.

'Honestly Gina, he is a changed man. Don't let it change us or how you talk to him,' Daniel pleaded.

'But what about Matthew? It obviously affects him,' I said. 'I'm not sure that I can handle having your dad around here to be honest.'

'Maybe talk to him and you'd see-'

'See what?'

'For fuck's sake, Gina, you let Charley off with everything she did.'

I'd had enough.

My stomach was in a fluttery panic as I stormed up the stairs and slammed the bedroom door. He didn't follow me.

* * * * *

Twenty minutes later, he appeared at the door.

I took out my headphones and put down the papers and photos in my hands, none of them what I was looking for.

'I said, can you come downstairs for a minute?'

When I saw who was waiting in the living room, I almost turned around and ran out. Daniel made me sit down on the sofa and then shuffled in next to me. We sat in silence for a few minutes.

'I need to explain myself.' Bob's stone grey eyes were directly on me. I wrapped my arms around myself, glad to be on the other side of Daniel. It was hard to imagine this shrinking man with the scruffy face being violent. But then I remembered the punch that floored Ken at the party.

'I was a bit lost back then,' Bob said finally, his knuckles white from tensing up. 'I know what a monster I was, and I tried every day to look after Tina once I righted myself again.'

It was hard to meet his gaze. Daniel kept his head down. I couldn't see his face properly. Bob was crying, shaking with it and wiping his eyes manically.

'Please…don't blame Daniel…I've tried so hard over the years to make up for it.' He fell over his words. I wasn't sure what to do. Daniel got up and went over and the two of them hugged. When they'd finished Bob looked at me, half-scared and half-warily.

'Will you talk to Matthew?' I asked, my eyes dry.

'I'll talk to Matty,' Bob said. 'I'll make him listen to me this time.' The last part was said with anger but I let that go. I left getting involved in the hug too.

'Gina, I honestly regret how I was when I was younger.' He got up and came towards me extending a hand. 'I was defending myself against Ken at that party. You can't blame a man for that.'

I took his hand as Daniel was watching and felt the dry chalkiness of his skin on my own.

I exhaled as he left the room with Daniel, and the front door closed behind him.

'I can't find my mum's letter anywhere,' I said quietly as Daniel sat on the sofa in a sort of daze. I wasn't ready to talk about Bob yet.

'Don't stress out. They'll be somewhere. We're going to be late for Karen's.'

'We're still going?'

'Of course we are. I told you not to let this change anything between us. You've listened to me dad now haven't you?'

'Yeah but-'

'But what?

'I don't think I'm really in the mood for another bloody party.'

'Fine.'

* * * * *

José was the first person we saw when we arrived on their ridiculously long driveway. He was sipping a bottle of sparkling water and looked pleased to see us.

'Daniel,' he pleaded as he jogged slightly ahead of us towards the house, 'you need to help me with the decorating. I am so useless! Karen, she is going mad.'

'The main guest room needs plastering,' Karen said greeting us at the side gate that led to the football pitch garden. 'I want José to do it with you, so he can learn.'

I didn't understand why… when they had so much money. Then again, Karen was also going on about how a real man can fix taps and stuff. She should marry Daniel really. I hugged his arm even tighter at that sick thought.

Karen found time to turn around and give me the once over. I didn't care as I was wearing a beautiful blood red dress which fell below the knee, with a white laced over-sized collar. 'Come on G, I've got something for you,' she said, pulling me through the garden and into the kitchen. It was crowded with 'her girls', including Lydia and Jemma. 'It's a pre-hen

130

party prezzie for you!' She pulled a wooden penis out of a box. The Tropical Fish all dissolved into laughter.

'What the hell is that for?' I asked, sober and embarrassed.

'Hen parrttay – love, we've talked about nothing else all week!' Karen screamed.

'But we haven't even set a date for the wedding yet.'

'Why haven't you set a date yet?' Lydia asked, as though this was innocence and not shit stirring. A 'look' passed between her and Karen.

'And I've been meaning to talk to you about the hen,' I took a large drink of wine to gain confidence and ignored Lydia, 'my friends Jennifer and Jo wanted to organise it.'

'Listen that's by the by, babe. We can have a little holiday, I mean hen party part one, and then another one for your mates to organise including the one who's preggers, in Liverpool. That way no one loses out. It's not like you're going to be waiting pure ages until you do book the wedding is it?'

I was going to put up more of a fight, honest I was, but then Karen showed me the accommodation. It was completely amazeballs, like, proper gorgeous. It was a private villa split into two parts. The secluded terraces looped out into blue sky and soft sand below - you could actually see the waves. The beds were massive and each bathroom was like a wet room. I'd never seen anything like it.

'How many sleeps is it until we go?' Jemma clapped her hands and danced around.

'I've booked it for the twelfth of July and Daniel's paid for it.' She nudged me at this. 'There's a Facebook group and I did invite your little friends too.'

Oh, I knew about that, I wanted to say, remembering Jo's pissed off face.

'I'm going to keep this for the younger group and do something for erm, Mu-, I mean aunties and that at mine,' she finished awkwardly.

'It's so sad that neither you or Daniel have your Mums.' Jemma said.

I hadn't expected her to say that. I hadn't expected anyone to say that. She looked genuinely close to tears at her own observation. I appreciated it. Especially as Karen and Lydia did what everyone else always does and averted their eyes and changed the subject, in their case to nail varnish. When the opportunity for anyone else to discuss dead mums passed, Karen carried on with her plans. As she spoke I realised I was too close to her, after years on the sunbeds, the view wasn't a good one. Her skin was like withered tangerine peel which had curled up at the edges.

'…and the best bit is that Daniel and all the others will be going on their stag there at the same time. I sorted that with José.'

That didn't sound like a hen party to me. I left the kitchen making the excuse that I needed to find Daniel. Taking a walk to an upstairs bathroom to look for him, I passed one of the spare bedrooms and saw it. Piles of it on the bedside table, like soft chalk chippings and white ashes.

I creaked the door open carefully. Lydia, Karen and Daniel were in there. Daniel jumped up with a look of panic.

Each one of them held a straw. Lydia's was up her nose at one end while the other moved across white lines of powder on an old CD case. She glanced at me and sniffed. I hadn't unsettled her, even for a minute.

'What are you doing?' I said, looking at Daniel for support. He was holding a straw too, wiping a hint of white from his nose.

'Chill out – you're a proper stress head.' Lydia said and looked at Daniel who paused for a moment and then laughed. 'Daniel said it's ok, doll. Why don't you have some too? C'mon, it's on me. Proper good stuff.'

Daniel came over to the door and wrapped an arm around me tightly. My head and neck throbbed again and the fish did some victory bites at my uncomfortableness.

'Well he shouldn't have.' I tried to loosen his grip but, as usual, his arms were too strong.

'Come on, chill out – it's not a big deal,' he said.

'It is a big deal to me. You know why-' I said, still trying to shrug him off. 'Can I speak to you outside?'

His face was dark, unsmiling but he came with me. 'What?' he said, almost like a threat.

'I'm not really comfortable with that,' I said, unsure of myself now. He was usually on my side.

'It's no wonder I want to get twatted when I can't even get you to set a date. Because it is you, Gina, not me.'

Taken aback, I stumbled on my heels.

'I'd marry you tomorrow and you're not even arsed. Even the bloody hen do has been booked first,' he continued. I could hear the others giggling inside.

'I'm sorry…I didn't think,' I said. 'It's so difficult to organise. There's loads to do.'

'We could go abroad, only invite close family or even up to Gretna Green,' he had his hands on either side of my shoulders. My body felt drained, like I was almost unable to stand.

'I'm sorry. I should have thought more of you but it doesn't affect everyone the same way you know.' He gave me a long kiss. 'I won't do it anymore. I promise you. I'll get my phone and we'll go downstairs.' As he went back in my phone vibrated. It was Anthony.

Haven't seen you since that party. You ok? Daniel's brother's a tool isn't he?

For a moment I saw the situation through Daniel's eyes and stopped my fingers from moving over the touchscreen. This was someone I'd obviously once had a crush on who turned up at nearly everything we did. No wonder Daniel lost his rag about it at times.

'Do you know what – forget getting married at home. I want to do it abroad,' I said when he came back out.

Daniel looked at me steadily. His pupils were spinning.

'Really?' His face spread into a massive smile.

My heart might have felt like it had been used as a punchbag over the last few hours but the hammering of the fish had temporarily stopped.

CHAPTER TWENTY-SIX

MAD: 11.45 Saturday 30th August 2014

A plastic bag and a bottle of water.

He threw the bag and rolled the bottle across the room. Both landed next to Gina's feet, but the water hit her foot and headed back towards him across the cold floor. She didn't move. Terror had made her immobile, stiffening her bones and influencing each breath. She must have slept, but it was impossible to tell what time it was.

She hadn't touched anything he had left. The jug of water had been kicked over and spilt out onto the floor. She must have done it in her sleep, unless he had been in during the last few hours. The thought made her shake uncontrollably.

'Open it.' He pointed towards the plastic bag. He looked clean, shaven and a hint of soap came off him, a light jasmine scent.

With trembling hands she pulled out a sandwich, packet of crisps and an apple.

'Eat it,' he said, a slow smile appearing on his face, 'and relax. I haven't even tied you up. You can move around all you want.'

'How long are you going to keep me here for?' she asked, her voice croaky.

'Why don't you drink some water?' he said, almost kindly.

She ignored him.

He sighed and picked up the bottle of water from his feet, opened it, sipped, and rolled it across.

'I don't trust you either you know,' he said, sitting down and opening up his own sandwich. The smell of cheese and pickle filled the room. 'That's the problem.'

He scratched at his face, took a bottle out of his pocket and gulped from it.

He was mad, completely and utterly mad. Sitting here eating a sandwich like they were having a picnic together.

'No police search for you yet,' he said.

'But someone is searching for me?'

He shrugged.

'Charley?'

'Drink some water.'

'Don't hurt her.'

'I won't, he said, 'if I don't have to.'

CHAPTER TWENTY-SEVEN

Mum(s)

~ Don't always do what they should

~ But not having one is worse than having a bad one

~ Do I even want to be one?

~ At least Jen has a Mum to make up for the horror that is Mark - him and Matthew should be friends

May 2014

Would I ever be the type of person who kept a faded red shoe the size of my hand in a box?

They were the first shoes she'd bought me. I put one against my nose. I'm always looking for traces of Mum, thinking something might be left from when she last touched it, but it smelt old, eau de 1990s or something. She was too many smells ago now.

I kept a jumper of hers for a while. It was brilliantly horrible, black and white striped. She looked like a zebra with cancer when she wore it towards the end. The smell didn't last on that either.

I often thought about future plans too. All the things that never happened with Mum in my life, like my first proper job, passing my driving test, getting engaged. Then there were the things, still to happen, like my wedding and having kids of my own. That's the thing about loss, you end up with a weird relationship with time. It's like a thick line gets drawn across your life from a time that comes 'before' and then everything after that. Before the line I had my Mum and afterwards I didn't. Time moves on, of course it does. But it stays still too.

'Our Daniel will be pleased to see you broody.'

I dropped the shoe and nearly jumped out of my skin as I turned around to see Bob in the doorway.

'I'm getting ready for Jen's baby shower,' I replied, blushing.

'Won't be long until you have one yourself.' He stayed in the doorway, taking up nearly the whole frame and holding a cup of tea. I thought Daniel had taken the key off him.

'Not for a while yet.' I laughed.

'You'll be having kids soon after you get married won't you?'

'When I'm thirty or something.'

Bob spluttered out his tea. A few splashes hit his shoe. 'Daniel won't be liking that at all. Waiting four years after you get married? That's a bit selfish isn't it?' He looked at me again. 'Why would you wait so long? Don't you think Daniel would be a good dad?'

'I never said that.'

A loud crash on the landing distracted him. Matthew's thin face poked around the door and forced Bob even further into the room.

'You'd defo be a better Ma than ours was,' he said. 'Not hard that though.'

'Leave it, Matt,' Bob said in a warning tone.

'Oh yeah, sorry, I forgot she wasn't in on the cancer crap.'

'The what?' I asked.

But Bob had slung Matthew out of the room. I heard Daniel shout from the hallway and by the time I got downstairs, they were both leaving and my fiancé was standing, smiling, holding the gift bag he'd been to get.

'What's up?' he asked.

'Nothing.' I forced a smile but I couldn't do it. 'Actually Matthew mentioned something about your mum.'

Daniel's face darkened. 'What did he say?'

'He kind of…made out that…'

He was staring at me. 'What?'

'That your mum didn't die of cancer.'

For second I wasn't sure what he was going to do.

'He's full of shit,' he said finally, each word through clenched
teeth.

'But why would-?

'Let's go, ok?'

I managed to get the present and my bag before he marched
me out of the door.

'Daniel?' I tried in the car.

'Leave it.' His face was like thunder. We took every corner
Formula-One style. My stomach heaved but I didn't dare open
my mouth again.

When we got there I didn't feel any better. Jennifer's baby
shower buffet was enough to make anyone vom. There were
little cupcakes with prams and baby faces and dummies and
the like. Someone had decorated the wall above the table with
photos of Jennifer as a baby. She was buzzing around the
room, all bumped up.

'Me Aunty made them.' Jennifer screeched. 'Aren't they
fab?'

I nodded and picked one up although the fish were going for
my vomit buttons. Unfortunately, it was one of the most
extreme creations: a baby's face staring back at me in cream
and yellow.

Real life babies scrambled across the floor, drew squiggles on
a chalkboard and played with a plastic kitchen. A little boy in
a blue and white checked shirt edged past me with a grinning
pink kettle in his hand. I thought it was him making a
whistling noise until I realised it was the general rabble of all
the kids making sounds together. I couldn't concentrate.
Daniel wouldn't look at me.

Most people who Jennifer had grown up with had kids by now. It was me and Jo who were in the minority.

Daniel was examining a cake too, picking a nappy off the top. He caught me looking at him and turned away. Jennifer bumped over to us amongst the madness, excited and flushed before I could get to him.

'Does anyone want a drink?' She was loving playing host.

'I'll have a beer.'

'Daniel, it's a kid's party.' I couldn't help myself.

He glared at me. 'Exactly, I need something to take the edge off.'

'We need to talk,' I said quietly.

He walked off.

Mark joined Daniel on the sidelines of the party, handing him a beer. As usual Jen's lovely boyfriend was hiding premature balding with a weird bowler type of hat, but that couldn't disguise eyes that reminded me of a hen's; they were so small and close together. The worst part about him was his triangle-shaped body. He had a big top frame that kind of went down into spindly legs like a frog's.

'What are you two doing over here?' I decided to be upbeat and make an effort with Hen Eyes so that I could see if Daniel was ok.

'Avoiding the sprog stuff, like.' Daniel took a long glug. Mark sniggered like this was the best comment ever.

'Coming for a ciggy?' he asked Daniel, who nodded and put his beer down.

'Let's get going when I get back.' When Daniel said things as statements, I knew that there was no point arguing, and if we left then it would finally give us a chance to talk.

'At least we got a few bevies out of this, eh, lad?' I heard Mark say as they walked toward the back door.

Jo was picking at a plate of crisps and cheese sandwiches while defending her decision not to have kids by the age of

140

twenty-five to a group of girls from Jennifer's old road. She jumped when I touched her arm to announce I was back.

Jen came over to the table and set down a pot of steaming chilli.

'Me mum made this. She's been cooking for us loads. I'm so tired after work, proper nightmare customers going on at me all day.' She was wearing a stretchy blue and white dress and a pair of flat boots that were a bit building site, but I suppose were comfortable. 'I don't know how I'd cope without me mum.' She gave me a startled look. 'Sorry, Gina. How's you? How are the wedding plans coming along?'

'Erm, ok you know, not much decided yet.' No way was I telling them about the Gretna Green idea today.

'When do we get to pick out our bridesmaid dresses then?' Jo said, giving me a glance that told me she was on to something. Thankfully, Daniel came back in then.

'Ready to go?' he announced.

'You're going?' Jen screeched.

'We have to, sorry girls,' he said, giving them a smile and ignoring me. 'Got loads of work on at the moment. I sorted your Mark out with some work on a few contracts too.'

I followed him to the hall. 'We need to talk about what Matthew said.'

'Actually why don't you stay and enjoy yourself?' he replied. 'I need some time on my own.'

Before I could say anything else, he was gone, shutting the door in my face. I heard footsteps. Mark's beady little eyes came towards me, shining out of his moon face.

'You ok, Gina?' he said, leaning in so that his breath was all over my face.

'Fine, yeah.' I skirted around him back into the main room, leaving him and his stupid legs in the hall.

'I'm not surprised you dropped out of Uni, love, waste of time. I went to the university of life meself, ASDA and

141

having kids is my education.' One of Jen's mum's friends was talking to Jo when I got back.

'You ok?' Jo whispered, her eyes in the direction where Daniel had left.

'Gina will probably be the next out of all of us to have a baby. She's getting married soon!' Jen was telling the group.

It must have been the spices from the chilli, slicing my emotions open and gutting the fish, but I felt on the verge of tears. It wasn't only because of how Daniel was being. The old feelings were coming up my throat. I couldn't exactly say to Jen, I haven't had a Mum for so long that I'm not sure how to react, and I've got a hole of emptiness that my mind tries to fill with irrational fears. So I nodded and smiled. My phone rumbled in my bag.

When u coming back?x

'You sure you're ok?' Jo said.

'Fine.'

What u up to?

This time no kisses. The phone started ringing in my hand. I cancelled the call.

Please Gina come back or I don't know what I'll do

'I'll have to go.' I said this louder than I meant to. Everyone looked at me. Jen's face fell into her tanned neck. She came over as a hush descended over her minions.

'Why are you going? You're my bezzie mate and this is my baby shower. It doesn't matter if Daniel isn't here. Youse aren't joined at the hip.'

'Listen, I'll ring you and explain later-' I began.

'You always put him first,' she cut in. 'We hardly see you anymore because of him and now you're getting off because he told you to.'

'There are things going on that I can't tell you about at the minute.'

'Yeah ok, whatever. That boy always has things going on.'

'Well, bye then.' I called over sarcastically.

'Yeah, bye.' Jen said, without seeing me to the door.

* * * * *

When I got back to ours I could smell the drink in the hallway. Daniel lurched out of the living room, a thick shadow against the light. He caught hold of me. His eyes were blank, emotionless. The TV was blaring in the living room.

'Take your fucking time then.' He leaned against the wall. 'What have you been doing, chatting up Mark's mates?'

'What the fuck Daniel?'

'Who goes to a baby shower dressed like a little slag anyway?'

'Don't take it out on me. Tell me what Matthew meant-'

His fist made a harsh sound on the coffee table. It was only an Ikea effort so the legs buckled. So did mine. 'You know what we need to talk about? Commitment.'

'What are you on about?'

'These could go for a start.' He brought my pills out of his pocket and slammed them down on the table too. The little green packet that made sure I stayed just me. I didn't say anything as I picked them back up. I wasn't ready for a baby yet.

He knocked a glass off the table that smashed on the wooden floor. His face changed. 'I didn't want you to find out about me mum like that.'

'Daniel, I don't know anything. I want you to talk to me.'

But he didn't answer. I went to walk out and that was when he lost control.

* * * * *

Afterwards, he took a deep breath and sat down. 'I need to make you understand.' The room was in devastation all

143

around us. The skin on his arm was rubbed raw. 'I want to tell you how my mum really died.'

CHAPTER TWENTY-EIGHT

WEEDS: 13.30 Saturday 30th August 2014

There was a gentle shuffling sound coming from the front garden, the source of it hidden behind the hedges.

All Charley could see was a glimpse of the red door over the top of the greenery shield, until she reached the edge of the driveway and saw Daniel's dad working busily with a small shovel, on his knees, with his bald head roasting under the sun. He was intent with his work, pulling stray weeds out of the soil and preparing it for the stack of little red and orange plants he had lined up on the grass. From the few times she'd met him, Charley couldn't tell if he was big boned and powerful or a small, fat man whose body kind of lumped itself together and looked muscled in certain lights.

As he worked, his biceps bulged and then became flabby when he relaxed again. He didn't seem to have noticed her. It would have been so easy to walk away but she had to be brave.

'You looking for Daniel love?' His voice came at her suddenly. He didn't look up from his task.

'Yeah…him and Gina. Have you seen them in the last couple of days?' she asked, hovering on the driveway.

'Saw him yesterday morning. He mentioned something about being away for the weekend.'

'For work?'

'Not sure, sorry, love,' he replied, kneeling up for a second and shaking the mud from his t-shirt. His stomach stuck out and wobbled as he moved. 'He runs the business now after all.'

'Was Matthew meant to be going with him?' Charley had to ask all the questions she could while the courage was in her.

'You ask a lot of questions,' he said. But it was in a gentle way with a kind smile. 'If you have any more, would you like a cuppa?'

She found herself nodding.

'Hope you don't mind if I finish this bit first,' he said. 'I'm not much of a gardener but Tina always liked it to look nice out here. It'll only take me a few more minutes.' His big, calloused hands moved gently around the plants, tucking them into the soil. Charley watched, strangely settled by it. Eventually he sat back satisfied. 'The house is a bit of a mess at the moment, so I'll bring the tea out if you don't mind waiting here,' he said and indicated towards the side of the garden. 'There are a couple of deck chairs there.'

The chairs were dusty and Charley had to shake them out. He came back soon after with two cups of tea and a plate of biscuits. She nibbled at one politely. It tasted of ginger and staleness.

'I don't shop much,' he apologised. 'Gina's very good at looking after me.'

Charley nodded.

'You two close as sisters then? Gina's mentioned you a lot.'

'Yeah.'

'Where's your dad again lovie?

'Hong Kong.'

'Did he get married again, after your Mum died?'

'They split up years before she died, but yeah.' Charley didn't want to go into her dad's love life.

'Any other family up here?' Bob asked.

Charley shook her head.

'And where do you live now, pet?'

'My own flat,' she replied vaguely. Not even her counsellor asked this many questions in a row, but Bob spoke in an easy tone and his voice, combined with the sun beating down on

146

them, was making her tired. She wanted to finish this so she could take her medication, have a quick lie down and think about what to do next. Bob would have her chatting about her life all afternoon if this carried on. It was a bit like talking to a Granddad, and Charley never had a Granddad.

But one of the definitions crossed Charley's mind, *Who started the fight, Bob or Ken?* Daniel's dad was violent, recently violent, and he had cheated on their mum and was sitting here talking about how she liked the garden kept nice. It didn't seem like the same person.

'Gardening has always relaxed me, taken my mind off things. You know how it is, the need to keep busy.' He stretched his back and grimaced slightly and then gave her a pat on the shoulder.

'Gina will be fine, pet. They are very in love you know,' he said. 'Daniel is also very proud and your sister is the same.'

'So you think they're away together?'

'I imagine so, yeah.'

He started to put the deck chairs back, waving away her offer of help.

'If you're ever feeling a bit down, lovie, pop in for a cup of tea. You can always help me out with some gardening.' He smiled.

Charley reached the car and sat down. Her hands shook against the steering wheel and she started to cry.

CHAPTER TWENTY-NINE

Non-negotiable - not open to discussion or alteration

~ No matter what his mum did there is no excuse for what he did to me tonight

May 2014

We sat in silence. Mum's gold clock ticked on the mantelpiece. My cheek throbbed.

'You have to listen to me.'

I didn't answer. He went to brush his hand against my face but I turned away.

'I lose it sometimes. I don't mean to do that. You got in the way.'

I placed cold fingers on my skin to try and dull the pain in my face. It could have been a lot worse, for the living room and for me.

'Are you going to let me out of the room?' I tried to get up, but dizziness and Daniel's strong arm pulled me back down onto the couch.

'You have to listen to me, please.' He took my silence as an answer.

'I found her,' he said. His hands found the dry patch on his arm and scratched until the skin went raw. 'That night, I opened our front door and found her at the bottom of the stairs. I thought she was dead.' He pulled at the stubble on his cheeks, creased his skin up with his fingers. 'She might as well have been. The next two weeks she was in a coma anyway. Her liver had packed in.'

He got up and started pacing the room. Within minutes Daniel had gone from a mad rant that ended with him trashing the living room, to a sad, lost little boy. His eyes found mine.

'I felt relieved you know,' he said, 'relieved that it was all over because I was sick of it, sick of her.'

I flinched.

'Before that, Mum was drinking all day and crying all night,' he continued.

'I'd even called our doctor, hoping he might make her go into rehab or something. And it was horrible having to phone someone and tell them your mum's a fucking alchie.

'Your mum is the person who is supposed always to be there for you, but mine wasn't, for any of us.' He leaned against the mantelpiece. 'She did stuff to all of us, got all aggressive and angry. Every night she'd be slurring and ranting. She'd never let us in the kitchen, saying there was no room, but really it was because she wanted a drink.'

'What did your dad do?'

'Had affairs, stayed out late, went away a lot.' He laughed bitterly. 'Thanks, Dad.'

'Is that why he gave you the business,' I said quietly, 'because he feels guilty?'

He hesitated. 'Matthew didn't want it. He hates Dad more than he hated Mum.'

'And you don't hate him?'

'I can't.' Daniel breathed out slowly. There was something new in his eyes that I wasn't following.

'What do you mean?'

'I owe him,' he replied. 'I owe them both. I did something stupid and he sorted it out for me.'

'Like what?' I leaned forward. 'What did you do?'

'Nothing really, childish stuff,' he said, turning away from me. 'I got into a fight.'

'What happened?'

'Someone was taking the piss out of Mum, a lad from school. We were sixteen. It was down where we used to live before we moved here. She'd-' he stopped for a moment, rubbed his hand across his face. 'It sounds so fucking stupid now, but at the time I wanted to kill her.'

He continued: 'At parents evening she turned up pissed and sat on Mr Melia's lap. He was my Maths teacher and all the girls fancied him. He was always dead flirty, but she was off her head and took it the wrong way. Everyone saw and the next day some lad was taking the piss and I hit him.'

'What did your dad have to do with that?

'I hit the lad hard, broke his jaw,' Daniel said, looking at the floor. 'His Mum and Dad wanted to press charges but my dad talked them out of it. She never said sorry. She blamed me, always did, especially if me dad wasn't there. We got it in the neck even more then.' He wiped his eyes. 'There was one time she got so mad, she had this plank of wood and smashed it into my side. I hadn't done anything wrong. Mum was angry and I was the only person in the house to take it out on. I've never told anyone any of this apart from my family.' His eyes found mine again.

'I...I had no idea.' I couldn't look at him. 'You should talk to someone properly, professionally...'

'What about? Cleaning up my Mum's piss? Helping her up the stairs and into bed, and then trying to make me and Matty tea but setting the pan on fire? When me Dad finally came back, the kitchen was black and the whole house stunk of smoke and he blamed me. Is that what I should talk about?' he shouted, getting louder and louder. 'Talk to someone about always feeling ashamed to bring mates home because they'd see the state of the house or the state of her. Or how about she didn't love us enough to bother picking us up from school, and how she'd go on about us ruining her fun? Where the fuck would I start with that?'

He fell on the couch then, hands over his face, sobbing. His whole body was shaking. He reached for my hand. I touched it lightly.

'I understand, I said slowly, 'but I need time to think.'

'Gina, you fell and hit the cabinet.'

We both knew I hadn't.

The throbbing in my cheek, from where it had hit the coffee table as he threw me across the room during his earlier rampage, was getting worse. I stood up.

'Daniel, I'm leaving.'

CHAPTER THIRTY

STRENGTH: 14.30 Saturday 30th August 2014

The door swung open.

'Brought you an early tea. I might not be able to get back in time later.' His voice had become sing-song false. Somehow, this was worse than the menacing threats and the dark tone he'd had at the start. He placed a tray down on the floor. On it was a plate covered with foil. The smell of chicken seeped out and added to the chemical mix of the room. She ignored the tray as he slid it towards her across the cold floor.

'Charley?' That was all she could manage, one word, the most important one.

'You don't need to worry about your sister. I have that all under control.' He took slow steps towards her until he was so close, she could see the dirt under his fingernails, smell weed on his breath. 'Thinks she's tough, but she's easy to break.' He emphasised break, making it sound like he was snapping something with his tongue.

'Stop panicking, I've brought you some sweets.'

She looked away.

'Haribos, tangy jelly ones? Everyone likes them.'

He started to clear the remnants of lunch up. Gina had tried to force down bites of the sandwich and the apple, but each piece felt like it stuck in her throat and made her choke.

'Big day tomorrow,' he said. 'You need to eat, keep your strength up.'

He had gone mad. Either that or he was trying to send her mad. She stayed bunched up in her blanket, being careful not to move too much.

'Now, I told you that I wouldn't hurt Charley if I didn't have to,' he said. 'She's making it difficult, but I do have it under control. I bought you a new phone.'

'Please, leave her alone,' Gina begged. Her heart felt like it was being sliced open.

'Shut up, you stupid bitch.' The menacing and dark voice was back. He recovered himself with a few breaths and the false happy tone returned. 'As I said, I've bought you a new phone.' He held it up.

Gina prayed that he wouldn't come over to where she sat on the blankets. She couldn't risk that.

He looked at her expectantly. 'Don't I even get a thanks?' A dark cloud of anger passed over his face again. 'Of course I don't. You're an ungrateful bitch. Could have had a nice life and you threw it all away.'

'Please let me go. I won't tell anyone about this.'

'You are a fucking gossip, of course you will.' He stared at her and then took a seat on a stool he'd dragged in. It screeched across the floor. 'First though, there's a few things I want to say to you, while you have to listen.'

They heard a noise then, a thudding from a distance like someone was banging on a door somewhere. He jumped off the stool, knocking it over, swearing before leaving the room. He came back a second later, fussed about with something in his pocket and then pulled out some tape. She resisted the urge to move too much but reflex made her shrink back anyway as he pulled some over her mouth and then to her hands behind her back and her bare feet. Luckily, the blanket stayed in position and he didn't notice what she was hiding beneath it. He shut the door carefully and then his footsteps grew fainter. She couldn't hear much after that, only the sound of muffled voices. It seemed to go on for ages and then he was back, untying her. She gasped for air and rubbed at her wrists and ankles.

'That was close,' he said. There was sweat on his face which he wiped away quickly before taking her tape off.

'Who was it?' she dared to ask. There was some hope that she might tease something out of him.

'No one,' he sneered at her. 'I need to send this text for you.'

He scratched himself, lifting his top to do this. There was a patch of red, freshly rubbed skin on his arm.

'Who would you run to if you needed a break?' he asked. 'Someone that you turn to but doesn't live here and isn't in touch with you anymore.'

'Callum.' It had come to her in a flash, a dangerous idea that would only work if Callum was still the same man he had always been.

'Who?'

'Callum, an ex-boyfriend,' she said steadily, looking right into his eyes. 'He doesn't have a Facebook. You can check on my friend's list on my phone. Callum Peers.'

'If you're lying then you sister will pay,' he said.

'Charley will remember him.'

'Why?' he asked.

'She knows I loved him.' Gina hoped that Charley would get the message.

He gave her a look of contempt. 'I'll be back later. We have to prepare for tomorrow. Eat your food.'

The door slammed and he was gone. Gina felt under the blankets. She'd lost her nerve. Next time he came as close as he had then, she would put her plan into action. But even if Charley did get the message, what could she do? Time was running out.

CHAPTER THIRTY-ONE

Oversized ~ above average in size or number or quantity or magnitude or extent...

~ Am I blowing things out of proportion? Everyone else seems to think so even Jen.

May 2014

I arrived in my oversized sunglasses with an undersized smile.

'What are you doing back, love?' Jen's mum opened the door.

'Only popped home for a bit,' I said with forced happiness like everything was light and easy.

'What do you want?' Jennifer appeared, giving me a filthy look until she saw my face and hers fell. 'It's ok, Mum, you go inside and make sure everyone gets taxis and stuff.'

Her mum gave me another glance, and headed back to the party.

My phone tinged. I'd sent Daniel one text in response to his fifteen. I'd asked him to pack his bags and leave. He'd begged me to meet and talk, tell him where I was. Even as I typed it, I wasn't sure if leaving him was the right thing to do. It was making the fish gnaw away at my stomach and send shoals up to my head so that it was impossible to think straight.

There was also a text from Charley.

How was baby shower? How are you? Xx

I hadn't checked in with her yet today and she was probably panicking. Pangs of guilt were released by the fish too as I imagined her alone in that poky flat thinking I had a cob on with her. But there were things I couldn't expose her to, although she'd argue that she'd seen a lot worse.

'Gina,' Jennifer called me softly. 'Do you want to go upstairs?'

'Where's Jo?'

'She went home already.'

'Good.' I started crying, proper snot-ragged tears as well. I couldn't be arsed with Judgemental Jo at this time. 'I had nowhere else to go, sorry.'

'You can *always* come here,' Jen said gently and then started climbing the stairs, leaving everyone laughing and enjoying themselves in the living room. I wished we were back in Jen's old house, where her room was small but cosy, the walls filled with photos of me, her and Jo. Longing for simpler times is normal when present times are a mess I suppose.

But Jen obviously didn't have her own room these days. The smell of Mark was on the pillow, an awkward mix of expensive aftershave and real man's sweat, as he would call it. A pair of his boxer shorts were on the floor, far too close to where I stood. There were a few photos of him and Jen around the room, on holidays together, all smiley and Facebook friendly. I'd seen them all online but I hadn't been in this room before. Mark usually made upstairs strictly off bounds. We even had to wait downstairs when Jen was finishing getting ready - with Mark giving us the evils because we were off on a night out. He was probably made up when she got pregnant and cut down on spending time with us. Come to think of it, he was probably jumping, cartwheeling happy, when Daniel took over my social life.

'What happened?' Jennifer asked. I took off the sunglasses and she winced. This made me dissolve into a full-on blubbering mess.

'Did he hit you?'

'He pushed me and I fell into the side of the coffee table,' I managed to say when I'd calmed down a bit.

'On purpose?' she asked, still staring at the red mark which had appeared so quickly and which was only going to get worse.

'He was tearing the living room apart and he pushed me out of the way.'

'Did you think it could have been by accident then? Why was he tearing the living room apart?' She placed a hand on my arm.

Mark appeared at the door with a sly grin. 'Daniel's here.'

'I'll go and talk to him, doll. You stay here. I'll give the twat a piece of my mind.'

'Wait.'

She turned back and looked at me.

'I want to tell you why first, because he won't tell you. But don't let on that I've told you ok? Please don't.'

She sat back down on the bed. I gave her the quick version of what he'd told me about his mum. It was almost down to Twitter characters I was trying to get it out that fast.

'Didn't you feel bad leaving him after all that?' she said after a long pause.

'Jen, he hit me.'

'You said he pushed you. It could have been an accident as you said.' She sighed and turned to look me in the eye, never a good sign with her. 'Listen, babe, Mark and me, we've had similar fights, not physically since I'm carrying this little one, but it can be normal for couples as long as he hasn't full on hit you or anything, like he didn't slam you in the face or nothing?'

I nodded, for the first time thinking it might have been good if Jo was here, but then I couldn't face the shame. The fish danced liberally after she left, taking the piss out of me until I collapsed on the bed, exhausted.

Not long passed before I heard Jen's footprints coming up the stairs, and I could sense what would have happened before she even opened the door, came back in and looked me in the eye again.

'He's devastated, babe. I haven't always seen eye to eye with him, but after what you told me about his mum, and seeing his face then - he's in tears and everything. Mark had to get him a shot of whiskey.'

Even before she said all that, I knew my decision had been made.

CHAPTER THIRTY-TWO

ASSAULT: 16.00 Saturday 30th August 2014

'Bloody hell, you again.'

Jen's stringy purple-red hair hung around her orange face. She was wearing a big, blue smock thing with paisley patterns and elasticised leggings. She casually licked a packet of tangy jellies, her fat fingers covered in sugar.

'Do you even care where Gina is?'

'Go home and have a rest, Charley. You need it, babe.' Jen went to shut the door but Charley put her foot in the way and stopped it. She was becoming an expert at that.

She'd tried to rest, tossing and turning for about ten minutes before she gave up. The guilt of doing nothing had started to sweat out of her as the medication lay unopened on the bedside table.

'I want to talk about Daniel's mum.'

'Love, it's absolutely none of your business. It's horrible what he had to go through, so you can excuse the lad losing his rag at times,' she said.

'It doesn't matter what his mum did, it still doesn't excuse what he did to Gina.' It was important to act like she already knew everything.

'I wanted them to work it out. Poor Daniel having a mum like that. It was heartbreaking what Gina was telling me. Some things you can understand making people go a bit mad,' she replied. 'I mean, you both lost your mum but imagine if she'd drank herself to death.'

Charley hid her shock at this revelation. 'Did Gina stay at yours after the baby shower?'

'No, not then. Listen, Charl, Mark is still really upset about losing that contract when we let Gina stay, so I think you should go. Gina will rock up soon with Daniel and you don't

161

want to look like an utter crank when that happens.' She selected another sweet and sucked it.

'Why did she stay here?'

'Not being funny or nothing, but why would she tell you her every move?' Jennifer said with a look of disgust. 'You've only been back in touch, like, a year?'

'Didn't Daniel throw a hot drink over Gina too? Do you think that's ok?'

'Charley, you're on one. Where's all this sudden information come from?'

'I found more definitions,' she said, deciding to be honest, thinking that might scare Jen into telling her even more. The latest ones she'd found in the house, after realising Gina's extra scrawlings on the back of M 'snow day' and 'happy', meant that the next set of definitions were hidden in the back of Gina's favourite photo of their Mum. It still wasn't enough for Field to do anything with though. She needed people like Jen to tell her more.

'Well whoop whoop for you going through your sister's things you weirdo.'

Charley had forgotten about Jen's cruel side. She used to be one of those girls who shouted 'eeeeee' at anyone across the playground who didn't look like a plastic princess in their navy blue uniform. Even though she was two years younger than Gina, Charley had seen this regularly before she got into the private school, which her mum was certain would sort her out.

The three little bitches, Jen, Jo and even Gina, who was ashamed of her bullying, scally past, and had changed. Gina had stayed friends with Jen long after Charley thought she would. Mind you, she wasn't one to talk about choosing good friends.

'Go and ask his fucking family instead of harassing me.'

'You're her best friend and you let her down. At least now you could give a shit and help me find her.'

'I stood up for her at that party. It's not my fault she got back with him.' She was roaring now. Charley half expected a neighbour to call the police if this carried on. And how would that look, pregnant girl versus someone like her?

'I mean it, Charley, fuck off.'

But Gina was more important. Charley stood her ground until it was taken from underneath her. It was like a black force came from behind Jen and threw itself at her.

'Get the fuck out of here.' Mark spat at her as she lay on the floor. He pulled her back up with one arm. His hooked nose and small eyes were burning right into her face. 'Your sister had a really good life off him, didn't have to work, loads of money, nice house, the lot and she threw it all back in his face and fucked everyone else over as well. We're skint because she couldn't sort her life out.' He gave Charley a lingering look. 'The silly bitch deserves everything she gets.'

Charley wiped the gravel from her arms and stood up. She knew exactly where she was going next.

CHAPTER THIRTY-THREE

Proper ~ truly what something is said or regarded to be; genuine

~ I'm a proper grown up and I'm finally in a proper relationship getting proper looked after - can I handle it? Yes I can.

~ Proper happy at the moment!

June 2014

I didn't think I'd ever be the type of person to do this, go back on all my principles and give in to someone else, let them persuade me on what's right and all that.

But looking around me now, I thought about the whirlpool of stones in the driveway at my old house. They were dark grey and there was a well in the middle filled with bigger stones. It had been a joint front garden once, when the neighbours liked us, but then they didn't, which was Charley's fault. They had planted big shrubs to keep us out of sight and out of mind.

It really was an ugly garden which we didn't have much time for as kids, but one winter it had all been covered with snow even all the trees and high bushes. Mum had got everyone in the road together and we'd built snowmen.

'Yours has got a bogeye.' Charley pointed out. The two grey stones I'd picked were different sizes.

'So's yer ma,' I said, using the language of the playground.

'That makes no sense.' Charley retorted adding a perfectly trimmed carrot and matching buttons to hers. I moved the buttons under the carrot to make a different picture all together when she wasn't looking.

The snow disappeared from my mind. It was space and cold bricks after all. The memories were the warm things you could take with you. I had the photo, the favourite one I have of Mum, hair all tousled, cheeks pink and eyes gleaming. I didn't need my old house to think about them.

In front of me was a beautiful cottage with an original fireplace in the living room and the country kitchen I'd always wanted. At my side was my very capable fiancé who could do amazing things with his hands - house-wise I mean obviously! - who was walking around pointing out all the potential. I loved it anyway, potential or not. I'm making this all sound very easy. But ok, it hadn't been the easiest process for me and there had been some 'heated' discussions.

'If we get a joint mortgage isn't this well past our limit?'

'It's not past my limit,' Daniel said, and then added, 'Look, I don't mind. I have the money and I want us to have somewhere amazing that will blow everyone away.'

'Can you at least wait until the house sells? I'll be getting a share off Dad towards the deposit?'

'But how much will you actually have?' Daniel knew about my credit card debts. 'And it might take years to sell in this market.'

'I'd have something,' I insisted. 'I want to pay my way. Please, let's look at what we could both afford equally first, even without the house selling.'

* * * * *

There had been the other houses, the ones in *my* budget. I swear there are some terrible places out there. There was one with half a bathroom and ten sheds in the garden. The walls seemed to be trying to get rid of the old wallpaper themselves, like trees shedding leaves. Even the estate agent, Jim, an ageing man who drove an ageing Vectra and looked constantly disappointed, was pissed off.

He had sweat patches under the arms of his unironed blue shirt, his thick grey head of hair all over the show from where he kept scratching it, trying to promote the houses but having

166

no answers on why anyone should want to buy them. He took us to three, with each seeming to represent its own decade.

I got a full waft of the 1970s when the door opened to the Penny Lane one I was pinning my hopes on. A phone from that era sat in the middle of the room, the only piece of furniture to be found. I went upstairs alone to catch my breath and maybe find a renovated bathroom. Instead, there was some burnt orange monstrosity, like someone had taken revenge on the colour and tortured it slightly. I had to look away.

I walked back down the stairs. Jim grimaced as the rail buckled and I ended up stumbling into the living room. Daniel had the phone held to his ear with a serious expression.

'What?' I asked.

'The 20s called. They want their house back.'

'Oh haha.'

'What's up?' asked Daniel. He noticed that I was on the verge of tears.

'I thought Penny Lane would be a bit more, I don't know, glam than this.' I was disappointed even though there had been some really cheap houses here.

'John Lennon would turn in his grave,' Daniel offered.

* * * * *

Then there was this house, the Alderly Edge one Daniel had shown me on the laptop. It was exciting to be in this position with someone, buying a house. It had helped us to sort a lot out, and now we were happy. My 'proper' fiancé gave me a long, lingering kiss. We weren't looking back on past mistakes. We both knew that didn't help anyone.

I'd even got used to my new job. Daniel gave me time off whenever I wanted it, like today, to come and visit this house, which was pretty cool. And there were no more visits from Natalie either. Hopefully she'd been sacked, the little cow.

There was one thing about the house – something I'd only then found out about - that bothered me.

167

'You didn't tell me you knew the owner,' I said, as Daniel pointed out how we could landscape the garden quite quickly with some cheap decking his mate could get a hold of.

'A friend of our Ken's owns it, and the old woman who lived here died. I don't have to give the keys back for a few days. He said I can get a real feel of the place first. It's a dead good deal.'

A hefty grunting nose that sounded like a trapped pig came from the front garden. I walked around to see what was happening and found it was Ken moving a fridge on a roller thing. He stopped and nodded at us, his big red face dripping with sweat.

'Why are you moving things in if we're just viewing it?'

'We should make an offer on this now,' Daniel said, ignoring me. 'There's no chain.'

'Is this definitely the right place for us?'

'Why wouldn't this be the right place for us?' Daniel demanded.

'I can't afford it,' said quietly.

'I fucking can, as I keep telling you,' he shouted back.

'Don't talk to her like that,' Ken bellowed. 'You sound like your dad.'

Daniel put his head down and pushed past us. Ken sighed.

'If our Dan's investing in this place, kid, he doesn't want to be messed around,' he said.

Ignoring his comment, I turned away. Karen was legging it up the pathway, pink rollers still jammed into her head. She'd was wearing a beige leather jacket with silver studs on the arms (the girl loved to dress for battle), black leggings that led into soft brown Ugg boots and a bag which said 'scouse boutique' as if she needed to remind Manchester where she was from

'Love, this is proper amazing!' she seemed to say to the house rather than me. 'Where's our Danny? I've got some ideas for changing that shit kitchen.'

No way was she getting her 'interior design' hands on the place. Her kitchen looked like a brothel, all red and black in sinister shades and sharp edges. But I didn't have the energy to argue right then and there.

'I'm on my way to see our Charley,' I lied as she gave me an air kiss. As I got in the car I decided that I may as well actually go and visit my sister.

* * * * *

'I'm a proper grown up now, getting a mortgage and all that.' I swung back on the rocking chair in Charley's flat, nearly taking my eye out on the corner of a picture that fell off the wall, unsettled by my swinging. It carried onto the floor and the glass smashed into pieces.

'I'll get you another one,' I said quickly.

'Don't worry about it,' Charley said, looking at me and not the chaos I'd caused. *Did you not feel like a proper grown up when you got engaged?* Her eyes said to the ring on my finger. Or maybe that was me.

'Not in work today Charl?' I hastily changed the subject.

'They're letting me cover a residential soon, so I get time back for that.'

'That's brilliant.' I thought it was great that Charley was working with troubled young kids. Dad wasn't too sure.

'Come over then if you're so worried about her,' I'd said on the carefully arranged time-difference phone call.

'I'm busy with work, and Kathryn has another exhibition on,' he replied.

Making an exhibition of herself, I thought.

'Do you ever think that things are a bit intense with Daniel?' Charley said out the blue, eyes down to the floor. It must have taken her a lot to say that. She never challenges me anymore.

'What do you mean?' I said, although I knew exactly what she meant.

'Sorry, it's not really my place,' she replied.

A buzz from my bag saved us both. I answered it.

'Come back to the house. I want to show you something.' Daniel's voice had something in it that made my insides feel warm.

'I'll have to go Charl,' I said, glad to avoid the upcoming conversation. 'Got some stuff to do at the house.'

'So you're definitely buying it then?' she said at the door.

'Yes, you're going to love it!' I screeched which only made her raise an eyebrow.

I rang my dad on the way. Something I should *never* do when I'm excited but somehow I never learn.

'Dad, me and Daniel are buying a house!'

'How are you affording that?'

'It's fine,' I lied. 'I've been saving.' I left out the part about the mortgage being solely in Daniel's name until I could contribute.

'How long will it all take to go through?'

'There's no chain, and Daniel knows the people selling, so not long. Think we can move in as it's all going through-'

'Great – we've been looking at a holiday home for when the old house sells-'

My turn to interrupt. 'Me and Charley get equal shares.' I always felt sick confronting my dad, but this was too important.

Silence.

'I have Mum's letter, and a copy of the will was in it too,' I added, also thinking, *I know you had to buy her out when you landed back on your feet, but you got us into that mess.*

170

'Well, we'll sort that out, yeah.' There was an awkward cough. 'As long as Charley doesn't use it for-'

'She's ok, now, Dad.' *As you would know if you came and saw us now and again.*

'Well we've got some other news.' He sounded excited *now*.

I could hear the smile in his voice.

'I'm going to be a granddad.'

Fish plummeted from my stomach down to my feet. My first thought was *what the fuck has Charley done and why had she told him first?*

Dad had started talking again. 'Georgia is very excited and Kathryn and I are already planning a trip to London. You'll have to drop down and see us when we're there.'

Oh Georgia. Kathryn's daughter. He should have been offering to come up and see us when he was in London, leave Kathryn's family to deal with themselves for a bit so he could see his daughters. I rang off without saying any of that.

* * * * *

When I finally got back, the front door was open and candles were set in a trail leading to the living room, where a new sofa, light blue and wide, and thick with cushions, lay next to a coffee table. There was a bottle of champagne, two glasses and some chocolates. The sofa and table were ones I had picked out online the other day as options for our new home. I felt his arms around my waist.

'Sorry about before. I should never have spoken to you like that,' he said, taking my hand and leading me fully into the room.

'I want,' he started lifting me up against the wall, 'to christen every room.'

The fish danced as they always do at these moments, but then disappeared. Even that part of our relationship was good at the moment.

'You help me,' he murmured. 'You calm me down.'

171

And with that, he laid me down on the floor.

After we were finished, the iPad came out. It seems that the modern day post-coital thing is to get iPhones and iPads out and we sat playing with ours. Daniel smiled and then showed me his screen. It was the website for Gretna Green.

'Let's do it as just us, and then surprise everyone with a party in September,' he said. 'Come on, we keep talking about it.'

'Isn't it too late to get a booking for this September?' I asked.

'I reserved it, in case, when we first talked about it,' Daniel said. Sunday 31st August 2014.'

CHAPTER THIRTY-FOUR

ALIBI: 18.00 Saturday 30th August 2014

There was no one behind the desk. A middle-aged man in a cap kept dinging the bell, standing back and swearing for a minute, before resting his finger back on it.

'I've been here bloody ages,' he said, turning around to look at who was behind him. 'There's no one even here!'

He stormed past, almost knocking Charley off her feet and was out the door. Moments later a policewoman appeared and stood by the bell.

'Yes?' She looked straight at Charley, folds of face fat hiding her neck.

'Could I speak to Officer Field please?'

'He's not in for another hour,' the policewoman replied. 'You can report to another police officer who's available before then?'

Charley hesitated for a moment, 'I'll wait for him.'

She checked her phone again to see if he'd replied and moved to the waiting area with all the other disgruntled people.

The posters on the walls were an unwelcome distraction. They were like advertisements for successful crimes, a car-jacking gang to be aware of, drugs on the street to stay away from, domestic abuse to watch out for signs of, all interspersed with smiling community officers who were ready to save the day.

Charley felt the sickness in the pit of her stomach rise with each second that ticked by on the large clock. A few more people came and went. There was an interview room right next to where she sat, and every word from a distressed sounding woman came out through the door, muffled but understandable. There was an ex-boyfriend threatening her, turning up at the house, leaving her angry voicemails. The woman was worried about what he might do. Charley wrapped her arms around herself and tried not to listen.

* * * * *

Finally, Officer Field came in through the door. He towered over the desk, hiding the chinless woman behind his wide frame. He glanced in Charley's direction and narrowed his eyes slightly before walking over.

Charley stood up. 'I want to report an assault.' The words tumbled out.

'Would you like to come this way?' he replied, leading her towards a room on the other side of the station.

'She's not fucking next,' a man muttered as they went past him.

The door squeaked open. Inside was a table with chairs scattered around. He left Charley sitting on one of them, the coldness of the plastic seeping through her clothes, and came back moments later with a stack of paper. He went through the formalities of her details as the blood rushed to her head, and then became absorbed in reading some of the notes he'd scribbled in handwriting she couldn't decipher.

'I got your missed calls and texts and came in straight away,' Officer Field said in a low voice while he carried on reading.

'I think Mark Murphy is involved in the kidnapping of my sister.'

'Charley-'

'He assaulted me, pushed me over, spat in my face and said Gina deserves everything she gets.'

'Any witnesses that *he* assaulted you?'

'Only his girlfriend,' Charley replied. 'She said he was upset about losing some contract and blamed Gina.'

'Have you been to the hospital?

'Well no, but I will have bruises. I tried to ring you and then came straight to the station.'

'I'll be back in a minute.' He stood up suddenly and left the room.

174

She sat confused until he came back around fifteen minutes later. He studied the papers on the desk and wouldn't look at her. 'I think you're going to have to be careful here.'

'What do you mean?'

He tapped his pen on the table.

'We had a call from a Mark Murphy reporting you for assault in the last hour,' he said. 'That's what's in the file here.'

'What?'

'I spoke to him and he isn't going to take it any further.'

'But it's only his word against mine,' Charley said aware that there were cracks in her voice.

'He has an independent witness.'

'But no one else was there apart from Jen and-'

'Charley, I am going to help you, but I would advise that you don't report this officially.'

She couldn't speak.

'Is there anything else you think will help us find your sister?'

'I also found some other definitions, but only to R.' She took them from her bag and let them spill out onto the table.

He read through them. 'But none of these imply that Mark has kidnapped your sister. They don't really show anything in fact.'

'But they show how badly Daniel was treating her.'

'You can't accuse both Daniel and Mark at the same time.'

Charley's phone vibrated in her pocket. As she read the text, her blood ran cold.

'Who's that?' Officer Field leaned over.

'It says it's Gina, but it's not.'

'Miss Ellison you said that last time-'

175

'You don't understand. It's saying that she's with someone called Callum. The only Callum she would know is my ex-boyfriend.'

'Why don't you try and call the number?' Field asked.

It rang without going to voicemail. The phone flashed in Charley's hand.

Another text, *leave me alone for a bit*

'Can you trace the number?'

'Are you sure this isn't your sister?'

'Callum…he's dangerous. He's angry with Gina.'

The door opened making Charley jump.

It was Officer Thompson.

'Excuse me for a minute,' Field said and left the room.

'Get it sorted.' Charley heard as Field came in again and sat down.

'What's going on?' she asked.

'She thinks you're wasting police time.' He wouldn't look her in the eye.

'But why would she-'

'We've discussed why she wouldn't trust you before,' he snapped. 'I've had to tell her that you're here about some anti-social behaviour by your flats. I told you not to come here.'

'Why would you say that? Gina's still missing!'

'I've told you that no one will treat this as a missing person's case yet.'

'What if he hurts her?' Charley whispered. 'You have to help me.'

'We have to figure out what is going on,' he replied, 'get some real evidence. Don't worry, I won't give up.'

CHAPTER THIRTY-FIVE

Query - problem, matter, issue, inquiry, doubt

~ Yes doubt!

~ Ever question what you're doing with a group of people? This was meant to be my hen!

~ Ever question what your fiancé is doing with these people?

Doubt ☹

July 2014

'Daniel, get over here, lad!'

Lydia was waiting with a pile of Louis Vuitton suitcases. 'What the hell?' she screamed in our faces when we reached her. 'What have you got on, lad? Is that Next?'

'Yeah, and what?' Daniel replied.

''kinell is it?' Lydia belonged to the breed of scousers that used a weird combination of fucking and hell to make a new word. She must have known my cardie was from Next too, the bitch.

Karen ran over in full holiday mode, wearing a fuchsia pink dress with straps. 'Lydia, wait there while I get this selfie sorted out, girl,' she said. When they finally had the right shot, they looked down at my case - a Primarni flowery offering, half the size of their smallest one.

'We invested in these ones cos we travel a lot,' Lydia said, although the only places I'd known them to travel to were Glastonbury and Ibiza.

'Who's looking after the baby, Lyd?' Jemma appeared and gave everyone a lipgloss kiss. Lydia had done the standard build-up to leaving the baby Facebook updates, like every good Mum does. Her last emotional offering from the night before had been. *Chillin with the bby ♥ with our cover on the couch :D gunna miss him :'(*

'His dad,' Lydia replied in an uninterested voice.

I didn't know her ex's name. In fact, I'd started to believe it actually was 'The Baby's Dad'.

I looked around and held in a sigh. These were my girlies for the weekend. Daniel's boys consisted of Matthew, José who had some free time between pre-season training, and a few lads from work.

* * * * *

The flight was pretty quiet as me and Daniel ended up sitting away from the others. It was when we got to the accommodation that the problems started. Karen and Lydia hadn't booked enough space in those magical apartments they'd blagged.

'Oh shit, four people are meant to be staying in the hotel round the corner. There aren't enough bedrooms here,' Karen said and looked pointedly in the direction of me, Daniel, Matthew and Jemma.

'Not a problem. We'll only be sleeping there anyway, won't we?' Daniel spread his arms out like he was taking it all on board. 'We'll launch our stuff in and come over to chill by your pool.'

'Arr thanks, babe.' Karen kissed him on the cheek. 'There's a room each for you two, don't worry,' she said to Matthew and Jemma. Melissa couldn't make it. She was looking after the kids and probably using the opportunity to have a break from Matthew.

Problem number two came almost straight away. The hotel room was on the tenth floor.

'I'll take the stairs.' I was scared of foreign lifts after getting stuck in one with Mum years ago. We were in there for ages, trapped with people and their luggage. It even went pitch black for the last five minutes. I was thirteen and crying like a baby while Mum massaged my hand and talked to me in a calming voice. It wasn't until we got out that I realised her face was as white as a sheet.

'Are you mad?' Matthew asked, lugging a case towards the iron doors and jabbing the button. The lift doors opened and revealed a tin-can coffin.

'I don't know why anyone gets bothered about lifts. Even if it gets stuck you're safe,' Jemma yawned and went in, putting her best carefully painted toenail forward in her strappy sandals. I shook my head and turned back towards the stairs, but a sharp tug on my arm hauled me in the opposite direction. The doors closed in the reflection of the lift mirror.

'Stairwells in places like this are proper dangerous,' Daniel said. His voice seemed miles away.

'Are you ok, babe?' Jemma touched my arm lightly. Her orange face was unusually pale looking.

'She's fine!' Daniel snapped. I gripped the wall to steady myself as the lift moved.

'Listen, I'm sorry! Chill out!' Daniel said as we reached the room. 'No way were you walking up those stairs on your own.' He stood uncertainly in the middle of the room as I walked past him and launched my case onto the bed. 'Are you going to sulk about this?'

I ignored him and headed for the bathroom, locking myself in. I ran the shower, keeping the water that little bit too hot so that it stung my skin. I heard the door slam. My arm throbbed from where he'd grabbed at it. As I turned the water off, I heard a rustling noise from the room. My heart lifted for a second thinking that Daniel hadn't really gone out, but was instead waiting to surprise me with a proper sorry.

But when I got out there was an old woman with a head full of rollers going through my suitcase. I turned the light on and saw it was Karen with no eyelashes on.

'Only checking what the theme should be for the hen night,' she smirked. 'See you over there. Gotta get me face sorted.'

Before I could build up the bottle to have a go at her she left, and Jemma came in wearing a bikini, which was slung down low on the knicker line, with little bows collected at the sides. The blue bounced off her skin and made it look firmer.

'Come on, darling, let's go to the pool,' she said, linking arms with me.

I went back into the bathroom and put on a sissy frill and floral cut out swimsuit. Not quite a bikini and not quite a swimsuit, it was designed to frill up the love handles and meet over my stomach to hide that too. I added a shawl thing so that she wouldn't see the mark on my arm from where Daniel had grabbed it in the lift.

'Sure you're ok?' she asked.

'I'm fine.'

We walked slowly across the road to the sound of club anthems. The apartments were amazing of course. The others, the ones selected for this upper class accommodation, were lying on stripy padded sun loungers next to a pool. Karen was sprawled across on what could only be described as a sun 'bed', which set her apart from the others.

She dropped the magazine and folded her arms, placing her chin on her hands and carried on reading it from the floor. 'Need me back to be brown to fuck,' she explained as a greeting to us.

'Karen, this is proper amazing!' Jemma gushed.

'Have a look inside, girls,' she muttered. I could detect even through her sunglasses that she was already a bit sick of the sight of us. Jemma didn't need telling twice. We walked over the peach tiles and past the vanilla-coloured columns. There was a lot of wickety stuff, baskets with trees forced into football shapes, as if José had to be reminded of his career everywhere he went. Someone had gone overboard on the pink flowers, but it did give the air a nice sweet scent, mixed in with that warm holiday smell you always get.

'They've got a courtyard for fuck's sake!' Jemma whispered. She danced over to one of the plush white sofas and threw herself down onto it.

We went back outside where the pool had become a menagerie of colours, from the bikinis to the lip-gloss, and even the cocktails that Karen had arranged for people to serve to us. This was a Tropical Fish tank at its best. I sank into my gills, my bad colouring and my badly shaped body suddenly becoming all the more apparent. I felt better after about five raspberry mojitos.

* * * * *

I didn't see Daniel all day but Karen told us not to worry as all the boys had topped up enough at the sunbeds before we'd left. I'd naively thought Daniel had been working outside more. The boys and the girls were dividing. Karen instructed us all to tan like our lives depended on it, but she had some St Tropez mousse to top us all up later if the worst should happen.

'Girls, it's our night - I mean Gina's night.' Karen threw a silver sash over me embodied with the initials D & G, like I was a bottle of perfume. She was wearing a pink, sparkly cowboy hat - the type we used to wear on nights out in sixth-form ten years ago.

'I decided to go all retro,' she explained. 'To fit with the clothes you've brought.' I opened my mouth to ask what she meant by that, but Karen plonked a version of her pink cowboy hat on me and turned away to do the same to all the others.

'Where are the boys going?' I asked innocently as we strode on like stragglers from a gay pride march. That seemed to bring Karen back down to earth. Jemma gave me a wide-eyed warning.

'Oh they'll be fucked off their faces already,' she answered. 'José can't even get it up after an afternoon session.' I digested this unnecessary information.

* * * * *

181

At the port, the boats packed tightly together as posh-looking people fizzed about. The air was rich with the smell of sizzling fish and car fumes. Every so often we'd have to move out of the way to let a Mercedes or some other flash effort get past.

A lad walked past looking like something off Made in Chelsea. Many of them did, but this one stuck out because Karen said 'Fit' without pausing in her stride. Anthony would have said something funny here, but I had no sarcasm allies. Jo would have taken the piss out of Karen to her face, then played the dumb card to get a laugh and would have pulled it off. Even Jennifer would have challenged the 'fit' statements, especially when they referred to cars. Charley would have cast an eye over the whole thing and left quickly.

It was a relief to hobble into a bar and clutch at a cocktail menu. After a while, and about three of the pink cosmos, I even started to enjoy myself. Karen and Lydia got into a heated debate about the better mascara to use, so it was me and Jemma left talking. She was much better without them, telling me about her ex who'd cheated on her, and how she'd known Karen for years and she was the best boss ever, 'but only 'cos she never comes in, like, so I get to run the place.' I started to relax more so that the euro-trash bombastic music from the bar sounded tempting. I did a shoulder shuffle dance, my usual warm-up.

'What's that, hun?' Jemma touched my bruised skin lightly. I'd let the shawl fall away from the top of my arm. She said it quietly even though Karen and Lydia were now shimmying with their respective mascaras out in some kind of tribal scouse make-up dance.

'Babe, I won't say anything, but you need to get away from him.' Her fingers running across my skin felt so kind that I had tears in my eyes. 'He's not... he doesn't treat you very nice. The others won't dare say it 'cos he's, like, Karen's cousin but you shouldn't put up with that. I don't care if you're engaged and that. You can get out of it.'

'He didn't mean it though.' I pulled my arm away, pulled the shawl thing back over the bruise. She looked doubtful and I could feel my face burning under all the make-up and the lights.

'Where's Karen?' I asked to break the silence.

'She's there,' Jemma said in a strange voice, like despair and boredom at the same time. I looked in the direction of Jemma's smokey-eyed gaze (she'd done a great job with silver and black eyeshadow). I could only see what looked like two people grappling in the corner, and then a strobe bounced off Karen's engagement ring and almost blinded me as she grabbed the hair of some randomer. I moved my head further out to get a look. They were kissing furiously, her and some lad with long hair and an expensive looking shirt opened a button too far.

'She's always like this,' Jemma said. She was shaking her head and jabbing at the ice in her cocktail with her straw.

Lydia tried to entice us into a dance, not seeming one bit arsed about Karen's behaviour, and I did a half-hearted shuffle until the harlot came back and threw her arms around us. Her eyelashes ran down her face like little spiders. Even her curly blow had given up - the hair around her face was all frizzled, like the curls had been blown up out of her head.

'Gina, sorry to tell ya this on ya hen night, babe,' she paused dramatically, letting another spider take its place on her cheek, 'but ALL men are twats.'

Jemma jumped down off her chair and the other girls got their bags and moved in unison.

'What's going on?' I picked my bag up and whispered to Jemma. I got my answer before she could open her mouth.

'He's in a fucking strip club, innee?' Karen launched at us. 'Come 'head girls – we're not being made a show of by our fellas in another country.'

'She only does it 'cos she hates José being in strip clubs.' Jemma sighed, retelling a tale she didn't sound like she believed.

'Does he go much at home?'

'Yeah, all the time!' She lowered her face closer to mine and pretended to play with the strap of her shoe. 'Last Christmas there was even a rumour that the footie club organised a night with a load of lap dancers for the players. It was a converted warehouse thing they set up as a party place. Karen was fuming for weeks but José denied it – said they had a casino night.'

The fish froze around my heart. As I was such a disappointment in bed, would Daniel take the opportunity to pay for a better experience? Did they actually do more than dance? I wasn't sure what happened in those back rooms.

We got to the place within minutes. Karen was on her phone and storming the steps of the club, legging it past the bouncers. Lydia tried to follow her but was pushed back by the big arm of an angry looking one. It didn't really matter because Karen was out two seconds later shoving José down the steps.

'Why aren't we fucking getting married, aye? Is it because you'd rather be getting private dances from slags? Yer a fucking cunt.' She started punching José in the back then, and he curled up into a standing ball.

Daniel and the lads followed them out.

'Karen…Karen, leave it, calm down.' Daniel gripped hold of her wrists, firmly but gently in a way that wouldn't leave bruises. She fell into him, sobbing her heart out. The rest of us watched until Karen span off her heels and fell into me.

'Are you starting, you stupid bitch?' She pulled at my hair and dragged me down to the ground. 'Yer a lucky cow havin' someone like 'im – you remember tha.'

Her nails reached for my face as I tried to fight her off. Eventually she was dragged back and Daniel appeared in her place and helped me up.

'Don't you ever touch her again,' he said, his face right against Karen's. 'Get her to bed.'

He turned back to me. 'Come on.'

I followed.

184

'I'm so sorry I forced you into this. They're all mad,' he said as we headed away from them. Karen had turned to hysterics, her cries managing to drown out the music of the nearby bars until we got far enough away. He kicked at the sand that had been blown onto the pavement by the beach. 'I've been a total dick.'

I didn't reply.

'I shouldn't have let Karen organise this and…I'm sorry about the lift thing before. I thought that, like, it would help if you faced it.'

'It didn't.'

He stopped and took me back into his arms, grabbing the bruised part as he did. I winced.

'Did I do that to you?' He slipped the material away from my skin. 'Jesus Christ.'

A couple walked past, arms around each other, laughing.

'Bet you're questioning what you're even doing with me.'

'It's not your fault what Karen's like,' I murmured. 'But it would have been nice to feel like I had a choice about my own hen.'

'I know,' he replied. 'Why don't we go and get our own hotel and make this a holiday for us?'

I smiled. 'Great idea. We walked along the beach, heading away from all the others. 'Will they split up?'

'Karen and José? No.' Daniel shook his head. 'He'll never leave her.' He laughed then added, 'no one gets away from this family alive.'

CHAPTER THIRTY-SIX

ESCAPE: 20.30 Saturday 30th August 2014

She'd waited hours for this.

With every noise, possible footsteps or a distant sound of a door, she gripped under the blanket and strengthened her resolve.

There was no mistaking his heavy boots gaining ground towards the room now.

She clung to her weapon. Her plan was so obvious. He mustn't have been thinking straight, taking her shoes and leaving a more dangerous option behind.

The door swung open and there he was; a thick, heavy figure in the doorway illuminated by the light inside the room.

* * * * *

'Your sister doesn't give up,' he said, scratching at his arm. Gina noticed it had become a red mosaic of scaly skin. 'Gets very obsessed doesn't she?' He moved further into the room and Gina strengthened her hold of the object under the pillow. 'Well, maybe 'obsessed' isn't the right word. Would 'addicted' be better?' He laughed, which sent a hollow, echoed sound around the room.

Gina took a deep breath. He needed to move a bit closer. 'You'll never get away with this. Charley will go to the police and they'll find out everything. You'll be locked away for years.'

She was terrified inside, but there was also a strange calm that had come over her, like this was her chance and she had to go all or nothing. 'And you should be, you and all your fucking psycho family - the ones left who didn't drink themselves to death.'

He was in her face then, screaming incomprehensibly and spitting. Now. It had to be now.

She caught him fully in the eyes, taking him by surprise. He fell backwards into a noisy heap on the floor, flailing about like a crab on its back. The taste of the chemical spray drops hit her own face as she ran through them. She dropped the bottle of disinfectant on the floor. He made a grab at her but she jumped lightly and made it out of the room.

Outside was a corridor with doors either end. The only light came from thin slits of windows, too high up to see out of. Both doors looked the same. She had to make a decision fast. She ran to the left.

Her bare feet hit the ground hard as she raced to the door and pulled at the handle. It wouldn't open. It was locked. Fighting back the urge to cry, she ran towards the other door.

He came out at her, throwing his whole body over hers and forcing her to the floor with a heavy thud. She cried out in pain.

'You fucking bitch.'

The smell of chemicals was choking as his face stayed close to hers. His weight was too much on her. She couldn't breathe. Her heart was beating hard and fast against the cold concrete beneath her.

Finally, he pulled himself off her. Instinctively she tried to get away, clawing at the ground, snapping her fingernails as she scraped desperately at the floor. He held onto her ankle, lightly, teasingly and then started to drag her back slowly. She shouted out, knowing it wouldn't make any difference.

Marks of her blood and tears stained the floor; something had caught on the front of her t-shirt and ripped it across the front. She twisted her head, tried to look up and watched the door getting further away from her. He scraped her back along the floor towards the room.

Things soon went dark again.

CHAPTER THIRTY-SEVEN

Real - used to emphasise the significance or seriousness of a situation

~ Anthony doesn't understand how very 'real' my relationship is now.

~ What Daniel wants is normal. Isn't it?

July 2014

It was like an undercover operation.

The bar was only down the road from the office but I couldn't be seen. There was too much at stake. I tottered over the cobbles in my killer heels, nearly toppling over when I saw Anthony had bagged a window seat. Jesus Christ, did he not get what I was risking here?

I stormed in and stopped in my tracks as he flashed me one of those smiles.

'Why are you sitting in full view of the world?'

'Hi then, Gina.' He smiled and ran his hand through his hair which made me realise he was nervous.

'Yeah, hi,' I said, a whole bunch of fish feeding on the nerves in my stomach. 'Can we move?'

He shrugged but stood up, catching my arm loosely. 'You ok?'

'Fine, why?' My face was heating up so I turned away from him and headed up the stairs.

We sat down at another free table away from outside view. The sun streamed in through the skylight and warmed us up a bit too much. I looked up at the clear ceiling. It was a Goldfish bowl sauna, annoying but safe from the outside world at least. Sweat trickled down my neck and I could feel beads of it down my bra too.

Anthony was wearing a blue shirt, purple tie and grey suit pants. He never dressed like that. Maybe the hoodie or print t-shirt days were finally over.

'We could sit outside instead?' he suggested.

It was a hot day and I could see the sun dancing off the tables outside. There was a holiday-feel across the city. Office workers with their legs out, blouses a button further down and a sense of smiley hope about life that would be taken away again when the clouds inevitably returned. Sitting outside would have been heaven, but I couldn't risk it. You never knew when someone random would walk past and see you.

'What's happened with work then? Why did they make you redundant?' He pretended to read the menu.

'They didn't. I left.'

'Why? I thought it was one of those jobs that paid well and you could still doss about a bit.' He still didn't look up.

'I'm working for Daniel's company.' I wanted to meet his eye but he didn't give me the chance to. He didn't answer that but carried on staring at the food list like it was the most exciting thing he'd ever seen. The waitress came over and took our drinks order. I ordered a bottle of Pinot Grigio, which arrived almost immediately. I sloshed some into my glass and offered him some.

'I'm sure bottles of wine used to be bigger,' I joked. He didn't smile.

'How you getting home?'

'Daniel drives me. Saves on petrol and everything. Or if he works late I can drive in or get the train.' I took a sip of my drink. It was hardly going to replace the sweat I was losing, but it felt nice and cool running down my throat.

'There was an article in the *New Scientist* that said you only need two days off a week from drinking.' I said to lighten the mood, or maybe justify myself, I wasn't sure. The wine was making me hazy already.

'You drink five nights a week?' Anthony was turning things around again when I thought he'd ask what the fuck I was doing reading New Scientist, or at least their Twitter feed. Same thing.

'I really want to get chips,' I announced, changing the subject.

'Order chips if you want them.' Finally, he looked up at me.

'You'll only take the piss.'

'When have I ever done that?'

I realised it was Daniel who made comments about my overeating, not Anthony.

'I want to have a flat wedding stomach.' I smiled. He didn't.

'How are the plans going then?' He said it like that was a hard question to ask. Obviously, I couldn't tell him about Gretna Green.

'Great, fine.' I took another sip of wine and looked at how he was dressed again. 'You got a job interview?'

'Something like that.' He took a drink of the coke that the waitress had put down on the table. When did he get so cryptic? A horrible thought crossed my mind. Anthony could be dressed for a date, not an interview. He even had a slight air of nervous sweat about him. The fish were hammerhead sharks, tapping against my heart. I told them not to be daft.

'To be honest,' he started, sighing in a way that I didn't like the sound of, 'I've been really worried about you.'

'Why?'

'The last time I saw you properly was months ago.'

'Don't be daft,' I said, 'I've seen you loads since then.'

'You give me what looks like a subtle Nazi salute from your driveway and then keep your head down,' he said. 'Oh, and the odd text.'

'It's a bit hard when you hate my fiancé.'

191

'I don't *hate* him,' Anthony said. 'I think that he's a bit, controlling, sometimes.'

I didn't answer. I was fuming.

'How you getting on with his family?' he said. 'That fight between his dad and uncle was mental. And his brother is a bit of a twat.'

'His family isn't his fault, Anthony,' I replied in my best higher moral and fairer person voice, although I did agree with him about them.

'You wouldn't mess with them though, would you?' he pushed.

I looked out of the window. The waitress came and took our food order.

'So, where are you going after this, all dressed up?' I asked, again to try and lighten the mood.

'If we were still friends on Facebook then you'd know what today was.'

'We are still friends on Facebook.' We were today anyway. I activated and deactivated my account daily and only looked at what people did, never commented. Daniel had kicked off when I'd said things on lads' photos or statuses so it wasn't worth the hassle.

'What is today then?' I was determined not to be put off.

'Going to meet the cast for my new play.' He said it as casually as he could, but there was a light in his eyes when he looked up. The waitress came and I didn't order chips. Daniel was giving me a lift home, and I'd end up cracking and telling him that I'd stuffed my face. I'd also have to pretend I'd done it alone, which would be weird.

'God, that's amazing!' I said.

'Are you going to come?'

'Yeah of course,' I thought about the excuses I could make up to Daniel. 'Tell me all about it.' I was really pleased for him, but everything seemed hard to concentrate on these days, even his details of the play.

'How was the hen thing?' Anthony said when he'd judged that I'd zoned out slightly.

Maybe it was the wine but I kind of told the truth.

'I didn't really enjoy it,' I said.

'Why not?' he asked.

'Well...I don't feel like I fit in with that group,' I started.

'Daniel's close friends and family?' he interrupted.

I realised how that sounded. 'Maybe I need to get to know them all better. Me and Daniel had a great time together though.'

'Things have moved fast,' Anthony nodded. 'I think he wants too much, too soon.'

'He loves me,' I challenged. 'Everything he does is for me.' When did I start talking like a Stepford Wife?

'Including not letting you see your own sister?' he said. 'Or your friends.'

'What?'

'Don't worry, Charley hasn't said anything but I did ask her why she didn't call around to the house anymore,' he said. 'She said you preferred to call in at the flat. Then I asked her the last time she'd actually seen Daniel...'

'There are reasons why he isn't comfortable with her,' I said, but the guilt was nipping at me.

'Why is seeing Charley difficult for Daniel?'

'There are things I can't tell you,' I replied. 'He needs time.' I was working on that, getting him to believe people could change, and that all addicts don't end up like his mum.

'That's out of order. She's your sister,' Anthony was becoming more annoyed. 'You think you're in a normal relationship here?'

I didn't answer.

'I've seen him and heard him too,' he continued.

'What do you mean?'

'Telling you not to stop and speak to me when you're going into the house and that. It's not a real relationship at all, Gina.'

I was furious then. Why were people always making me feel like I wasn't in a real relationship? Anthony doesn't understand how very 'real' my relationship is now. What Daniel wants is normal. Isn't it? He did lose his mum because of her addiction and nearly lost himself.

'You can't judge me. Look at you and Lydia.'

'Me and Lydia?' he said. 'We're talking about you, so don't try and change the subject.'

The food came. The mozzarella and tomato salad stayed on my plate. The salmon and cream cheese baguette and wedges stayed on Anthony's plate. I wanted to leave even though I felt really sad, like proper deeply, hit you in the stomach, fish all over the show, sad.

I didn't want to lose Anthony as a friend, but we were behaving like this was a bad first date or a meeting between exes.

'Gina,' he started, 'I don't want to fall out with you.'

'Then don't.'

There was more trouble when it was time to pay. I'd brought the wrong card. Well, it wasn't exactly that. I had no money in my account anymore; my wages got paid into the joint account with Daniel, where the mortgage and bills came out of, or rather where my wages would be paid into once a figure was decided. It wasn't a joint account, yet, but in his name as that helped with his mortgage application, and we needed time to get an appointment with the bank

'Shit, I've brought the wrong card.' I played that game, even putting it down on the table and everything.

194

'What, is it an old one?' Anthony sounded disinterested yet still had a quick look.

'Yeah – forgot to cut it up.'

But I had it on the table and I knew from a quick glance that he had seen it didn't expire until next year. Anthony noticed everything.

'It'll be like working for yourself.' Daniel had said when selling the job to me.

Except I'll be working for you. I said to myself. These two lines spun around in my head until the golden outcome became the realisation that I was now dependent on Daniel.

* * * * *

We stood up and walked down the stairs. The uncomfortable silence was something I couldn't handle with Anthony. I think even he was surprised by the hug though; there was real emotion in it that took me aback too.

'Gina…' when I finally let go of him, he let my name hang in the hot beer air. 'If you ever need to talk-'

'Get a room, dickheads.' A drunk leered at us. I turned away from him and caught something that filled my stomach with fish.

Lydia was at the bar. Her eyebrows perfectly painted, in skinny jeans and high heels, an oversized top and curled hair. Her face looked like it had been painted on in permanent make-up.

'What are you doing?' Anthony asked as I pushed him towards the door, my head down.

'Did she see me?'

'Was that Lydia then? Why would it matter if she had?'

'Did she see me?' I repeated. My head was in a real mess.

CHAPTER THIRTY-EIGHT

THREATS: 21.00 Saturday 30th August 2014

The lift clattered down at such a slow pace that Charley decided to take the stairs, two at a time, phone clutched to her ear, still trying to ring the number Gina had texted from. Field had no trace on it yet.

The blur of grey came at her suddenly; she fought against strong hands that gripped around her wrists and pulled her into a corner, up against the wall.

'Hey, calm down, you mad bitch.' A pale skinhead appeared at the top of all the grey.

'Let go of me! Charley tried to bite his face.

'You ran at me!' The man held her back. 'I'm not going to hurt you or nothing. I shit myself to be honest. These stairwells are dodgy aren't they?'

He let her go. She recognised him from around the flats; the typical grey tracksuit, constant hood up, hanging around with a joint, looking to buy or sell after a series of 'clean days.'

'You looking for anything?' he asked, patting his pocket.

'No,' she said firmly.

'You're different aren't yer?' he said. 'Always thought you was a bit posh and that. How'd you end up here?'

She pushed past him.

'You in flat four? he asked, moving out of her way, his clothes thick with the smell of stale smoke and other substances.

'Yeah, why?'

'You had some visitors before, girl.'

'What?'

'Just warning yer, 'cos they didn't look too friendly, like.' He disappeared down the stairs.

She thought about calling the police or Field again, but then these things had happened before; small break-ins, people trying to see what they could get. She couldn't risk looking like a crank straight after reporting an assault. Anyway, Mark wouldn't dare, would he? And he didn't know where she lived, hardly anyone did. A horrible, irrational thought entered her head - maybe Gina was with Callum. Had he finally tracked them down? He'd never been the type to carry out his threats before.

The flat door was closed, so maybe no one had got in after all. She tried the lock and it was intact, requiring the usual few shifts of the key before it would open.

The smell was horrendous. It hit her nose at the same time she felt the sludge under her foot. The brown mess spread up over her white trainers. She ran to the sink and vomited. Desperate to keep control, she splashed water on her face quickly, took off her soiled shoe and threw it into the sink. She picked up a knife from the kitchen, taking in the small space with light steps. Whoever had posted the dog shit through her letterbox could have left other warnings, or decided that this little threat wasn't enough.

There was no one in the small room, no one in the bedroom, no one in the flat. She could only hear her own breathing, punctuated by sickening coughs that rattled her throat each time the smell got to her. She shut the front door.

Callum, Callum, Callum.

The last time anything like this had happened to Charley it was because of him. Gina was asking for help, but no one else knew about Callum. She couldn't track him down without going back into her old life, and seeing the people she didn't want to know anymore. But Callum didn't do kidnapping. That would take planning, precision.

The shit would stain the carpet if left for much longer. She picked up most of it in tissues and then scrubbed at the floor with soap and water. A sudden need to get out of the place overtook her as she finished. Grabbing a change of clothes and pulling on boots to replace the trainers, she left and headed back out.

* * * * *

The driveway was as dark and terrifying as always. Her phone startled her as it vibrated. It was Field.

'Any news?' she asked.

'Still no lead, but Mark Murphy has been back on about pressing charges.'

'What happens next?' Charley could feel her heart pounding.

'I'll keep you informed.' He was formal-sounding, with none of the sympathy she usually got.

'Oh-what can I do now?' Her voice wobbled.

'Don't hesitate to get in touch if you have anything new.' His tone softened. 'I'll keep trying.'

She went to end the call but he shouted. 'Charlotte, wait!'

'I don't believe that shit from Mark. I'll work on him, don't worry,' he added.

They came from nowhere, pushing her through the door, forcing their way inside and slamming it behind them.

CHAPTER THIRTY-NINE

Shock ~ a sudden upsetting or surprising event or experience

~ I can't do it any more

~ I don't mean that - is the shock.

~ Because he didn't mean it - was the shock.

~ Better off staying here, in Jen's, until feel safe safe - calm.

August 2014

'I've got a surprise for you!' Daniel called from the kitchen. The fish kicked off in my stomach. I hated surprises.

The table was laid out for a special breakfast. There was salmon, homemade pancakes with syrup, bacon with the fat cut off and scrambled egg. I sat down and immediately felt the urge to be sick, putting my hand over my mouth to try and hide it.

'What's up?' Daniel asked.

'Are you sure I'm ok to eat this? I picked at the egg with a fork and decided to use the wedding weight excuse. 'I mean with the calories and that?'

'Don't worry about all that. We're having a nice day off together, and that means away from everyone and everything,' he said, then added, 'and I made the scrambled eggs with the whites only, for your wedding stomach.' He leaned across and patted my belly when he said that. It wobbled. I had to stop avoiding gym sessions with Karen and the Tropicals.

'Thought we might go out for a drive, New Brighton or somewhere?'

'Well I kind of have work today.' I lifted a fragment of egg to my mouth.

'Not when you work for me,' he replied. 'Catch up tomorrow. There's not that much to do is there?' He kept saying that lately. And it was true.

'Are you sure you even need me working there? I asked. 'I mean, I could apply for something else?'

I was skinto minto. I had like, nothing. Daniel controlled the money at the moment 'to save me from myself and give us a good life'. I literally had to work for him to repay this debt five days a week. It was impossible to save for my contribution to Alderley Edge. Daniel kept saying it would be half mine when we were married anyway. Jen thought I was mad to care. She loved being a kept woman. I didn't dare tell Jo what was happening.

'Relax, Gina. Forget about work and have a few bites of the brekkie at least.'

Maybe I was just being a moaning cow.

'New Brighton sounds good,' I said, forcing some food down. I didn't want to piss him off. It was a week after Lydia had caught me with Anthony, and although nothing had been said, I still felt shards of fish fins hitting my insides whenever Daniel was in a bad mood.

'Do you mind driving?' He tossed me his keys. 'I might have a drink when we're there - need to relax.'

'Can't we go in my car?' I hated driving his. It was a big, black cube and was like trying to get a lorry down an alleyway.

'That shit tin?' he laughed. 'No chance I'm being seen in that. I'm always tellin' yer.' He was.

I looked out the window at my little car. I never used to think it was that bad. I'd saved up (for a change) and bought it myself a couple of years ago; chose it, negotiated a deal and everything. It was a Corsa, silver and non-showy. Daniel said I was ripped off for a 'little shit tin', and it did look a bit crap next to his BMW. My heart was beating against my chest as I said it, but I was too jittery to risk driving his car today.

'Please let me take the shit tin,' I said, faking a laugh. 'Come on, no one knows us over there.'

'Alright, but we need to get you a better car soon, like.'

* * * * *

New Brighton had turned into Benidorm. The beach was a barbeque, filled with perfectly grilled bodies. I mean, it was only the Wirral, but in the sun everyone had morphed into LA models. Two of them ahead of us, young girls, too post-teen to have too much cellulite, were knee-deep in the sea. One had her bikini bottoms hitched up deliberately. They had that tanned, blonde look that I never understood and always wanted. The sea dipped up and down their legs, as though showing them its admiration.

I tried to catch the direction of Daniel's gaze, but he was wearing sunglasses and lying further back than me. He probably wasn't even looking at the girls. There were plenty of women with desirable bodies in the 'magazine' he was reading.

I couldn't stop fidgeting, and the waves certainly weren't helping, fighting and crashing into each other every few seconds. This massive beach was giving me too much space to think.

Someone from a Special K advert walked across us, all clever diet and flat stomach. Alongside them were thin families with thick towels and matching golden tans. What was with this beach? My bottled tan was all I could rely on. I tried to stay in the shade of a rock, like a small creature skulking in the background and ruining the postcard setting. The sun was still getting at me, licking at my legs like flames. Daniel had gone blotchy.

'Do you want any cream?' I asked him.

'I'd rather have a tan,' he answered, shifting over. 'You probably need to put some more fake stuff on yourself.'

'Yeah,' I said, checking for blotchy bits.

203

'I'm going on the beds before the wedding anyway,' Daniel said. 'Do you want to come and stop me looking gay?'

'You know I can't!' He knew how worried I was about skin cancer, any cancer, after Mum. The umbrella shook in the hot wind as though nodding in agreement.

'Sorry,' Daniel laid a hand on my thigh, 'I think sometimes you're being overcautious. Everyone looks better with a tan.'

I looked around the beach. Everyone did look better with a tan, even the kids. A little boy was holding a bat that was bigger than his head, half the size of him. I imagined hitting Daniel over the head with it and leaving. I was shocked at how easily this image came into my head. A seagull went by squawking in hysterics, as though it was reading my murderous thoughts. I concentrated on my stomach instead of being angry with him, breathing in to make it dip the way I would like it to.

'Do some more sit-ups like you used to. I don't know why you stopped doing them to be honest.' Daniel cast a critical eye. Those late night splurges when I'd got so hungry I hadn't cared were catching up with me.

'Can we go soon?'

He looked up from his reading with narrowed eyes. 'God, relax will yer!' A few blonde bombshells turned to see what the commotion was. He took a deep breath. 'Will it help if we talk about wedding plans?'

'I've been looking at dresses,' I said brightly. This part of the wedding excited me at least.

'Our Karen will help you there,' Daniel said. 'She'll do your hair and make-up on the day too. I sorted it with her.'

'How's she going to do that? It'll be ruined by the time we drive up to Scotland.'

Daniel went quiet.

'She isn't coming, Daniel. That isn't fair at all!'

'It'll only be her and José coming as witnesses.'

'After the way they carried on in Marbella? If you're having Karen there then Charley is coming!'

'Oh alright yeah, like she won't cause any trouble.'

'You hardly know her,' I said. 'You never let me ask her round or to come out with us or anything-'

'I can't be arsed talking about it now. Let's go home,' he snapped.

The barbeque beach was filling up with fresh meat, with sand for charcoal and flesh for frying. A man, purpling in the sun, turned over with the efficiency of a kebab. The ones dipping in the sea and then running across the sand seemed to be salt and peppering their bodies. A thin teenage trio were reading Marion Keyes by a rock, their bodies golden and ready. We were the left overs meat - the ham ends. The fish were swimming rapidly now, showing off how much space they had in my big, fat tummy.

We got into the car and drove along towards the tunnel in silence.

'Are we even getting married next month, or are you stringing me along?' Daniel said out of the blue.

'What?'

'Well you sneak around my back constantly for a start, having little dates with that faggot.'

My insides froze.

'Lydia saw you, so don't fuckin' lie,' he said in that low voice that always caused my stomach to drop.

I placed a hand on his arm. 'I should have told you I ran into him and we went for lunch, that's all.'

He said nothing but stared straight ahead at the road.

'Anyway, if you think he's gay, why are you arsed?' I tried to laugh.

The car spun around and came to a sharp halt.

'You fucking stupid bitch!' he screamed as he got out, his body shaking with anger and absolute hatred. The door slammed and seemed to shudder right down my body and shake even more fish into being. They bit everywhere and wouldn't stop. My neck throbbed.

Cars beeped as I sat in the middle of the road. Some people looked like they might leave their vehicles to help, but then couldn't be bothered and began manoeuvring around me where they could. It didn't help that I was facing the wrong side of the road, my neck throbbing from the force of the sudden stop. The handbrake was up and locked.

As I sat with my head spinning, a woman with greying hair and a kind smile knocked at the window. She looked like she could have been one of my mum's friends - she had that nice but slightly wild look about her. I let the window down with a shaking finger.

'Are you ok, love?' Her voice was warm and comforting, a bit like a hug. I couldn't answer.

'What happened?' she asked, looking in the direction of where Daniel had walked off around the corner. Her voice was kind but pressing and she said the next part in a whisper. 'Did he do that? Did he pull up the handbrake when you were driving...' she trailed off.

Before I could get my head straight and form an answer, Daniel was back in the car. 'Right, let's go then.'

I steadied my hand on the wheel and took a deep breath. The beeping continued all around us. The woman at the side of the car looked ready to reach in and pull me out as Daniel leaned across and pushed the button to make the window go back up.

'That bastard is not fucking winning, ok!'

I drove us home, sometimes hitting the kerb. Daniel stayed quiet and solemn until we got to the house. Then he held my hand and grasped it, with a sweet smile like nothing at all had happened. I undid my belt and pretended to get out, waiting until he had shut the door before I sped off towards Jen's.

* * * * *

'Why would he do that?' Jen brought me a cup of sugary, milky tea and sat next to me on her sofa. The sound of a key turning in the door made me jump.

'It's only Mark.'

He walked into the living room and gave me a sneer that reached up to his hooked nose.

'What's going on?' he said to Jen.

'Daniel pulled the handbrake up in the car while Gina was driving.'

He turned to me, his patchy eyebrows raised, and laughed. 'What did you do to piss him off?'

'Mark!' Jen gasped. 'He could have killed them both.' Then she looked at me, '*Did* you do anything?'

'I saw Anthony in town and went for lunch with him. Why is that such a big deal?'

Mark's hen eyes flashed in annoyance. 'She needs to go home and sort it out with him.'

'Gina,' Jen said slowly, her eyes low, not meeting mine. 'Maybe you should go and talk to him, hun. We all know that Anthony fancies you. Think how jealous you'd be if it was the other way around.'

I clutched my tea which was too hot in my hands.

'What he did in the car was wrong but I think he saw red and you can get through it,' she continued.

'Jen, please let me stay here,' I said quietly. 'I've got nowhere else to go.'

'I'll be out on me arse if we let her stay. The lad's given me some great contracts,' Mark said.

The doorbell went.

CHAPTER FORTY

'Did you like our little present?'

The high-pitched voice went through Charley like a thin knife to her brain. They surrounded her, blocking any escape.

One of them looked uncomfortable, shifting on her stilted high heels, twirling her bright red hair around her finger until it must have started to cut off her blood supply. It was the girl Karen had practically dragged into her house earlier that day.

Charley got up, rubbing at her hand, which had burned along the hall carpet as she'd fallen. Her vision was blurry from getting up too fast.

'Look at her, she's scared shitless,' one of them said.

'Well, she *should* be.' That was definitely Karen.

Charley was pushed into the living room and forced onto the couch. The three girls piled in after her, the last slithering like a skinny snake around the door and running a hand through her long dark hair. They all sat down apart from the red-haired girl, who jittered up and down the room with her arms wrapped around her.

'How long will this take?' Snake girl yawned and snapped her pink-lipsticked mouth shut.

'As long as it takes for her to realise that she can't be going to the police left, right and centre, accusing people of all kinds because her sister has took off.'

'Karen, I think we should leave it. She gets the message.' The red haired girl looked around the room, chewing on a purple painted fingernail.

'No, she'll get the message in a minute.' Karen stood up and took out her mobile. She didn't take her eyes off Charley as she let it ring a few times and then ended the call.

'What have you done to Gina?'

Karen crossed the room until she was in Charley's face, so close that cigarettes and mints, mixed with a chalky make-up scent, made her choke.

'You kick off on Melissa about our Matthew, tell the police you think our Danny is up to something, even accuse someone he used to work with of attacking you, making it look like our family has done something. Well, you can fuck off!' Karen stalked back across the room, jabbing her heels into the well-worn carpet like she'd made a winning point.

All three of them looked at her. Charley stared back. They were nothing. She'd been in situations like this with far worse people, not three little flighty bimbos. There was a noise from the hall.

He walked into the room like he owned it, eyes on Charley as her heart stopped.

'If you know what's good for you, you'll leave this alone,' Karen said with a satisfied smile. 'Don't try and drag our family's name through shit for the sake of your stupid bitch of a sister.' She took a piece of paper out of her bag and threw it at Charley's feet. 'Open it.'

Charley unfolded the paper and there was a name and a building site address.

'If the police do give a shit and visit there, they'll meet a nice man who'll tell them how Daniel has been working with him the last couple of days,' Karen said. 'Oh, and don't try the Mark thing again either, love. We don't like the attention it brings on Dan's business as he's an ex-employee. I heard that a neighbour saw you going for Jen and Mark pushed you out of the way.'

Daniel hadn't taken his eyes off Charley. He crossed the room and leaned into her, his breath in her face. His nose was bent out of shape. 'My family always sort things out. Don't get in the way.' When he pulled away, Charley saw something unexpected in his face. It was almost fear.

'Right, let's go,' Karen instructed them all, giving Charley one last warning glare. 'If you do say anything, you know we

210

could all be witnesses to your little habit. Daniel, didn't you say she had a big fight with Gina over it in front of you?'

Daniel left the room. The red-haired girl turned back as she followed and gave her a pained glance. Charley looked away. The door slammed shut.

She sat for a moment, stilling her breathing and thumping heart. Seeing Daniel made every painful feeling from that night come back. She crawled down onto the floor, night drawing in, everything getting darker. Salty tears licked at her face, cold and hopeless, until she looked up and noticed the wall.

22.15

* * * * *

The bar was busy. Waitresses and waiters walked past with baskets of chips and fat burgers held together with cocktail sticks and decorated with little American flags.

Charley hadn't eaten for hours, and even then only grabbed a quick bit of bread and cheese, not even stopping to make a proper sandwich. She couldn't get away with not eating at all these days. The smells of the place were overwhelming to her now unblunted senses. She picked at some chips. Her hands were shaking as she picked up the jam jar glass of lemonade and read through the definitions on the table in front of her.

Lying on the floor in an almost comatose state, she'd looked up and seen it, the section of wallpaper slightly looser than the others at the top corner. It peeled back and there was the brick in the wall. She pulled it out carefully, remembering how it had fallen once and hit Dad on his toe. Inside was S, T, U, V and W. That is what Gina meant when she'd scrawled over R, 'a safe, unsafe place'. This had been their parents' hiding place for cash and cards.

Officer Field came in civilian clothes. It made him look younger. There was sympathy in her eyes when he sat down, but not pity. She didn't want it to be pity. She needed him to listen. He'd called to check on her at a key time, almost like he'd known she needed him.

211

'Daniel's turned up,' she started talking before he'd even sat down. 'He came with Karen and some of her mates and they attacked me after breaking into my flat.'

'Charley, slow down.' He settled into the seat and put his hand over hers. 'You're shaking,' he added, as she looked down at them. He moved his hands away. 'Tell me what happened. When did you see Daniel?'

'They warned me about going to the police. How did they know I'd told you? They must be watching me.'

'What did they do to you?' A dark shadow crossed over his features, closing them in.

'Nothing, I'm fine. It was only threats.' But she had to wipe a tear away. 'They gave me an address which is meant to be Daniel's alibi, where they'll say he was working the last couple of days, but you know they're hiding something if they even need to give an alibi, aren't they?'

'I'll check this out for you,' he replied, taking the piece of paper and putting it in his pocket. She had anticipated this and had kept a copy for herself. 'I'll do everything I can to get this taken up as a case. What are you going to do about their attack on you? Is there any sign of forced entry in the house?'

'No, they attacked me as I was going in and the stuff in the flat would be hard to prove.' She thought about the grey-tracksuit man. 'Someone who lives in my flats saw them though…' she trailed off. Whether she could persuade him to give evidence or not was another thing.

'Who?'

'He's always hanging around the stairs in a grey tracksuit, probably still a user,' she said the last part guiltily. 'Even if he would be a witness, what if I report them and they come after me? Can the police protect me?'

He hesitated. 'Only if there was enough evidence that you were in danger and now Daniel is back that would rule him out officially-'

'Daniel being back doesn't mean anything,' Charley cut in. 'He could be keeping her somewhere. And I think the whole

212

family's in on it. Look at these.' She spread out the pieces of paper covered in Gina's handwriting. 'She hasn't gone away. Look, you can see she wasn't feeling safe. She wanted to get away from *him,* and look what else she says, about Daniel and his family and how far they'd go with their vendettas, and there's also something about a punch and lots of wrongs.'

'I believe you.' Concern showed on his face. He was really listening. No one ever listened. 'But it'll be hard to convince anyone else with so much vague information. Especially with Mark Murphy's recent accusations.'

'Why?'

'Well, Mark has an independent witness as I said-'

'No, I mean why do you believe me?'

'You remind me of someone,' he paused, 'someone that no one listened to.'

The waitress interrupted them. She smiled and took an order of a beer from Field. As she scooped up the menu items, she gave Charley a sly smile. Field was attractive, the type who would draw glances, his large frame adding to the impression of power he gave. They looked like another couple, maybe in the awkward stages, but still a couple. She wondered how many other secret conversations and confessions went on in places as ordinary as this burger bar. All around them was the noise of ordinary life, a mix of loud and whispered voices.

'Who do I remind you of?' Charley asked when the waitress had brought over the beer and moved onto other tables.

He stared down at the table. There was an uncomfortable silence, set against the bursts of laughter and shouts from others around them.

'Do you want to talk about it?' she said eventually.

'Normally no, but…*you* would get it,' he said, looking up and then took a large slug out of the bottle before wiping his mouth self-consciously. 'The someone was my sister.'

Charley knew the implications of 'was'.

'What happened?'

213

'Classic case of getting involved with the wrong crowd,' he said. 'She was only twenty when she died of an overdose. The shit who gave her the stuff and took it along with her, he survived and got out of prison a few years after.'

Charley's hand froze around the jam jar drink. He played with the bottle of beer for a minute. The ebb and hum of the voices around them kept up as they sat silently.

'The police wouldn't listen when she reported her ex a few months before. He said he was going to kill her,' he continued. 'Mind you, we didn't believe her either. Who would listen to a smackhead?' His voice snapped on the last word. 'He planned the whole thing and gave her the stuff because he wanted her dead.' He dug his fingernails into the table.

'How old were you?'

'Fourteen.'

'You were too young to do anything.'

'I remember how helpless I felt. It was one of the reasons I joined the police, to try and make sure everyone was listened to, no matter who they are, or what they'd done.'

'You do help,' Charley said quietly.

The waitress looked over hopefully, as though they might finally settle the bill and leave.

'Let's see if I can get anything from this alibi you mentioned,' he said. This man, whoever he is, might trip himself up. I'll also keep an eye on you and call on a few friends, informally, to keep an eye on your flat and the family home. If they catch anything, we can use it against Mr Ryan and the others.'

'Thanks Officer-'

'Call me Mike.'

'Thanks Mike.'

'And remember, contact *me* when anything comes up, at any time.'

214

Their eyes locked across the table. Neither of them made a move.

'I should go,' Charley said finally.

'Ok, he said, 'but please look after yourself, and let me look for your sister.' He put a hand on her shoulder as they stood up. He was looking at her in a way that no one had in a long time, if ever.

'Could you stay for one more drink?' he asked. 'I won't be able to get to the address until tomorrow and I think you could do with someone to talk to.'

Her insides pulled with guilt, but there was no point going to find Callum this late at night. It would be dangerous enough in the morning. She sat back down.

CHAPTER FORTY-ONE

Trust ~ firm belief in the reliability, truth, or ability of someone or something.

~ Should trust myself, I know what I'm doing? Firm belief I have the ability to do it!!

~ M backed up all my beliefs, hard but had to trust her, although she clearly didn't trust me - why would she? I'm another her.

August 2014

'Come outside, I've got a surprise for you!'

It was like a groundhog surprise day in this house. But as it was also a house of eggshells at the moment, I did what I was told and hurried down the stairs.

After that night in Jen's when he turned up at the door, all tears and mad threats (against himself, not me), things had been different. I'd persuaded him to get rid of the bottle of antifreeze he'd brought with him and threatened to drink, and I made a promise to stay and try again. That was if he left me alone for one night to recover. I stayed in Jen's spare room and cried more than I slept. When I woke up there was something different in how I felt. I couldn't explain it, except to say that the shock of what he'd done yesterday had opened up a new way of thinking for me. I saw him differently. I saw me differently. But I would have to bide my time.

* * * * *

Outside, the muggy August air hit me like a blast of bad breath. There was a white Audi in the driveway, a huge, monstrous thing with a pink bow around it. Ok, in normal times I did kind of like these cars and the idea of driving around in one looking down at the world, but with everything going on, this unsettled me.

'What do you think?' He cheddar-grinned at me.

'Is this for me?' I asked to make sure. 'Where's the shi-, I mean, my car gone?'

'Oh I sold it for parts so you wouldn't have any hassle with it,' he said. 'It's yours, although I'm insured on it too so I'll use it as well.'

'Thanks, this is amazing,' I forced myself to say.

'I've also got you something else white. He gave me a wink and took my hand, leading me back inside and upstairs to our bedroom. For one horrible minute, I thought this was a trick and he'd found the secret stash of money and the real destination for the clothes I'd started packing, pretending to sort out to take to the charity shop. What was laid out on the bed was almost worse.

The doorbell did its stupid ding-dong, letting me off the hook and giving me time to take the horror off my face. Daniel raced off to answer it.

'Come in, Charley.' I heard him say, over-loudly.

'I invited her round,' Daniel whispered proudly, a huge smile on his face as he came back up the stairs ahead of her.

Oh fuck, fantastic timing there. I didn't have time to bundle the dress into the wardrobe before she came up. Charley hovered at the edge of the room, unsure of her next move, wearing her standard 'uniform' of jeans, hoodie and Conversey-type trainers. She was chewing on a fingernail like a five year old.

'Leave you two to catch up then - going to test out that car!' Daniel kissed me quickly and flew past Charley. We heard him bounding down the stairs and then the door shut.

'That Daniel's new car outside?' Charley said breathing out and moving over to the bed. 'Is *that* your wedding dress?'

'Erm yeah. Do you like it?'

218

'It's not what I'd expect you to pick.' She touched the net-curtain style lace lightly with her fingers, as if it might bite her.

It was fucking hideous. And I couldn't tell her that she'd never see me in it. I was so near the end now that it wasn't worth the risk. The other night, after telling me we'd always be together, Daniel had said, *I'll always find you Gina. There's nowhere you can go.* It sent shiver fish up my spine - something that was happening more often.

Daniel not knowing exactly where Charley lived (because he'd never taken an interest) was a good thing, but I couldn't tell her about my plan yet.

'Charley, I'm really sorry but I'm on my way out for a hair appointment,' I said. 'Daniel didn't tell me you were calling around.'

She got her usual disappointed-but-I-suppose-I-deserve-it look on her face. After making promises to call around later on and have a proper catch up, I could finally set out to do what I needed to.

* * * * *

The cafe was warm, cosy, homely and all that, and at a different time I might have liked it. The air was choked with coffee fumes, making everyone in there a bit high, even if they stuck to fruit smoothies like me.

She was pretty, in a skinny little rabbit way, running around the small place like a blue arsed fly, collecting empty cups and wiping table.

'Megan,' I said, when she came to take my empty glass. She had massive bug eyes helped out by a little bit of mascara that clumped at the end of her eyelashes.

'Do I know you?' she asked, already backing away.

'Daniel.'

The glass smashed on the floor.

'What do you want?'

219

The man serving behind the counter shouted at her, some of the customers were looking at us, sensing the tension and hoping to see a fight.

'He doesn't know I'm here.'

'Karen sent you? I haven't said anything, I promise.'

'Jemma told me where you worked,' I said, not wanting her to realise that I didn't know what she was talking about.

'Oh,' she relaxed slightly, in time for another member of staff to come over and give her a dustpan and brush, nodding their head in the direction of the man behind the counter, who was red in the face. She bent down and started to clean up. I leaned down next to her.

'I'm going to leave him,' I said.

'But you haven't left him yet?' She looked at the ring on my finger and then stood up fully, the dustpan of glass shaking slightly in her right hand. 'Why are you here?'

I didn't exactly know myself. I needed reassurance, back up if you like, for what I was going to do. I wanted something over Daniel.

'What did you mean you haven't said anything?' I asked.

She considered me for a second and then shook her head slowly. 'You probably won't leave him.'

'I will. I've already started planning it.'

'You started working for him yet?' she asked. 'He's probably told you I lost my job so that's why he gave me one.' She let out a deep breath. 'I didn't lose my job. He didn't like the fact that I worked in a team full of men. I'm back in Uni now. Daniel-' She stopped, put her bug eyes right in line with mine. 'I can't trust you at all.'

I'd come along thinking we'd both be on the same side, but she was still his ex, with straggly blonde hair and wrists you could get your hand around, and she seemed to be winning.

'I *am* going to leave him.' I noticed that her ears had two long scars either side where earrings should be. She rubbed them lightly, self-consciously.

'He always says sorry doesn't he, so that you feel bad? Buys you presents?' Her voice was cutting through me. 'If you knew what you were in for, you wouldn't be talking to me. I can't get involved in all this again. It's too dangerous.'

'We're on the same side.'

'Yeah alright,' she laughed but it came out a bit like a choking sound. She went to walk off and I grabbed her arm, shocking us both.

'What do you want me to do?' She shook me off.

I was surprised to find myself on the verge of tears.

'Get away from him before it's too late,' she hesitated, 'are you on the pill?'

'What?'

'He swapped mine with some fake ones once, not sure how, but I think Karen has a mate who works in a pharmacy and can get placebo packs. Has he persuaded you to put them in those Monday to Sunday cases, like he really cares?'

I stared at her in horror. The fish in my stomach came flooding back as I thought about the case by my bed; the one Daniel had bought me a few months ago. He'd organised the pills for me, so I wouldn't forget to take one.

Everything was closing in on me. I couldn't see Megan properly; her face was blurred. Those stupid skinny fingers were on my arm. I heard her shouting after me as I knocked into tables and people until somehow I found the door.

Town was packed but I ran through the crowds. The woman at the till asked me if was I ok and I ignored her.

Sitting in the toilets of the first shitty pub I found, I tried to clear my head and think. When was my last period? Why didn't I pay attention to things like this? My periods had always been all over the show, turning up around the same time each month but not to a strict schedule or anything.

I dipped the stick into my dribbles of wee and held it there, ignoring the fact that most of it went on my hand. The stick didn't do anything at first. Then I got my answer.

CHAPTER FORTY-TWO

GUILT: 9.00 Sunday 31ˢᵗ August 2014

Three places to go. Three sets of people to see.

Her head was heavy and foggy as she woke up. But for the first time in as long as she could remember, that lonely, desperate feeling hadn't been there when she'd crawled into bed.

It wasn't the drink, which never usually eased her mind. It was the getting rid of time, making it pass by having someone to talk to, someone who got it. They'd talked a lot.

At first she'd alternated between feeling giddy and then guilty; the latter had faded the more open she'd been. To understand her story, you'd had to have lived it in some way, and in his own way, Mike had. They mainly talked about her, not him. She knew he had an apartment by the docks, that his parents were still alive, the story of his sister and about him joining the police. Not much else.

She'd been up for two hours already and the bad feelings were back. Thinking about Gina, wondering where she could be and what was happening to her, regretting their whole relationship, and especially their last conversation. What if the unspeakable had happened and those were the last words they'd ever say to each other? She was finding it increasingly difficult to remember the good times; the mind was so much better at recalling a slap or a sharp word. That couldn't be the lasting memory.

'It won't be,' Mike had said, holding her hand across the table and this time not letting it go. 'She will be fine. I promise you.'

She'd been vague of course, pretended the argument between her and Gina had been at the party, left out a few details, despite what Mike already knew about her. He couldn't think she was still a liar. People always believed the worst, no matter what they said.

What she also couldn't admit was that the temptation *was* still there, that easy get out clause she'd always used in the past when things got too hard. It was only ever a few phone calls and a short drive away, that life she could instantly sink back into. She had to close her eyes to it until it got too much and she got up, went to the kitchen and took a knife from the kitchen drawer.

She stared at the blade for a long time, considering what she could do with it and everything that would follow. Her wrists looked fragile, incapable of resistance.

That drive was happening today. But she wasn't doing it alone. The knife went back in the drawer.

* * * * *

Mike was waiting outside in the car, like he said he would be, exactly on time. It was still a surprise to her when people stuck to their word.

Charley took a deep breath and gulped all the feelings in. Her emotional energy had to go into finding Gina.

Mike only knew about the one visit. He didn't need to know about the Facebook message on her phone from an account she didn't recognise. The profile looked hastily made up, with a picture of a bunny and the name 'raving rabbits'. It gave the name and address of a cafe and the words 'speak to her', followed by **Tell no one.**

The café wouldn't be open until eleven. The hardest journey would have to be done first.

'Ready?' Mike smiled at her as she got into his car.

'Yeah,' she lied.

* * * * *

The soft sun of the last day in August did little to lighten the village that Charley had always thought of as a place of tragedy and open wounds, barely hidden behind half-hearted housing projects. She took several deep breaths to try and unclench her body, which stiffened further with each speed bump and roundabout turn.

'Are you ok?' Mike asked, taking his eyes off the road momentarily.

'I'm ok.' She forced a weak smile and looked out of the window.

This was a place no one ever really wanted to get to, and if you did, chances were that you wouldn't have the incentive to leave. There were no trains and buses were rare, and when Charley lived here, she hadn't owned a car. She didn't mind at the time. It was only when things got really bad that she realised how trapped she was.

She wondered how Gina had felt doing this same drive, only a year ago, also coming to put herself in danger and not knowing quite what she would find.

Charley's chest was so tight when she pulled up outside the house that it hurt to breathe. The place tattered, with an overgrown garden which looked like an ill-conceived frame rather than a pathway. Callum had sold it to her as their little haven, although it was more like a hovel, to do what they wanted and live how they pleased.

'It's us now doll,' he said, 'just us.' But even that part wasn't true. It was never just them. The 'business' they ran meant people were in and out all the time; lounging around, paying off money, taking it, threatening, pleading, arguing, crying. It was a house of hell. She knew that from the moment Callum had picked her up, mock wedding style, and carried her over the threshold.

He might have been skinny but Callum had surprising strength. Charley got to see that quite a few times. Callum with his thick, fish-like lips, heavy eyelids, mop of brown hair and his thin body which was so long that it caused his unwashed t-shirts to ride across his stomach. Callum could twist her arm behind her back until she thought he would break it. But she could do it back to him, twice as hard.

* * * * *

Before they had the chance to get to the door of the house, a woman wearing a faded blue tracksuit opened it. She was painfully thin, with long dark hair straggled over her face. She placed a hand on her hip and looked Charley up and down, then cast a warmer glance at Mike. The other hand held a cigarette. Her neglected face was marked with dry skin and sections of sores. The woman was what she could have become, her own Dorian Gray.

'What do yer want?' The woman drawled, revealing missing teeth.

Charley licked her tongue across her own set. Well, not exactly her own, the ones Gina had reached her credit card limit to pay for.

'We're looking for Callum.'

'Why?' The woman blew smoke in Charley's face. This added to the scent of weed and other substances that clotted around them.

Mike stepped in front of her. 'We have money for him.'

'Money you owe him, darling, or for something you want?' The woman smiled at Mike and leaned back against the doorframe.

'No,' Charley said, 'money if he does something for me, a quick job.' That had always made Callum go to the door for people in the past. He was known to break a nose for a tenner. The judo classes his wealthy parents shelled out for in the hope of teaching their unruly son some discipline could come in handy at times when he needed quick cash.

The door swung open behind the woman and a man stepped into view. He had a beaky nose and a scrawny frame. He was familiar. Charley remembered the knife in her bag.

'What do they want?' he barked.

'We're looking for Callum,' Mike said, standing a little in front of Charley and squaring his body up. 'I need him for a quick job.'

'Callum fucked off ages ago. Someone grassed him up and he scarpered.' The man looked closely at Charley.

'I know you.' He spat onto the floor and wiped his mouth roughly. 'Fucking hell, yer the grass aren't yer? Fuck, I wish

226

Callum was here, he'd fuckin' kill yer. Didn't you and your sister take his last stash and grass him up to the bizzies?' He stepped out of the door and Charley moved back behind Mike. Fear coursed through her veins.

'If I 'ad his new number I'd call him and say you were back.' The man glared at her. 'So, girl, I wouldn't be trackin' im down if I were you.'

'You can't call him, you tit,' the woman said, 'he's in jail.'

'He's in jail?' Charley was already mentally working her way further back towards the gate she had left open, car keys in her hand.

'What the fuck do you care?' The woman shouted.

'Yer one cheeky bitch!' The man spat again.

'Right that's it, out of the way!' Mike grabbed Charley by the hand and forced his way past the man and woman and into the house.

Inside the smell was putrid. The wallpaper hung off the wall in limp strips, a never-ending pile of mail spread across the floor, unopened. They went through to the kitchen, where dishes crusted onto dishes and the back door was blocked by a stack of bricks.

'Stops the bastards breaking in on the sly,' a voice said behind them - one that was deep and familiar to Charley. Callum walked past them and sat on the plastic white garden set that served as a dining table and chairs in the kitchen. 'Morning Charl.' He was halfway through rolling a joint. He wore shorts that cut above his dirty knees, showing a fresh cut on one of his shins.

'Where's my sister?' Charley found herself saying in a low growl, more suited to how she used to talk when she lived there.

'Who the fuck's this?' Callum ignored her and nodded towards Mike.

'Never mind who I am, mate,' Mike replied. 'If you know anything about where her sister is, you'd better tell us.'

'There was a time,' Callum started and then paused to lick the paper into shape around his weed. 'a time when I would have wanted to know where she was myself, so I could teach your sister a lesson.'

Mike pulled him up by the neck of his t-shirt. 'Listen, you little shit. If you know what's happened to Gina, you will tell us.' There was no reaction, as Charley knew there wouldn't be. Callum was never scared by violence. He was well practiced in it. Mike let him down and Callum rubbed at his neck, a smirk on his face, before taking his place back on the plastic chair. 'What's happened to her, Charl?'

'I'll knock your fucking block off.' Mike's voice was low, angry and not at all like him.

'No you won't,' Callum answered, eyes still on Charley.

'She's been kidnapped,' she said, looking straight at him.

'Kidnapped? Shit.' He let out a low whistle and went back to building his joint. 'You don't think this has anything to do with me do you?'

'We could get the police around here right now-' Mike started.

'You know what she is right? You know what she did?' Callum interrupted. 'Or has she fooled you with all her clever shit? I met her at Uni you know. She's not that clever.' He paused, curling his lip up at Charley. 'The things I know about her would interest the police more than anything I've got in the house, for medicinal purposes I might add.' He laughed and then lit the joint, taking a long drag. 'Not my way of doing things, kidnap. You know that, Charl. Yeah, I said I wanted to kill you both at the time, but I'd only really do that if there was something in it for me. I'm not putting myself back inside again, or letting *someone* put me back in again. Nobody wants that. You know what I mean, Charl?' He gestured the joint towards Charley. Mike looked at her. She hadn't got around to telling him about that part of her life yet.

Bile rose up in her throat. She ran out of the kitchen, past the man and woman who were still outside who shouted threats

228

after her. She got to the car before Mike caught up with her. His arms were on her shoulders as she took deep breaths.

'Don't let him get to you,' he said. 'I think he knows more than he's letting on.'

'I don't think he does,' she replied. That was one thing that Charley was certain of. Callum didn't know anything. If he had then he would have asked for money. Kidnap wasn't his style. It was messy effort. He liked quick jobs.

'Then why would Gina text saying she was with him?'

'She was trying to tell me that she's in danger.' Callum was the second most recent person to tell Charley they wished she was dead. That was what Gina was trying to tell her by texting his name. Whoever had Gina, wanted her to die.

'Don't take me back to the flat,' she told Mike. The family home would feel safer somehow, if she could keep her wits about her.

'I still think we have enough to get a case on him, especially if we use the text.'

'No, it hasn't got anything to do with him.'

'The lad basically admitted he had something against you and your sister. There's loads we could get him on.'

'It'd be wasting time, I-I know him well,' she admitted, although it was hard to say this in front of Mike. She'd passed off Callum as an old acquaintance the night before, someone from her darker days but not an ex-boyfriend. 'If he had her, then he would have tried to strike a deal with us ages ago, and if he knew anything about her, he would have taken money for information.'

Mike didn't answer. Charley knew she'd lost his trust in some way.

* * * * *

As they left the main part of the village through the last set of lights, Charley's vision began to separate. The air around the house had been sour and suffocating, and it seemed to have stuck to her clothes. Her skin pricked and sweat formed on her upper lip. By the time Mike pulled the car up by the house, a tidal wave of nausea resulted in her being violently sick. She steadied herself against the wall and wiped her mouth.

'You need to have a rest,' Mike said. 'I'm going to get something on that little dickhead and go back around there to find out what he really knows.'

She didn't have the energy to argue. He led her into the house, even going so far as to make her sit on the sofa while he fetched a blanket and water.

'I'm going to check out that alibi too,' he said. 'But if you need me, ring, and I'll be straight back.'

Twenty minutes later she got up, splashed some water on her face and left.

* * * * *

The site was bubbling over with rubble and felt unstable as she walked across to the loosely locked gate. Mike's car was nowhere to be seen. He was probably off wasting more time on Callum.

The door to the security hut was open, and she could hear the voices from within. She approached cautiously and knocked lightly on the door, pushing it slightly as she did. A man spun around in an office chair, still talking into his mobile phone, his dark and large features set into an annoyed expression. The desk behind him was covered in paperwork.

'Just a sec,' he said into the phone. 'What do you want?'

She knew how she must have appeared to him. Her face was clammy despite the quick wash, and the smell of sick drifted from her.

'I want to ask a question.'

'I'll ring you back,' he said into the phone and then gave her a hard look. 'What?'

'Are Daniel and Matthew Ryan working this weekend?'

230

He pulled a face that knotted his thick eyebrows together. 'Why - you need them for a job?

'Are they working in Liverpool?'

'Yeah, but they can't fit no more work in love. It's Sunday and they're finishing off.'

'I don't need them for a job,' she swallowed. 'I'm looking for my sister.'

'What?'

'You probably know her. She worked in the office for them.'

He shifted in his chair.

'I haven't seen her since Friday,' Charley tried to catch his eye.

'Love, I don't know what you're asking me for. I don't work with your sister or anything, I'm based in this office,' he said and scratched at his head, revealing a tattoo of the Everton Football Club crest on the inside of his wrist.

'I've got work to be getting on with anyway.' He practically pushed her out of the door and slammed it shut.

It was only as she walked towards the cafe, her third and final visit that day, that she realised where she'd seen that tattoo before. It was the Ryan family stamp.

Chapter FORTY-THREE

Unsure - not feeling, showing, or doing with confidence and certainty

~ Of my life, my relationship, myself...how much trouble I'm really in.

~ Of how far Karen and the family would go for Daniel.

~ Of how far Daniel would go for me (to keep me)...

August 2014

'Should we order food?' Karen's talons, which were painted a coral pink today, rapped on the table.

'No,' Daniel said, 'get a drink here and then we'll have to move on.' He gave me a wink from across the table.

'Oh yeah,' Karen laughed shrilly. 'I keep forgetting.'

'About what?' I said, even though I'd asked loads of times what all this was about.

Daniel had called it his final 'surprise' although I somehow doubted that. I'd said I needed to talk to him as soon as I got back to the house, but then they'd all piled out behind him; Bob, Karen, José, bloody Ken and even Matthew and Melissa. I had no idea what was going on but it was the worst timing ever. They all glared at me like they knew my secret.

I didn't want to eat. The smell of over-salted and vinegared fish and chips, along with some special or another put on in this dingy pub, was making my insides rock and roll all over the place. Everyone ordered their drinks. I went for a lime and soda. I had to talk to Daniel alone and get this out there before I was actually sick.

'You not drinking, Gina?' Karen arched an eyebrow at me, which was a bit like a facial exercise for her. I ignored her.

'Daniel, could we go for a walk?' I tried to keep my voice normal. Across the waterfront, outside the pub, the clouds were stretching themselves out after a long day and it was calming me down. That's the type of thing our Charley would say, clouds stretching out. I wondered if I should talk to her first.

'Great idea, we'll all go after these drinks,' Bob said heartily. I sat back and tried to concentrate on breathing as the talk went on all around me. I couldn't understand a word of it. The pub lights seemed to dim and then brighten. I had to shut my eyes.

'You ready?' Daniel nudged me. He looked happy, possibly due to the pint he'd had; his eyes sparkled. He helped me up and kissed me on the cheek. When things were like this, I still felt that pull towards him, like it was me and him against everything. Maybe this would go ok. Maybe he would get it.

Outside it was chilly for August, so I didn't mind Daniel pulling me towards his warm body. He was wearing the nice aftershave I'd bought him a while back - a dreamy, musty kind of scent. There was also the river air, that slightly weird – not quite sure if it's good or bad for you - sea smell.

I tried to walk us ahead of the others, but Karen was a master of high heels and was always right behind us, close enough to hear anything we said.

'Is like the clouds are jumping across the sky,' José said.

'Arrh yer so poetic, babe. Isn't he?' Karen poked me in the back. It shocked me enough to step out of Daniel's grip. In a second, José had taken my place. Well not exactly my place obviously, him and Daniel weren't walking arm in arm or anything.

Karen became my new walking partner. Matthew and Melissa were whisper-arguing behind us.

'Dan's like José isn't he?' Karen said. I couldn't really find a way to answer that. 'I mean, like, they'd do anything for us. Like, if someone was taking the piss or needed sorting out.'

'What?'

'What I'm saying is, I won't have our Danny screwed over again. He chose to marry you, and some proper little bitches he sacked off in the past will be jel over that. They'll say anything.' I stopped cold but Ken interrupted us. 'Should get a move on,' he said, lifting his arm up to look at his watch, and giving me the full view of the horrible, filthy little tattoo that looks like a crest of dirt scribbled into the skin of his wrist.

'Yeah you're right,' Daniel turned around. 'You lot go ahead and we'll follow you.'

There was the sound of a scuffle behind us. Bob had Matthew by the scruff of his jacket, hissing words into his ear.

'I still don't think it's fucking fair,' Matthew said before crashing into me.

'Watch it!' Bob warned, pushing him away. 'You ok, love?' His face was all old and kind-looking again.

'Family comes first and I always wanted a daughter,' Bob said. 'I can see you calm Dan down. You're good for him.'

'Thanks.' His words had only made me feel worse.

Karen's heels took lumps out of the cobbles as she ran back from eating the face off José by the railings. 'Wait!' she shouted, her eyes as sparkly as her lip gloss. 'Can I give her the package now, Danny?' She pulled something out of her massive handbag. It was a lumpy looking parcel covered with pink tissue paper and wrapped with a bow.

Daniel nodded.

'Yes!' Karen grabbed my hand, her nails scratching across my palm and pulled me back towards the pub.

'What's going on?'

235

'Aren't you ever grateful?' she hissed, dragging me back through the door of and into the stale-beer-stuck-in-the-carpet-since-the-1980s smell. When we got to the toilets, she started pulling out make-up from her bag and muttering that I never wore enough eyeliner. The package seemed to have become an afterthought as she flung it and pushed me into a cubicle. Before I even opened it, I could hear her shouting through the door, 'isn't it fucking fabulous?'

It was a beautiful, floaty pink dress, the exact colour I was always telling Daniel made me look good in photos and the exact style which hid my fat wrestler arms and took the attention off my stomach on non-skinny days.

'It's gorgeous,' I shouted. 'Did you choose it?'

'No, our Danny did,' she called back. 'I got you these though.' She pushed a pair of silver shoes under the door with heels that a trapeze artist would have struggled to balance on. 'Anyway, hurry up. I want to do a quick job on your face.'

The fish fluttered in my stomach again, which was already feeling a bit swollen. I hurried to put the dress on, knowing the sooner that I did all this, the sooner I could get Daniel on his own.

Karen fussed about me, spinning my hair around her fingers and pinning it with jabs to my scalp before setting to work on my face and using every size brush known to man (or woman) to blend my eye make-up right. When I looked in the mirror, I realised I had been completely Tropically Fished.

'You should always wear these colours, babe,' Karen stood back, admiring her five-minute makeover. 'And wear your hair up. It takes the attention off your nose.'

Daniel was waiting in the white Audi.

'José's taken our car home so I'll jump in with you two,' Karen got in the back and slammed the door. 'God, I'm proper excited.'

Daniel took my hand. 'You look really beautiful,' he said, and my head was a jumble again. Why was he making it harder? I sat back as we raced along the roads leading out of Liverpool

236

and towards the motorway. Everything blinkered past too fast; streets lights, other buildings, cars, they all became one bright mesh.

'Maybe you should slow down a bit,' I risked saying.

'Relax,' Daniel said through gritted teeth. Karen didn't seem arsed at all, flicking through her phone and ignoring everything else.

'We're showing you how quick it is to get here.' He smiled secretively.

'Where?'

Eventually I recognised the shops, the bars and the little boutiques as we were forced to slow down.

'It's finally ready, babe,' he said as we pulled up in a dark street which didn't look ready for anything at all. Karen giggled and leaned across the seat, and before I knew it, she was tying something around my eyes, really thick so that I couldn't see at all.

'Don't!' I snatched weakly at her hand. Waves of panic moved up and down me. They laughed, even though I'd explained to Daniel loads of times that I had claustrophobic eyes.

'Calm down, you crank!' I heard Karen say; her voice was all disorientated. There was something not right about the way they were both acting. I grabbed at the blindfold but my hands were smacked and then held down roughly with something that tickled my skin and clasped them into place. I bit my tongue in panic and felt blood start to build up in my mouth. The car shook as Karen got out of the back and slammed the door. I could hear the faint sound of her scuttling away from the car before it started up again and the doors locked. It was then I found that I couldn't move my hands.

CHAPTER FORTY-FOUR

LOYALTY: 10.00 Sunday 31st August 2014

He'd won.

She didn't have the energy to fight back any more, even if the opportunity came up. But it wouldn't. Her hands were bound behind her back, tied with thick ropes to the wooden chair, while her bare feet were stuck together with tape so tightly that she couldn't even move her toes.

She'd drifted in and out of consciousness and had no sense of time. Every bone in her body ached, from her neck where she'd strained it, slumping to one side when she'd slept, to her kneecaps and chin, which were bruised from smacking the floor. She tried to concentrate now that the lights were back on and he was in the room again.

'You're disgusting, Making out you're some kind of princess, and look at you.' He pointed at the floor.

Gina already knew that she'd wet herself at some point. There were too many strains around her body to care. The main thing she noticed was that the object reflecting in the light was a knife. In his other hand was a large sheet with what looked like a coat hanger poking out of the top.

'Bet you're wondering what that is.' He placed it carefully over the back of another chair he must have brought in at some point.

Gina could guess what it was as her eyes adjusted to the light. The hideous lace was creeping out from the bottom of the sheet.

'Yes,' she croaked, her lips cracking as she spoke. 'I'll do it.'

'You don't even know what I'm going to ask yet!' He laughed. 'Silly cow.' He took something from his pocket. It was a small can. 'Antifreeze,' he said and then took out a bottle of pills and shook them in her face before putting them both down on the floor.

'Or maybe you could slit your wrists.' He ran a finger across the blade until it drew blood. This made him jump back and a hissing sound escaped through his teeth. He sucked at his finger, watching her.

She could still taste the chemicals she'd tried to use as a weapon. There was a harsh dryness at the sides of her mouth. The skin on her stomach and breast felt exposed through the rip in her t-shirt. Dry blood and tears stuck to her face.

'And don't tell me I'll never get away with it again,' he said. 'You think I've never hidden evidence before? Or blamed someone else?' He used the knife to point at the smudge of a tattoo on the back of his wrist, 'You see this, that's loyalty that is. Something you don't know the meaning of.'

He brought the knife close to her face. She closed her eyes.

CHAPTER FORTY-FIVE

Vendetta - a bitter, destructive feud

~ This family are big on them, apparently if I mess up there'll be one against me?

~ Probably have loads of vendettas against them too, Mark for a start although maybe not any more.

August 2014

'I'm really sorry!' Daniel repeated. 'It was only so you wouldn't take the blindfold off.'

'Drama queen,' Karen muttered, loud enough for me to hear. She put a smile back on her face for Daniel. 'What should I tell everyone?'

'Tell them to wait!'

I was shaking like a leaf. The furry pink handcuffs were off my wrists and on the driveway, with the black sleep mask that had been over my eyes lying next to it. Daniel rubbed his arm, scratching at the skin. 'I'm honestly so sorry, babe. I didn't know it would scare you so much. I had to park around the corner so you wouldn't see the gazebo or fairy lights. Then everything else-' he put a hand in the direction of the cuffs and mask, '-was meant to be for effect...so, like, it would be a better surprise. Karen thought it was a good idea. I should have realised you wouldn't be into it.

Suddenly I felt a bit stupid. As if my own fiancé and his bimbo cousin were going to kidnap me. I wiped at my face again, getting rid of the last of the panic tears.

'I've had a team of removal men taking all our stuff here tonight. The house is finally ready.'

'All my stuff is here?' I croaked. It was then I finally looked up at our new home, the same beautiful cottage, licked with fresh paint.

'A few boxes couldn't fit in, but most of it, yeah.'

I'd sat in a pub while my whole life was moved around.

'Ready?' Daniel didn't notice my shock. My feet crunched over the gravel and as we turned the corner. There in front of us, in the wide open garden, was *everyone*.

'What's this?'

'Here she is!' Daniel shouted to the crowd instead of answering me. They cheered back like an X Factor audience who'd been given a 'cheer or die' cue card.

Even our Charley was there in the crowd, shuffling in jeans and a t-shirt (too hot for a hoodie). She gave me an awkward thumbs up. I mouthed that I was coming over to her but Jen was headed towards me, fighting against grass and an eight-month pregnancy belly.

'I want a word with you,' she said, wagging her finger in Daniel's face. Her purple-red roots were practically down to her chin.

'Jen, you look really lovely,' Daniel said kissing her on the cheek. Her face automatically went into that glowing smile she gets when the attention is on her. 'Sorry about what happened with Mark. It was a bit of a cash flow problem and I didn't think we'd have enough work in but a major job could be back on,' Daniel continued and then looked around. 'So, is he here so I can let him know?'

'Erm, well he's not here.' Jen said.

'I'll text him then.' Daniel took out his phone while heading towards one of his friends who was waving from across the garden.

'What's that about?' I asked.

'Oh, erm, nothing,'

She looked very glam in a bump-hugging orange dress, but her scouse brows were wonky with worry. 'Are you ok, though?' she turned to me. 'We've been really worried about you.'

'Jen, you didn't tell anyone about the night I stayed at yours did you?' My heart was pounding. Jo appeared at the edge of the garden. Her pink billowy shorts and black strappy top made her look thinner than ever.

'Jo!' Jen called out, glad of the distraction. I followed and then we all stood there in the middle of my new garden, party noise all around us, three awkward friends. Jo scuffed at the grass with her ballet pumps, ruining them I might add.

'Well if you're not going to say something to her, I am.' Jen said finally.

'Say something to *me*?'

Jo took a breath and stopped the scuffing. 'Can we get a drink or something?'

'What's up with you?' Jen nudged her. '*We* agreed to talk to her.'

'You've both been bitching about me then?' I asked.

'Not bitching at all Gina,' Jen shook her head violently. 'We're worried about you and all the stuff that's been going on. That's why we came.' She stared at Jo again. 'You not going to say anything then?'

'I don't think I want to hear what you've got to say,' I said. 'There are things I trusted you with, Jen, and I can see that I was wrong to.' My eyes were stinging, and I knew if I didn't walk away from them soon I'd start crying. I didn't look back but I could hear Jen kicking off at Jo. They didn't try and come after me.

A gin bottle on a table winked at me under the fairy lights outside the house. It offered me a way out. Sometimes getting the fish completely fucked subdued them, made them pass out, whereas at other times it got them worse.

I resisted and headed inside. Daniel hadn't let me see the house over the last few weeks, although I'd emailed him paint colours and wallpaper patterns I liked. He'd obviously ignored all the suggestions.

The gorgeous country kitchen had turned into a modern monstrosity, complete with blood red walls. I walked through the hall where the garishness continued. The original fireplace in the living room was gone, and the large staircase in the hall now featured a thin red carpet, ready for any sudden influx of celebrities. Hideous. The ring on my finger suddenly felt tighter.

I went and found a bathroom, apparently there were three, and washed my hands with boiling hot water. The ring on my finger was a swirling, ugly weight . I took it off and put it in my bag and looked at myself in the mirror. I was like one of those Picasso paintings of a sliding, melting face, only done in make-up.

Sometimes looking at my reflection is like emotional suicide, other times it helps. I try and see what's left of Mum. I have more of her than Charley, who is like Dad physically, with a snub nose and oval face, although she hates to admit it. Today was an emotional suicide day so I looked away. I had to find Charley. It was time to tell her what I had planned.

It was Karen who led me to her. I could hear her whiney tones, made worse by the patronising voice she usually keeps for children and those with special needs. She had my sister held conversation captive.

'You need to eat more, girl,' Karen was saying as she held an untouched plate of sausage rolls under Charley's nose. 'Fatten up a bit and take advantage of being so skinny.' She turned to me. 'Doesn't she?'

Before I could answer, Lydia stormed over with a face like thunder. Behind her was Anthony, wearing a light blue shirt with rolled up sleeves, slim black chinos and grey plimsolls. His hair was subtly styled with lacquer so it moved to one side. Karen gave him an approving once over.

'What's up with you?' Karen asked Lydia. 'He binned you off again?

'It's always the same bleeding story with him,' Lydia, who was usually an expert in being high on her heels was swaying slightly and smelt like a wino. She swirled the glass in her hand. 'He fucking loves her, doesn't he?' She pointed a bony finger at me. This created a horrible silence that even the noise of the people partying around us couldn't sort.

'I'm getting some scran,' Lydia said and took the plate of sausage rolls off Karen stuffing three of them in her mouth as she swaggered away.

'Fuck's sake,' Karen said as she poured herself a lethal cocktail mix that had cherries like red eyes running through it. She stared down at my finger. 'Where's your ring?'

'In my bag,' I said. 'I took it off. My finger's got a rash on it.'

She gave me a *look*.

'What's up?' Daniel shouted, prompting Karen to back off and head after Lydia. 'I love you,' he whispered into my ear, tingling cider and breathy blackcurrant and beer against my skin. I flinched.

'Anthony's here you know,' he said loudly, taking a swig of his drink. 'I invited him.' The last part was said with some kind of weird pride. 'There he is. Anthony!' Daniel's shout blasted down my face. The light blue shirt moved towards us from across the garden.

'House looks great,' Anthony said when he reached us.

'Ta, mate, worked so hard on it these last couple of months,' Daniel's voice was booming, 'wanted to have it all ready for Gina to move in and not have to worry about anything.'

'How are the wedding plans going?' Anthony asked politely.

'All sorted. Booked for Gretna Green on 1st Sept,' Daniel replied.

Anthony and Charley looked like they'd both been smacked in the face. Daniel took a sip of his beer, a victory sip.

'I need a drink,' I said, walking off. My head was spinning. Charley followed me.

'Are you ok?' she asked.

'Yeah, fine.'

'Are you getting married in Gretna Green?'

'Charley, you can get angry with me sometimes you know!'

She didn't say anything. I wanted the Charley back who wasn't scared of offending me because she felt like she owed me a huge debt.

'And no...I mean I don't know,' I admitted. How much could I tell her? 'I need to talk to you properly-'

'This is so exciting, love!' A loud screech interrupted. Melissa ran over and hugged us both. 'We were dying to tell you in the pub but we weren't allowed to.' She smelt like the cheap perfume shop in St John's Market. 'Dan has done amazing though. Did you have any idea?'

'Proper little princess you aren't yer?' Matthew whispered into my ear as he hugged me. He reached into my hair and I froze - I'd forgotten about the tiara that Karen had plonked on my head on the driveway while I was still panicking. Matthew stepped back and smiled like a normal person then. The tiara was in his plaster-ridden hand.

'Big plastering project at Karen's at the mo – can't get the stuff off. Your Daniel must be the same,' he said. Melissa gave him a kiss on his stubbled cheek. 'Me hard working boy,' I almost laughed. Luckily, they walked off.

'What did you want to tell me?' Charley asked.

'Oh nothing, only stuff about dad selling the house and that, boring really,' I lied. 'I'll meet you back in the garden. I'm going to...sort some of these bottles out.' I pointed to the growing stack of cans and empty wine bottles littering the pathway.

'I could help you,' she offered.

'Go and get me a water and that will be a start.'

I had to be on my own for a bit, even if it was spent down the side of the house listening to the whoops of a party. I took the lid off the bin as Anthony shuffled down towards me.

'Gretna Green?' he asked.

I mumbled a yes as I tried to shove wine bottles into a bin already full with all kinds of crap. I pulled out a few things, recognising boxes of old bank statements and notebooks I'd been meaning to throw out but had left in the old house. Then something caught my eye, a section of familiar, sloppy handwriting. I pulled it out and my heart dropped.

'You ok?' Anthony put a hand on my arm. I didn't brush it away. I kept looking at the words from Mum I thought I'd lost. A rush of red mist seemed to float in front of my eyes.

'What the fuck are you two doing?' A voice echoed down the thin pathway. Lydia's eyes were glistening and dangerous; the sequins from her dress bouncing off them in the security light.

I stormed past Lydia, knocking her against the wall and headed for Daniel, but Karen stood in the way.

'Last girl who took the piss out of our Danny,' she began, swirling her drink slowly with her free hand as she kept hold of me like some kind of expert gangster, 'we went out in Lydia's car, 'cos she thought we didn't know and then we locked her in.'

'She was screaming, broke all her nails trying to open the car door,' Lydia added.

'It was hilarious wasn't it?' Karen said.

'You gave her a proper hiding didn't yer?' Lydia laughed from behind us. 'Did you keep the earrings in the end?'

'Well she won't be wearing them again will she?' Karen replied with a grin that made my stomach turn. 'That Anthony will be wearing his balls around his ears if he ever tries it on with you again.

'He didn't try it on with me.' My heart was pounding.

'You see if you were thinking of leaving our Danny after all he's done for you, well, like where would you go? Your

247

sister's little flat by Lark Lane? Anthony's house, where they never lock the back door?'

'What?' A chill came over me.

'Do what our Dan wants and make him happy - then you don't need to worry about anyone.'

'I've had enough!' My shout echoed. I was away from her, heading towards Daniel. The fairy lights to the green carpet-like grass became a hazy grey. I pulled him away from the party, back down to the driveway. He followed me like it was a game.

'I've had enough,' I said again when we were out of earshot of anyone else.

'Don't drink any more then.' He laughed.

'No,' I said, ' I've had enough of all this.'

His face changed. 'I haven't done anything apart from sort out a bigger house for you, and a job.'

'Throwing out my mum's letter and swapping my pills for fake ones. I don't even want a baby yet, but you didn't give me a choice.'

'Are you pregnant?' There was a horrible kind of hope in his voice.

'Why did you hide the letter and then throw them out?' I avoided his question.

'I forgot I'd even put them in that box.'

'But you still threw them out.'

'I didn't mean to. I was angry. You were swallowing all me dad's bullshit about being lost when he was younger and all that.' He put his face close to mine. 'I'll kill myself if you leave me. You know that.'

He stood back. 'Are you pregnant?'

A loud scream came from the party. It was Jen. We found her on the floor, sprawled awkwardly and crying.

248

'I think she's going in labour,' Jo said, standing rigid looking over her.

Anthony pushed past us and got down on the floor with Jen. 'I've rang an ambulance.'

'Someone phone Mark. Where's Mark?' Jen cried.

'I'll ring him,' Daniel said.

'Don't you help me you twat!' Jen shouted between short breaths as Daniel crouched down on the other side of her. 'Laying Mark off because we let Gina stay after you scared the shit out of her. ' She spat out the word shit.

'What?' Daniel said. Everyone was looking at us.

'It was an accident,' I said. This could ruin all my plans.

'You'd be better off with him!' Jen pointed towards Anthony.

'Fuck this!' Daniel stormed off.

I stood, uncertain which way to go. I knew what Daniel was capable of, what would come next, but I could take the risk for my friend.

'Don't…I don't want you to come with me,' Jen said to me as I sat down next to her and we heard the ambulance sirens, 'unless you leave him.'

'Jen-'

'I'll go with her,' Jo said, not meeting my eye.

The paramedics arrived, green uniforms blending against the grass, and we all stepped back as they helped Jen.

'You can come with us,' Anthony said, taking my hand. I held on as we headed to the driveway.

My phone moved in my pocket. The text was from Daniel.

You go with her and I'll do it. I'll fucking do it.

'I'll follow you in my own car,' I said. 'I haven't really had anything to drink.'

'Gina, we're not leaving you here,' Charley spoke up.

'I need to see if Daniel's ok and then I'll follow. I'll be right behind you-'

'Don't be ridiculous,' Anthony said. 'This is your friend having a baby. Get in the car.'

Karen appeared by my side and put an arm around me as though in support. 'Get them to leave,' she whispered, digging her nail into my arm. 'If anything happens to Daniel, it would all be your fault.

'Don't stay here with him, please, Gina,' Charley pleaded.

'I love him! Why don't you get that?' I replied.

'Gina, come on,' Anthony said.

'I said *no* ! What do you think I'll be an easy lay or something because of what Jen said!'

His face was like thunder. 'Do what you want then!' He got into the car. Charley stood with her hand on the door. 'Please come with us,' she said.

'Make sure Jen is ok and I'll follow you, I promise.'

'Are you sure-'

'Go! Let me sort my own life out! I'm sick of having to deal with everyone else's!'

She gave me one last questioning look and then thankfully got into the car. They drove off.

'Good girl,' Karen said. 'You can't leave our Danny for the sake of them and that other slag Jen. You're with us now, our family, and if Danny has told you stuff that could come back on all of us, you'd best fucking not tell anyone. Do yer know what I mean?' I got a last warning in my ear. 'You tell anyone and I won't hurt you, I'll hurt *them*.' She pushed me towards the side of the house. Daniel was waiting in the shadows.

'You need to listen to me.' He dragged me roughly into the garage. 'You need to know.' He stood in front of the door, blocking the way out. His tears were on my face, his nose touching my cheek. 'I killed someone.'

CHAPTER FORTY-SIX

The café was too warm, creating a claustrophobic air which belied the lack of customers. One man stood behind the counter. He was strolling up and down past the pastries and wrapped up sandwiches, too settled in their packets to be as fresh as the sign behind him promised.

Charley looked at the clock again. She had done this almost as many times as the man in the apron had. They both looked up when a girl burst through the door, blonde highlighted head with dark roots. She ran towards the counter, mumbling apologies and then stopped to put down her bag and sweep the hair off her face. It was then that she saw Charley and went pale. She muttered something to the man, who narrowed his eyes, before she disappeared through the kitchen doors.

'Would you like another drink?' The man asked Charley warily as she approached the counter. He was young, maybe around Gina's age, and had a 'manager' badge pinned onto his uniform of a plain white shirt, dark trousers and a stripy apron, that hung loosely on his thin frame.

'I was wondering if I could speak to Megan.'

'She had enough trouble in her last place. I don't know how you people track her down but-'

'It's ok,' Megan interrupted from the door behind him. 'She isn't one of them.'

The man stepped back as Megan came to the front of the counter.

'I'll be fine.' Megan turned back to the man, who shrugged and gave Charley a warning look.

They sat down on a table away from the window. Megan fiddled with her hair, twisting it around her finger.

'You don't look anything like her, really,' Megan said. 'It was the expression on your face. It was like hers when she came in.'

'She's gone missing,' Charley forced the words out. Her throat felt so dry that she took a sip of her insipid coffee.

Megan's head snapped up.

'When did you see her?'

'Last week.' Megan sat back and ran her hand through her hair. 'She came in here. I didn't think that she would really leave him and then she ran out and-'

'Ran out?'

'Yeah…I…listen, it's her business,' Megan continued, avoiding Charley's gaze.

'She's gone missing,' Charley said sitting up, 'and I know that Daniel's family has something to do with it.'

The door rang nosily as it opened and they both jumped. An old man with a newspaper sat at a table on the other side of the café.

'Why did she run out?'

Megan looked out the window.

'Please, *you* know what Daniel is like.'

'She thought she might be pregnant,' Megan replied. 'I told her that Daniel had swapped my pills for placebos and I thought I should warn her.'

Charley's blood ran cold.

'I didn't think she was ready to leave him until I saw her face when I told her that. It's hard to leave. You convince yourself it's all normal, the way he is, especially when he tells you about his past, like, everything he went through with his mum.'

A definition echoed in Charley's head. *What Daniel wants is normal. Isn't it?*

'The family only warned me off.' Megan tucked stray strands of hair behind her ears now. 'And they won't harm her if she's pregnant. They might just scare her a bit.' She pressed at her ears when she said that and Charley noticed the torn skin, still healing.

'What did they do to you?'

'They called it a *warning*,' Megan replied. 'They do have people who stop them going too far, like Jemma. She has a conscience, took me to the hospital after they locked me in the car that time.'

'Why did they do that?

'I'd threatened to leave Daniel, changed my mind, wasn't ready. I didn't think they knew, but they did.'

'Did you go to the police?'

Megan shook her head. 'Karen always said if I went to the police that would be the end of me.'

'You believed that?'

'Apart from the torn ear lobes, what else could I say? The police wouldn't listen to the fact that my boyfriend made a few nasty comments, took away my self-esteem, and that was before I found out what they were all so concerned about hiding, that awful…anyway, it was my word against theirs…for what Daniel told me he'd done, and what they did to me because I knew.'

'What did Daniel do?'

'Did they do that?' Megan was looking at her finger, bandaged but still awkwardly positioned, an obvious break.

'Please.'

'I don't want to be…I can't be dragged into this again.' Megan stood up, scraping the chair back across the cheap tiled floor. 'I didn't trust her. I didn't think she'd leave him. God!' She sat down again and put her head in her hands. 'I thought she was safe because she obviously didn't know then, or she would have said.'

'Know what?'

'I can't, honestly-'

'You have to tell me.'

There was no answer.

'Megan, please. I only have her.'

Megan took a deep breath. 'They'll always cover up for him and they'll do anything to stop it getting out.'

'You have to help Gina. I don't know what they'll do to her.'

'I didn't think they would do anything to her, especially if she's pregnant.'

'Then you need to tell me everything you know,' Charley said, 'and I won't go to the police.' Technically that was true.

Megan lifted her head back up. He lower lip wobbled. 'Sorry, I can't.'

'Think of what they did to you and what they did to me. Gina could be going through much worse right now.' Charley took the bandage off her finger and Megan winced at the raw and mangled skin. Her hands reached towards her destroyed earlobes. 'They could even carry on and do it to other girls too. But we can stop them; we can stop them for good.'

CHAPTER FORTY-SEVEN

Wrong ~ unjust, dishonest, or immoral

~ But it was only one punch.

~ But that's like saying it was only one life.

~ So much wrong and no one has done the right thing; wrong, after wrong, after wrong.

August 2014

He locked the door and put the key in his pocket.

'What are you doing?' I tried to get back around him but he blocked me.

'You two having fun in there are yer?' Karen shouted from outside. 'Leaving us to clean up the party after yer mate wrecked it all, 'ey?'

Daniel clamped a hand over my mouth, snapping my head back as he did and stopping me from making any proper noise. When he finally let me go, I had no breath left and it had gone quiet outside. My neck throbbed.

'Fucking listen to me. I have to tell you what happened.' Daniel tried to take hold of my hands. I put them behind my back.

'You killed someone?' My heart was beating right out of my chest.

'No,' he said, 'I mean, yeah. I…you have to listen to me.' He paced back and forth, scratching at his arm.

'It was only one punch.' He started crying, his face quickly got slimy with tears, like slug marks on his skin.

I didn't say anything. I tried to think of how I could get out. There were no windows. The room stunk of chemicals.

'That fight I got into,' he said, sitting down on the floor, 'I didn't break his jaw….I killed him….I didn't mean to I-'

'How do you not mean to kill someone?'

'I was only fifteen. Everything else I told you about how it happened was true,' he said. 'He was one of the lads who was laughing when everyone was taking the piss out of Mum sitting on that teacher's knee.' He rubbed his hands across his face. 'He wasn't even one of them who said anything. He laughed.'

'How did you get away with it?'

'My dad sorted it.'

'What do you mean *sorted* it?' I asked.

'I dunno,' Daniel said, keeping his eyes on the ground. 'He got someone to give me an alibi when everyone in our school was interviewed by the police.

'Who?'

'It doesn't matter,' Daniel replied. 'I mean, I don't even know who it was.'

'But you must have known who it was.'

'He went down like a ton of bricks and I thought he was joking,' Daniel said as his eyes glazed over. 'If I confess now, yeah?' He pulled me down suddenly so that my knees knocked the floor. 'If I do that, right,' he said, looking all around like he was expecting someone to come out of the shadows. 'They all go inside with me, all of them. And… they won't let that happen.'

His eyes were bloodshot and wild under the light. 'But you know I've wanted to, since I fucking did it. I've wanted to. It's like carrying a brick around inside me, in my chest. You know when you were talking about fish and I laughed, I thought she really doesn't realise how lucky she is. Fucking fish.'

His face lit up. 'You could help me. I'd confess if you helped me. Then he shook his head slowly. 'No…he'll kill anyone you tell about this.'

'Who will?'

'You don't get it,' he said. 'How can I make you get it?'

I wanted to shut my eyes and block this nightmare out.

'Charley.'

'Don't hurt her!'

'I don't want to hurt her,' he replied quietly. 'That's the thing. I didn't even want to hurt him. I wanted to… punish myself or maybe even her, me Mum. I don't know. But I didn't want to kill anyone. It was a mistake, you know like when Charley-'

He didn't need to say anything else. His eyes locked into mine. 'So you see what I mean?'

I sat down on the floor next to him. He took my hand and I didn't move it away.

I never talked about what Charley did, what finally broke her. Of course everyone knew about it, being in the papers as it was, a smiling schoolgirl gone wrong making the front pages on a slow news day. Daniel hadn't brought it up before. We sat in silence with the light casting strange shapes on the bottles of chemicals on the white shelves.

'What would you have done for Charley if she-'

'I don't know,' I admitted, 'but I don't think you can carry on like this. It's sending you mad.'

'I know,' he muttered. 'But it's like there's too many things wrong now, and everyone else won't let themselves be dropped in it.' He turned around and his eyes locked into mine. 'You can't say anything. There's a lot of people involved, not just my family, and they'll do anything to stop it getting out. They might even…'

'What?'

'Hurt you.'

'Like they did with Megan?' I thought of the ripped earlobes.

'I didn't know Karen was going to do that,' he muttered. 'I can't control what they do, that's the thing.'

He took his hand back off me and I noticed that the skin was twisting off his finger.

'We've all got these tattoos right? Everyone who knows.'

'Melissa?'

'No, but she likes her life the way it is. She doesn't ask questions.'

'Mum never knew. Dad said she'd only get pissed and blab it, and I shouldn't feel guilty as it was her fault really anyway.' He scratched at his peeling fingers. 'The day after, when I woke up, it was like a red pain all over my body, like someone had ripped part of me away. Agony from my neck down to my knees.'

We were silent again. I could tell he was building up to say something else that I wouldn't want to hear.

'You never answered me before. Are you pregnant?'

It dawned on me what was happening when I saw the easy expression return to his face, only moments after he'd confessed to murder.

He was only reining in his temper because he thought I was pregnant. The anger and the danger was still there, in his flaking skin his jittery leg and the way he everything, like nothing was really his fault. Even now, when he was telling me about a *murder*, someone's life being ended because of him, he was doing it in a way to make me feel sorry for him.

'Yeah, I mean, I don't know. I feel like I am, but I need to do a test.' It was safer to lie.

'I know I'm capable of being loved when I'm with you. I'm sorry about how I treat you sometimes. I can be better. I will be better. And I'm sorry about the letter. I was jealous because you had a relationship with your mum and that she actually liked you.'

My skin turned hot all over. The letter. I had it memorised in my head, but I needed to have it in my hands from time to time. Daniel had known this. He kept doing terrible things and how long before he lost it again and did something else he didn't mean to do? Charley was genuinely sorry. That was the difference between them.

I stood up and forced myself to smile and take his hand.

CHAPTER FORTY-EIGHT

ALIBIS: 12.30 Sunday 31ˢᵗ August 2014

'I'm coming over to the station. Can you meet me there?

'What?'

'I've got something against Daniel we can use.' She was running towards the car.

'Where are you? I can't hear you properly.'

Charley took a deep breath and slowed to a walk. 'I've got something on Daniel. It's worse than we thought. Can you meet me at the station so we can report this and get them looking for Gina?'

'I really don't think it's a good idea for you to come to the station.'

'We have to.'

'Charley, calm down. I'll meet you-'

'Daniel killed someone. His whole family are covering for him.'

The line went silent.

'Mike, are you still there?'

'Who told you that?'

'I can't tell you.'

A pause. 'Where are you now?'

'At my car.'

'Don't go to the station yet. I have to talk to you.'

'About what? He killed someone. Isn't that enough?'

'You won't even tell *me* who your source is, so how is this going to work?'

'It'll be ok when it's all in an official report.' Charley struggled with the car door.

'I need to make sure that you have enough evidence to make this accusation and…something else has come up. Can you meet me at your flat?'

'I don't feel very safe going back there at the moment.'

'Even if I meet you there?' he replied. 'You know I would keep you safe.'

Her heart leapt at that, but there was no time for those thoughts.

'I'd rather meet at the burger place again if that's ok.'

'It would be easier to talk in yours.'

'I'd rather be somewhere public.'

'Don't you trust me?' There was more than a hint of hurt in his voice.

'It's them I don't trust. I don't know what they'll do next.' She looked down at her finger, the reminder.

Mike was waiting in a booth when she got there. He was engrossed in his phone but got up when he noticed Charley, embracing her in a comforting hug. They sat down.

'You need some food.' He grabbed the attention of the waitress and ordered a sandwich and some fries. 'You'll feel better for it,' he said, leaning forward on the table. 'Now, tell me everything this witness told you.'

'She wasn't exactly a witness to the murder itself,' Charley realised how flimsy it sounded without Megan, 'but she said Daniel confessed to her that he'd killed someone.'

'She?'

Charley swallowed. 'I can't tell you who it is.'

'Tell me what she said then.'

'That he punched someone and they died. It was when he was fifteen. The family covered it up. Gina must know. That's why they've taken her.'

'Did this witness have any details like places, names and dates?

262

'He was fifteen, you could look it up, see what school he was in, he didn't live around here then-'

'Will the witness come with us to give a statement?'

'No.'

'Your witness won't talk and you won't give her name in? How do you think this is going to work?' He slammed the table with his fist, a move that surprised them both. A couple at the next table looked over. The girl widened her eyes and the boy gave Mike a hard stare.

'Sorry,' he said, 'but it's important that I know who told you this otherwise it is useless.''

There were splinters in Charley's chest. They both sat back to let the waitress place the food down in front of her.

'You have to give me more, Charley.' He took her hand over the top of the bread and chips that couldn't have looked less appetising. 'Where does this witness live or work? I can go and question her, see if we can get some solid evidence. It's important you have everything in order as Daniel has enough, along with the assault allegation that came from Mark, to put you back inside.'

Charley's whole body went cold. 'How?'

'Apparently he's got a film on his phone of the night you last saw Gina, and it doesn't match up to when you told us you last saw her and…implicates you in more serious allegations.'

He'd filmed it?

'But what about what they did to me?' She rubbed at the bandage on her finger.

'I'm at the point of making a big breakthrough here, despite everything, and we can use what they did to you eventually, just not yet. Even Janet is starting to listen, but I need more time and more evidence,' he said in a gentle voice. She felt a shameful jealous pinch in how he referred to Officer Thomson as 'Janet'. 'Tell me where this girl is and I'll go and find out more.'

'I'll come with you.'

263

'You need to eat, rest. Go home and get a couple of hours and then I'll come to you.'

'But I can help.'

'Don't worry about any of them coming to the house or your flat again. I'll give my friend a call who's on duty around that area, make sure he keeps a lookout and passes by your flat and I'll do the same by the house. Anyone matching their descriptions comes near and I'll be straight there.'

'No, it's not that. I really want to come too. She told me not to tell anyone. I have to be there so that she-'

'Charley, I'll go as a police officer so she knows its official, and I'll tell her what's going on. I'll protect you both.' He picked up her fork and speared it with a chip and some salad. 'Now, eat.' He held it towards her. She smiled and took the fork off him. He waited until she'd eaten a good portion before talking again.

'Where can I find her?'

'Can't we wait and I'll go with you?' Charley replied, although there was a heaviness washing over her. She could hardly lift her fork.

'Charley, you're falling asleep in your food.'

'I could get a couple of hours sleep first.'

'You said there's no time to waste,' he said, taking her hand again and rubbing it gently.

Her head was clouded.

'I promised.'

'Charley, let me help you. We have to find your sister.'

'Ok,' she heard herself say. 'Take me home, please.'

Mike guided her back to the car through the busy streets. 'You can't drive like this.' He was holding her up by this time.

'I don't know what's wrong with me.'

'I'll drive your car home,' he insisted and took the keys from her.

* * * * *

'Do you want me to walk you up to your flat?' he asked as they pulled up, already taking off his seatbelt and leaning across to unbuckle hers. He opened the car door and helped her out, unexpectedly kissing her on the cheek. The warmth of it was still on her face as they entered the flats. They braved the piss-soaked stairs. On the third flight, the man in the grey tracksuit was slumped on the floor. Noticing them, he scrambled to his feet and fell back against the wall. There was a large cut down one side of his face.

'Don't!' he pleaded, jumping up, eyes filled with terror. Despite Mike's arm around her, she fell against the banister as the man ran through them.

'I hate you having to live here,' Mike said.

She couldn't answer. Everything was sloping as though she was running in a virtual reality game. All she wanted to do was lie down, or make herself sick. What if Mike thought she had taken something?

'Do you want me to stay, make sure you're ok?' he said, as they entered her hall.

'No, I'm feeling a bit better, you go. I'll follow you soon.'

'Should I wait?'

She wanted to tell him yes, but the guilt at wasting time was starting to ebb. 'No, go and find Gina.' The words span away from her.

She gave him the address of Megan's cafe. After he left, she went to the kitchen and vomited into the sink.

* * * * *

Mike's mobile kept ringing out. She sent him another text while pacing the flat, drinking glass after glass of water until her senses came back. Three hours had passed and she'd forced herself to stay awake, being sick a few more times. The dizziness was starting to fade. She should have gone with

265

him to the café. She considered going back there but it would have been closed by now.

Every noise from outside made her jump. A door banging, the odd burst of talking or laughter, the sound of footsteps near the flat door.

When the Facebook message came, announced by the buzzing phone in her pocket, her heart stopped for a second. She debated what to do before dropping the knife into her bag and running to the car.

* * * * *

The place that Jemma wanted to meet her in was shabby and indie. It was somewhere that Karen and Lydia would never go. The constant conversation around them was already making Charley's head ache as she sat down. She steeled herself and forced a blank, hard look onto her face.

'I had nothing to do with what happened yesterday,' Jemma said hurriedly, her head down. When she did look up, her eyes were in every direction but Charley's.

'Did you have anything to do with what happened to Megan?' Charley replied, making the effort to stare straight at her.

'I took her the hospital.' Jemma fixed her eyes on the table, which had old scratches all over it. She was adding another one with her nail.

'The thing is, they aren't like that, often,' she said. 'It's, like, they're such a protective family. They go too far over some things though.'

'Like breaking into someone's flat and trapping their finger in a door?'

'You did accuse Daniel of kidnapping Gina, and you went to the police.'

'So what they did to me is ok?'

'No! I'm only saying they're all about family, especially Karen, and the way she is over Daniel.'

266

'Where do you think Gina is then? What am I meant to do, let Daniel and everyone get away with taking my sister?'

'I don't think you can blame Daniel.' Her voice wobbled. 'He had a real go at Karen and Lydia over what they did to you.'

'He didn't stop them though did he?'

Jemma wiped a tear away from her eye. 'It's hard. Karen has some kind of hold over him.'

'Over you as well?'

'We've been mates for years. She helped me get a job and get on my feet when me mum and dad kicked me out and I had nothing. She's been there.'

'But you're still meeting me?'

'I think it was awful what they did to you, and I'm worried about Gina. I want to try and help - do what I can.'

'Go on then.'

'I overheard Karen telling José to make sure that they all keep an eye on Bob, in case he does something stupid. That was before Gina went missing.'

'Daniel's dad?'

'From stuff they've said in the past, I got the impression they were all involved in something, but they were all a bit scared of Bob.'

'Involved in what?' Charley asked, testing her reaction.

Jemma shook her head. 'I don't know.' She sighed and looked back at Charley. 'Daniel treated Gina like shit at times. Same as with Megan; he gets with lovely girls and then messes it, and them, up. I had an ex-boyfriend like that once. I don't like seeing it happen and-'

'And what?'

'Like, I don't know,' she paused. 'I think Gina's ok, but there's something different. That's why I told you where Megan was, even though I felt bad doing that. But I don't think it's Daniel who has done something, not after seeing him yesterday. He was all over the place after we'd been to yours and he was always really upset about splitting up with Megan.' Jemma clasped her hands around the cup of coffee. 'They won't tell me anything though. I always thought Megan knew more and maybe she could help you.'

'Do you know about anything about Bob that I should tell the police?'

'God no, don't tell the police again! I'm sorry but I've given you as much as I can. I don't know anything else, but that the situation with Bob has always been weird. She'll turn up anyway. They never go *that* far.' Jemma grabbed her bag, the chair scrapping as she stood up and left the bar without looking back.

Charley was out of breath when she got back to the flat. There were no texts or calls off Mike Field. Five minutes later there was a knock at the door.

'It's me!' he called through the letter box. She let him in, then closed it quickly behind them, clasping at every chain.

'Megan's gone.'

'Gone?'

'Her manager said she resigned yesterday.'

'Did you get her home address?'

'Tried that. No one in and didn't look like she was coming back any time soon. I had a look through the windows of her downstairs flat and it was all bare.' He took a seat on the red sofa, legs spread out awkwardly like the first time he'd sat there, and ran a hand through his mop of curly dark hair. He was wearing jeans and a striped t-shirt, as though he was a friend calling round. There were thin beads of sweat on his forehead.

'I also checked in with the station,' he said and then paused. 'Mark has followed up his accusation, saying he thinks you were on drugs at the time of the attack. I think Daniel is pushing him into it as he thinks you'll accuse him next.'

'Why hasn't anyone been to see me then to ask questions?'

'It's only a matter of time,' he replied. 'Daniel hasn't made a statement yet, but he called in and mentioned the video informally, and said you've been harassing him and his family.'

'Why hasn't he made a statement though?'

'Said he feels sorry for you,' Mike said, his eyes concentrating on the floor.

'I want you to know something,' Charley said. 'That night, he set me up to stop Gina speaking to me.' It mattered to her that he believed this. 'Have you seen the film he said is on his phone?'

Mike shook his head. 'I think it's unfair of him to try and use something like that when you've done such a good job of turning your life around. He must have something to hide.'

Charley's cheeks flushed.

'But I don't think Daniel has anything to do with your sister being missing.'

'He *must* do.'

'He has alibis for the whole weekend. I didn't need to follow up your source as he brought the same contact details with him.'

She opened her mouth to tell him about the tattoo on the man who'd provided that alibi, but by mentioning this detail she'd have to come clean about wanting to check the alibi herself. Mike was one of her only allies at the moment and she couldn't push it.

'It could still be him. He could have slipped back to work and have her locked up somewhere.'

'What you don't want is Daniel and Mark to team up and use what they have against you. There is more evidence against you than them at the moment.'

They were both quiet now.

'Did you find anything about the murder Daniel committed?' she asked finally.

'I've looked into it. There's nothing we can link him to.'

'But the alibi would be on record wouldn't it?'

'I'm doing everything I can,' he snapped, gritting his teeth slightly and then almost immediately his face relaxed. 'Sorry, I really want to help you here but feel like I'm getting nowhere.'

'I've thought about someone you could question and I should have brought him up sooner,' she said, sitting down carefully on the sofa next to him. 'Daniel's dad.'

'Why's that?' He shifted forward on his seat.

She hesitated, not wanting to drop Jemma in it. 'I've seen him lose his temper.'

'We can't make a formal accusation as it'll prove you're inconsistent,' he replied. 'But I will look into his background. I still think we should look at Callum again.'

'It isn't Callum,' she said quietly.

He took her hand, leaned forward and kissed her lightly on the lips.

'Sorry, I shouldn't have done that.' He moved away from her.

'I'm worried that Gina could be pregnant,' she blurted out.

He turned quickly back to her. 'Do you know that for certain?

'Daniel was swapping her pills. I know she had a scare.'

He was quiet for a moment and then his eyes locked right onto hers, 'I will get this sorted out for you.'

CHAPTER FORTY-NINE

X-ray ~ photograph, examine

~ They should invent one that shows up all the mistakes that you're going to make so you have a chance to stop them (including forgiving people).

~ Because people don't change, they just get worse, family or not, hard to make them see through themselves.

Thursday 28th August 2014

My stomach was boiling with nerves. The fish were cooked.

I made my way around the waxy corridors, with bright nursery-style coloured walls. There were no bloody lilies around but the place stunk of them. Maybe that was the smell of death again, although this was meant to be a hospital of life.

Jen was sitting up in the bed, holding what looked like a wrinkled ball of dough wrapped in a white blanket. She was wearing one of those shitty hospital gowns, and I was surprised (and relieved) to find her alone.

'What are you doing here?' she whispered, shaking the dough ball slightly. 'Mark has gone for a smoke. He'll go mad if he sees you here.'

'Can I hold him?' I asked, stretching my arms out. Her face lost its harshness and she passed over the bundle of softness. 'I thought you'd still be in labour.'

'It was dead quick, like,' she said. 'Too quick. But he's fine even though he's early.' She shifted about.

'Did you call him Jake in the end?' I asked. She nodded and leaned back on the bed, wincing slightly.

'Suits you,' she said as I rocked him, his little face all wrinkled, and tiny hands poking out of the blanket. He smelt fresh, new, like how being innocent must smell. Innocence. The thought knocked my insides.

'Why didn't you come with me? I would never have left you going the ozzie on your own like that,' she said, watching me carefully.

'You told me not to come.'

'You could come if you left him. Why didn't you leave him?'

'He threatened to kill himself again.' I couldn't tell her what else he'd told me, not now, and maybe not ever.

'As if he ever would!' she shouted. Jake moved in my arms.

'And Karen…'

'Karen what?'

Her threats were twisted in my head. I changed the subject. 'How come no one is in here with you?'

'Like I said, Mark's gone for a smoke. He needed a break. Me mum's on the way.' She gripped the blanket under her.

Mark would come back and blow ciggy breath all over his gorgeous new boy, and Jen would accept it. She'd let it all wash over her and tell herself she's grateful to have a kid before she got too far into her late twenties and hit that weird 'elderly mum' shelf that all her mates from around hers and her mum had created. Mark could say what he wanted, do what he wanted, call her a tit or a fat bitch, even when the baby was old enough to understand.

If I stayed with Daniel, even if I could accept what he'd done, and we had a baby, then me and Jen would meet up and moan so that we could feel it was all normal, and friends like Jo would give up and fade away.

Being with Daniel was like being surrounded by a mini hurricane, hurling everything out that was related to me and welcoming in all his shit, his family, his ideas.

272

I looked back at Jen. This couldn't have worked out better for Mark. Jen and Jake were how he wanted them, in the hospital, cooped up and watched, while he went off and did his own thing. It was only a ciggy for now, but soon enough it would be drinking and God knows what else. What would happen when Jake cried in the night or when Jen wanted him to change a nappy?

'What the fuck is she doing here?'

I turned around, still holding the baby, to see Mark, eyes like black bullets in his head, fists clenched, stinking of stale air and ciggies.

'She's left him, haven't you?' Jen said, looking at me.

Mark laughed like a cartoon villain. 'Why is he waiting outside for you in that big fuck off white Audi then?'

'You brought Daniel here?' Jen screeched. 'You're not splitting up with him? Give me my baby back!'

I handed Jake over, who'd started bawling with all the noise.

'Jen, c'mon-'

'Just leave,' she said, turning away from me.

'She went into fucking early labour because of you and that tit.' Mark shoved me away from the bed.

I looked back as I left, but Jen was engrossed in the baby and didn't notice the push or the fuck-off-face that Mark gave me, vicious and chilling.

I got in the car and slammed the door. He grabbed hold of my hand. I moved it away.

'Where are we going?'

He was driving in the opposite direction of my house, where I'd asked to be dropped off. The car was bouncing too fast down the dock road. It was starting to rain and everything became shapes and flashes of light outside the tinted windows.

273

'I want to take you somewhere, relive some better memories,' he said, spinning the car down a dark tunnel.

We came out into a well-lit car park which I realised was Liverpool One. He parked up. There was a smile on his face. We walked, or rather he walked me with a steady arm on my back, in the direction of that bar we'd first had a drink in, our first official (and only) sort of date. He didn't say anything as he delivered me to a seat, sticky fabric against my skin, and steady arms around me.

He came back with the same order as that first time. The cupcakes looked slimy and defeated, the drinks, unappealing, murky liquids.

'I don't think I can do this.'

'I thought you understood.' His face crumpled up and then went back into place again with a more certain look. 'After what your Charley did.'

'Yeah I know…but I've been thinking…I think…you should hand yourself in because this is never going to go away.'

'I've already told you why that can't happen.'

'You need to see through all the shit your family are saying to you,' I replied. 'I'll help you.'

'So, you'll make me confess, screw my family over, send us to jail and then you'll leave,' he said, eyes glinting. His hand gripped mine tightly and pushed it down onto the table so that I cried out in pain. It was loud in the bar. No one looked over.

'You can't leave me. I'll tell them that you know,' he said quietly, his hand still pressing mine down. Finally, he let it go.

'I'm not leaving you – I need time to think,' I lied. 'I'll get a taxi home.' I didn't think he'd let me go but I edged around him easily, ready to jump out of the way if he grabbed me.

'What are you calling home then?'

I didn't answer that.

'Take the car. I bought it for you.'

'What are you going to do?'

'I'm going to stay out and get smashed, aren't I?'

There were steps behind me as I entered the car park. It was another couple, the girl wearing clacking heels. I got to the car safely and let out a breath I hadn't realised I was holding onto.

* * * * *

The lights of the Cathedral twinkled in front of me. I'd pulled the car into a space overlooking it, all brown stone and proper massive. It was a powerful building. I needed power, strength, time to think.

Loss creeps up on you in waves. It can leave you alone for a bit, but then a random thought can pop up out of nowhere and take the breath right out of you. That's how it's always happened for me anyway. I was searching Mum's old words for anything that might help me. I hoped being outside one of her favourite places would somehow enhance our connection.

Brave ~ courageous and fearless
~ my daughter, Gina
November 2006

My beautiful baby girl,

I'm writing this before I go into hospital. I feel really ill. I'll do my best to recover, but I'm not sure I'll be able to. I love you and always will. You were the best birthday present I could ever wish for. You have blossomed into a beautiful young woman with lots of friends. You always get a lot of male attention, but make sure it's the right kind, and when you've finished 'playing the field' then I hope you'll meet someone who will love you forever, and will show you the loving care and respect you deserve. Don't forget your ambitions, dreams and career plans, and don't let anyone stop you from achieving them. Take in every experience and every word. Go for what gives you a buzz in life, and always tell yourself 'you can do it'. Positive thinking is all important. Don't ever feel like you're not good enough. Don't be scared or weighed down by regrets because *Brave* is my definition of what you are.

Slow down and enjoy life. But always do what you think is right. I wanted to write this so that you know how I feel. I hope it will help you through some difficult times. My love for you and Charley will never die. Make sure she reads her letter too. Lots of love, Mum

I thought about Charley then. I'd get her to come to the police station with me.

I scrambled through my bag for my phone, only finding my work one. It's always on silent. I was shocked to see five missed calls and a text, all from Daniel.

I'm in me dad's. You left your phone with me. Charley came around looking for you. You should get around here. Now. She's in a mess.

276

I drove as fast as I could but it was already too late.

The red door was slightly open. They were in the kitchen. Charley's forehead crinkled with confusion when Daniel told me to check her coat.

She pulled the bag out of the pocket herself before I could even do anything. Her face went white and she started to protest, looking right at me. But I'd seen these tricks before, when I pointed out Mum's ring in the pawnshop.

I shoved her out of the house, pushing her against the door. I said things I hope nobody ever writes down.

I told him to stay away from me too. The shock on his face matched Charley's when she'd held the small bag of brown powder, like dried up mud.

He was trying to reason with me. You'll change your mind. You'll see that we have to be together, he insisted, as I pushed him out of the door. I won't let you go. He'll make sure you don't go.

CHAPTER FIFTY

ME: 18.30 Sunday 31st August 2014

'You should have died.' Gina's words were still finding their way into Charley's head three nights later.

This hurt more than when her head knocked back against the door and the rippled carvings of wood dug into her back. The red paint seemed to glow outwards against Gina's face, displaying the anger all over it.

'You've never been grateful for being alive have you? You should have died, not Mum.' She meant every word. Charley could see it in her eyes, feel it in her grip, hear it in her tone. 'Why don't you take enough in one go to finally do it, so that I don't have to spend my whole life worrying about you!'

Charley tried to speak, but her tongue got caught. Gina let her go and she fell against the door.

Everything had happened so fast.

The text off Gina's phone told her to get to Daniel's dad's house as fast as she could. She had arrived to find Daniel standing in the doorway, swaying slightly, stinking of various types of alcohol. The hug he gave was weird at the time, but he hadn't given her much choice. The strength of him surprised her, and then he led her, or rather pushed her, right into the house saying he was worried about Gina. That's when he must have slipped the bag into her pocket.

She shuddered thinking about it again, and went back to the definitions that were overlapped on her steering wheel. They all pointed to one person. She sat, waiting, thinking.

Mike was taking too long. She'd waited all afternoon and he wasn't answering his phone.

That night Charley had wished she was dead, knowing Gina thought she was capable of going down that path again after everything that had happened. Her sister lived on tenterhooks waiting for Charley to slip back into being the type of person who could sell her dead Mum's ring at a pawnshop.

That time it really had been a text from Gina. One asking her to meet by Tesco, the one within walking distance of their house. Charley had already been setting off back to the house with Callum, having got what she needed under the pretence of a quick home visit.

As she saw Gina waiting at the entrance, she realised what was happening and made to turn around and get out of there, but Gina had seen her and came running, high heels clacking on the ground.

'You little bitch!' Gina had grabbed her by the arm and dragged her back to the pawnshop.

'Buy it back,' she demanded.

'I can't,' Charley replied. It was the truth; Callum had already taken most of the money the night before so they wouldn't lose out on the deal.

Gina shoved her head into the glass so hard that the ring became a crystal blur along with all the other bits of jewellery. 'I don't have a sister.'

She left as Gina stormed into the shop, and soon enough she was back at the house in the middle of that tattered little village, sharing the rewards with Callum. Gina didn't come after her for a couple of years, until after things had got much worse.

* * * * *

The incident with the ring wasn't the end of a journey which had started when Charley was thirteen.

While Gina had a more romantic version of a mother's love, Charley remembered disappointment more than anything else.

'You always have your head in a book.' Her mum would tell her, standing in the bedroom doorway, sounding critical, looking beautiful, with soft brown hair, perfectly formed cheekbones and a strong jaw line. Charley couldn't tell her mum or anyone, that she read because she was scared, and not

280

of the things other kids her age were reading. They knew nothing about fear from inside your own head. Sometimes she thought air particles were trying to get her, other times a song or a face would stick in her head and wouldn't leave. The stories in the books would take her momentarily away from this but then she would lay awake, terrified, body frozen stiff, hours after she'd been put to bed. She withdrew into herself, hoping no one else would notice.

The summer before dad left, taking all of their money with him, they went on a family holiday. Gina had made friends as usual, and they were dancing in one of those stupid kid's disco games that made Charley's head hurt.

'Why don't you get up and dance?' Her Mum had prodded her, red lipsticked half-smile. When Charley hesitated, she got an 'Oh Charley' sigh, and the smile became the usual thin red line of disappointment.

'Leave her alone,' her dad retorted. 'You're forever on at her.'

'I just want her to be more sociable,' Charley heard her mum say, despite her efforts not to listen to their arguments.

At thirteen, smoking weed helped to keep back the bad thoughts and her mum's negative comments. It started when she took a stolen cigarette on a walk to the shop and ran into a gang from school.

'I thought you were dead quiet and that,' a girl called Louise, one of the hard knocks of her year had said. 'You can sneak me joints into school 'cos I'm always getting them taken off me and I can't afford to keep buying more weed all the time.'

In return for her quiet geeky and quiet exterior, she got a cut of the weed every so often and her position as 'holder' gained her new friends.

Her mum was delighted with Charley's packed social life, and then she got diagnosed with cancer and got sicker and sicker, before she could look further into her daughter's activities. Only Gina tracked her, tried to pull her out of it and finally gave up, thinking she would grow out of it.

Despite bad friends and worse behaviour, Charley still got good marks in school, which worked even more in her favour. Even Gina thought things couldn't be that bad if Charley was still getting grade As all the time. It was the one thing their mum did seem to like about her youngest.

By sixth form, Charley was trying ecstasy, casually at the odd party, when the prodigal ex-husband/father returned to 'look after' them. Charley was still furious about being left by the one person she thought understood her so he could run off to Hong Kong and find a new wife.

In university things got even worse because, while life carried on for everyone else, for Charley everything had stayed unresolved since she was fifteen. The world had stopped at the moment she'd seen her mum's body, touched her cold fingers and realised they would never sort things out.

As time went on, nothing satisfied her. Dad went back to his other life, Gina got a job and rented the family home, and Charley went to university in Manchester. The books she'd counted on during childhood suddenly weren't enough to keep her from falling back inside her own head full of fears, and neither was the once or twice a week cocaine fix she'd get at parties or nights out. Charley used more and more to forget, until she actually couldn't remember how to live.

Before long she'd dropped out of Uni and into a life with Callum, who was even more fucked up than she was.

They met at a party in that first year. Over lines of cokes, he listened to the current worry circling her head, keeping her awake; her fear of becoming a 'cog', someone who kept the world turning but never enjoyed what they did. The idea had formed when others on her course had started deciding what to do with their lives.

She didn't want to teach. Whenever she walked by the local school and caught the outpour of swarms of unruly ants, she shuddered and picked up her pace. Then the worries developed further, as they always did, into the fact that she would never be a useful member of society, that no job would ever suit her. She would never even make it to cog level, with the ability to carry out a simple everyday task. She thought about this when she watched people working in shops, scanning food through tills, restacking shelves, hanging up clothes. The monotony of jobs that seemed like they should be easy would send her mad, and that would make her incompetent at them.

'So don't become part of it then,' Callum said.

'What do you mean?' she asked.

He smiled.

* * * * *

The drugs began to melt into an undefined cycle of thoughts. Callum introduced her to new ways of releasing pain, using harsher drugs they injected and smoked. They funded their increasingly costly habits by selling anything and everything. When they were cutting they would find white stuff that could be crushed; antihistamines, paracetamol, cleaning detergent and even some of Charley's contraceptive pills.

One night Callum accidentally cut his arm with a knife until it was down to the bone. Charley held his skin together for an hour-and-a-half until the ambulance got there. A pathway of blood had found its way down the stairs.

It wasn't enough to make them stop. Lying on the filthy mattress they slept on, absorbing the clichés that surrounded her, she didn't care about anything. So many awful things happened that should have made her leave that life.

Their 'friend' Gareth owed money to another gang. The gang found one of Gareth's close mates, who happened to have nothing to do with the debt, and kept him tied up as a hostage for a week. Every so often, he would be made to call Gareth, begging him to hand over the money. At the end of the week, he was released, but he was in a right state. Apparently, one of the ways his captors entertained themselves was by setting dogs on him.

Another young addict Charley knew also owed money to a gang of drug dealers. They drove her up to the woods and made her have sex with each of them once it became clear she couldn't pay them back. But by then, and despite all this, Charley couldn't grab hold of a cog if she tried.

That dark chapter finally ended for Charley in a skanky pub, with wallpaper stripped in sections, a sweaty carpet, and sticky tables.

When Charley looked at herself, she didn't think it possible that she could break a man's jaw. What no one would believe is, she really wanted to hurt herself.

A man she recognised as one of the gang members they owed money to wrapped his hands around her waist and whispered in her ear, 'maybe we can work this out another way'. She smashed the glass into his face.

The four months in prison was an experience she never wanted to repeat, but she survived it, and made plans. That was until she got out and realised there was nowhere to go.

* * * * *

Callum was waiting, wanting the Charley back who helped him fuck up his life and fund it. There didn't seem like any other option.

But then Gina came to get her. Gina who still cared, still believed she could change, even after all that had happened. Gina who she'd caught out of the corner of her eye when she was sentenced in court, who she'd refused to see when she was in jail.

* * * * *

Callum wasn't in that afternoon. Gina explained later that she knew this - she'd waited outside in the car and watched him leave. Charley thought the bangs on the door were Callum desperate to get back in because he'd seen someone he wanted to avoid. Instead, there was her sister standing on the doorstep.

Charley broke down, grabbed hold of Gina and cried like she hadn't done in years until her sister, who was usually the emotional one but was now stony-faced, pulled her up.

'Grab your stuff, come on.' Gina took control as she tried not to recoil at the dishes and mouldy cups on the floor, the stained sofa, the ash trapped in the carpets. Charley picked up a bag and threw all her stuff in it. Gina picked up something worse - the brown powder in tin foil that looked so innocent and small in her sister's hand.

Before Charley could stop her, she dashed for the toilet, flushing it all away in one go.

'That isn't mine!' she shouted, standing in the doorway of the stinking bathroom, littered with empty toilet roll holders that no one thought to throw away. 'He'll kill us.'

Charley was frozen with fear, and for a moment she thought Gina was too, until her sister said, 'fuck him.' They grabbed her things and left.

There was one text off Callum before she changed her number.

Ur dead if I find you, and so's ur sister

* * * * *

There was movement from the house which brought Charley back to the present. The light went on in an upstairs room. He must have got in around the back way. She got out of the car and hammered at the door with her fists until it opened and she fell into the hallway.

'I know she's here,' Charley forced herself up and headed to the little cupboard under the stairs and down in the basement they'd played in as kids. It had a secret door that had always reminded her of Narnia. Sometimes when they crept back up to the hall at night and it was dark, you couldn't see how to get out of the house. Anthony tried to grab her, but she squeezed past him.

A bare bulb was glowing at the top of the room. Apart from that, it was all white, no windows, a few shelves, with a writing desk and a single chair in the corner, and a sofa bed in the other.

'What have you done to Gina?' Charley asked as she felt him behind her. She studied his face, green eyes that she couldn't

285

read, ones that must have entranced Gina. She picked up the piece of paper from the floor marked with a large Y.

'Charley, you need to stay out of this.' Anthony was breathing heavily.

She looked at him directly, the definition still in her grip. 'What happened between you and Daniel the night Gina got kidnapped?'

CHAPTER FIFTY-ONE

You ~ Used to refer to the person or people that the speaker is addressing.~

~ YOU didn't listen (violence does not solve violence).

~ I hope YOU find this (and what happened between me and you won't happen again - don't treat me like a little woman you can fight for - you have known me too long for that). Thursday 28th August 2014 - Friday 29th August 2014

'Gina, what the hell?'

I stumbled into the doorway, practically falling into his arms. Mascara was streaming down my face.

'What's wrong?' he asked, helping me to stand upright.

'Charley-'

'She hasn't?'

I nodded my head. 'I've split up with Daniel.' I chose to change the conversation to the lesser of the two evils banging around inside my head.

He didn't say anything, so for reasons I can't explain, it was then that I decided to kiss him.

'My mum and dad are still in,' he whispered, holding me right against him, so my melting make-up rubbed against his t-shirt and his smell got right up my nose.

I let him usher me towards the stairs, shushing me as we went through the doorway. I could hear movement from the rooms upstairs and his mum's shrill voice outdoing his dad's mumbling one.

Anthony led me through the door under the staircase and down the other steps. I'd forgotten this little hideaway, and the sight of it, the memories. It even had the same firewood smell and the scent of random, rusty old bikes and house-fixing equipment his dad used to store down here that we'd play around with. It was cleared of all that now, less homely. The walls were white and it stunk of fresh paint.

'You have a bed in here?' I sat down on the striped Ikea duvet, and the springs of the sofa bed groaned. 'There's no windows or anything! Bit of a miserable place to sleep.'

'Peace and quiet to write.' He shrugged.

'But your mum and dad are like the quietest people ever,' I replied. They were a little diddy, dotty couple, a bit older than most of the other parents. Anthony was an only child.

'You know how my mum goes on at me.' He cleared his throat.

'About what?'

'About always reading and writing and not getting a proper job, being a disappointment, not manly enough, the usual,' he said, 'same sort of way your mum used to go at Charley for not being what she wanted her to be.'

There was a sharp pang in my stomach when he said her name, followed by an even sharper one when I remembered what Mum could be like with Charley. I tried not to think about that side of her. It seemed unfair now she was gone and couldn't defend herself.

'They're going on holiday in about ten minutes,' Anthony said.

'What?'

'My mum and dad,' he sighed. 'I can't be bothered with all the questions if they see you, so better stay down here.'

I thought that was a bit strange, they loved me despite their reserved ways, but I agreed and waited after he climbed the stairs again. Upstairs the doors were banging, his Mum was going on about nothing and Anthony was obviously trying to hurry them out. The door shut but I could hear the taps in the kitchen going.

Finally, he came back downstairs.

'Can't wait for the flat to go through,' he said, handing me a cup of tea.

'You've bought a flat? Where?'

'Sefton Park.' he said. 'We really haven't talked properly in ages have we?'

I shook my head.

'Drink your tea.'

'What the fuck is in that?' I spluttered after taking a sip and feeling something hot and bitter at the back of my throat.

'I put some brandy in it,' he replied with a small smile. 'Thought you might need it.'

I coughed on its burning aftertaste. 'It doesn't taste like brandy.'

'We didn't have any Gazpacho soup in, sorry.'

I laughed and that's what set us off. Like before, I didn't even know I was going to do it, but I did. A soft second on my lips was all it took. I should have lost my appetite for this, but I could feel the sparks coming off me, off us. They were nice sparks, not dangerous ones. A shot of desire came as I felt the pressure of his hand on my arm - it wasn't threatening, like I was used to. I wanted him so much. I wanted to forget what had happened so much. He pulled me against him.

My mouth opened slightly as he explored my skin, teasing and clever. I'd got a lot wrong but this was right. Spark, after spark, after spark. Then something extinguished it, a snarling face popped into my head.

'Aren't you with Lydia?'

'She's been stalking me for months.' He stopped kissing my shoulder and sighed. 'There is nothing going on between me and her.'

'Really?'

'I only went to those parties to look out for you.'

We sat side by side for a few minutes, and then he turned and ran his fingers gently across my mouth. I was holding my breath. He tasted sweet and comforting– his hands and lips pressed hard against me.

It felt strange, like we'd never touched before. The fish were liquidated.

'Are you sure?'

I nodded so furiously I thought my head would fall off. He pulled me onto the bed and it was then that I couldn't stop laughing. But he soon shut me up, unbuttoning my blouse and kissing me the whole time, struggling with the straps of my bra until he had to admit defeat and I had to do it myself. It's never like the films. I had a tan stained bra on and black bikini knickers. He smiled and told me I was lovely and stroked me all over, warmth rushing through us. We almost did the crazy, tear each other's clothes off thing. Our breathing was all over the show. It was almost too much to look at him.

Nothing else was important.

His beautiful long body, his eyes on me, gripping my hands and I moved up and down on him. I couldn't believe it was Anthony; he was here, we were here, finally. I was moving hard against him as his hands pressed on me, doubling the pleasure, then he cried out and pulled me into him. We hugged for a few moments, him still inside me; this was also new for me.

My heart was thumping, drowning out the fish - they were tapping so lightly now, with a new rhythm, which actually felt good.

We fell asleep.

* * * * *

'Are you ok?' He kissed me. I couldn't find my phone. I leaned across him and picked his up off the floor. Hours had passed.

'I should really have checked on Charley,' I said, getting up and pulling on his white t-shirt before realising it wasn't my own. I was in too much of a hurry to change into my blouse.

'You can only help her to a certain point,' he said, trying to reach me with his arm. 'People have to make their own mistakes.'

I didn't answer. My mind was working overtime and he sensed it.

'How do you know Charley is using again, by the way?' He sat up.

'I found stuff in her pocket.'

'Why did you check her pockets?'

I explained about Daniel's text.

'Why was Charley at Daniel's though, and why would she be daft enough to turn up with stuff in her pocket if she was back on it?' he asked.

'I know.' I was about to burst into tears. 'Where's my mobile?' The only night of my life that I hadn't thought about my phone. 'Shit. I need to ring her!'

'Where have you left it?'

'Probably in the car.'

'You can use my phone.' He picked it back up off the bed and handed it over. I rang until it went to voicemail.

'She might have tried to call me to explain,' I said, pulling back on my shorts and heels and rushing back up the stairs. 'Why have you locked the door?'

Anthony came up behind me with slow steps that thudded on the wood.

'Habit.' He moved me out the way to put a key in the lock.

My white car was still where I'd left it on the road. The phone wasn't there or in the house when we searched.

'Come back to mine,' Anthony said, putting his arm around me. 'We can keep watch on the house and keep trying to call her.'

'No, I need to find her,' I insisted. We got into the car. I drove us in a mad spin to Charley's flat.

Her little cube of a place was visible from the car park, and when I made it up there - she didn't answer the door. But her car was still gone and I knew she'd been driving around, calming down, forming a plan to make me believe her. That's how she was these days, a thinker. Maybe that had always been the problem.

I hated these flats. So many times I'd asked her to come back and live in the family home, but it's like she wouldn't allow things to be made easier for her.

I banged on the door until my hand hurt and Anthony led me back to the car silently, taking the keys and driving as I was in a state by then. He took me back into his house and we sat on the sofa, where there was a good view of my old home. Somehow I couldn't bring myself to actually wait inside it.

* * * * *

I kept checking the clock on Anthony's phone.

'A light's gone on in the hall,' he said.

'Did you see her go in through the front door? Where's her car?' I dragged my heels on quickly. I raced out of Anthony's, reached our family house and scraped the key against the wood, missing the lock completely, in my hurry.

'Charley-' I stopped in my tracks when I finally got the door open. The hall was full of boxes and bits and pieces that hadn't been there before. In the middle of them all, head in hands, was Daniel.

'What are you doing here?'

Daniel lifted his head up. His eyes were red, his hair and clothes dishevelled. 'I wanted to do it you know, to hand myself in. He went mad.' His fists clenched when Anthony appeared beside me.

292

I had Anthony's t-shirt on and no bra. Daniel clocked all of it. The alcohol was sweating off him.

'Why don't you leave?' Anthony said steadily.

'I brought some of your stuff back,' Daniel said through gritted teeth, ignoring Anthony. 'Some of the boxes are upstairs as well.'

'Come on, mate, get out.' Anthony stood taller.

Daniel didn't move from the floor. His eyes didn't leave mine. 'You told him then? You fucked him and told him all about it, didn't you?'

'I'm giving you another minute to leave, lad,' Anthony said next to me.

'Messing about with him and you're pregnant with my baby?'

'I'm not pregnant.'

His eyes went so dark they seemed to glare back black. 'You got rid of it?' His voice was low, dangerous, as he started to stand up.

Before I could say that there had never been any baby, Anthony launched himself at Daniel. They both went tumbling in a horrible, thudding heap on the floor.

'Stop it!' I screamed. Daniel staggered up towards the kitchen and Anthony followed him, murder in his eyes. I tried to grab hold of his arm. He shrugged me off.

'Are you listening to me? Don't do this! Leave it!' I carried on shouting. Anthony's eyes were blazing as he punched Daniel in the nose, causing a sickening crack. He fell to the floor clutching his face. I went to help him up but Anthony pushed me out of the way and dragged him up and towards the front door.

'He won't let you get away with this,' Daniel said as he regained his balance on the driveway.

'Oh fuck off.' Anthony slammed the door in his face.

I stood, unable to react, as Anthony picked up one of my bags at random, took my hand and led me back over to his house.

293

There was still a horrible light in his eyes when we got back in. I'd left my purse and bank cards in the basement. I went down to get them. Anthony came after me.

'What are you doing?'

'There was no need for what you did.'

'He's an idiot, Gina, and he shouldn't have been in your house.'

'You're no better than him.'

'He's fine. And he deserved it.' He tried to put an arm around me. I shrugged him off. 'Where are you going?'

'I can't stay here,' I said.

'Why?'

'I can't stay here with you after you acted like that.'

'Where are you going to go?

'Back home, or maybe I'll go to Charley's and wait for her to come back - I don't know. I need to get changed.' I could still smell him all over me and I didn't want to anymore.

'You have a bag, stay here,' he pleaded.

'I want to be on my own.' For the first time in ages, I genuinely did, unless I could find my sister and say sorry.

'I wanted to defend you.'

'Why?'

'Because, well, you know, we-'

'Had sex and now I'm all yours to look after?'

'That's not what I meant, but Gina you need looking after.'

'Like a little woman you can fight for?' I was shaking. 'If you find Charley first, don't involve her in any of this.' I wrapped my arms around myself.

'Gina, please!' Anthony tried to block my path but I pushed past him. He stepped aside, head down. 'Come back when you've calmed down.'

'I want to be completely on my own for once!' I shouted.

It was only when I got to the front door that I realised I'd left my purse on the bed. I turned around to go back when something came out of the hedge, heading straight for me. For a split second I thought it was a cat, a tick of shadows making it look larger than it was, but then a hand was over my mouth and I was gasping for breath. I was dragged down the driveway, my heels scratching against paving, leaving marks, plaster running down my throat from the hand on my face. A chemical smell, a taste, made my body so heavy that I couldn't move to fight back. Inside the car, a balaclava appeared in front of my face, blurry as it sealed something across my mouth and started tying my hands together.

CHAPTER FIFTY-TWO

PREPARATIONS: 19.30 Sunday 31st August 2014

It would be over soon.

Hours had passed since he'd teased her with the knife, bringing it so close to her face that she'd closed her eyes and waited for the cold, sharp bite of steel. Instead, he started cutting at the ropes which tied her hands and feet. When he finished, something soft but heavy landed on her lap.

He turned around to let her put it on. There was white underwear with the tags on, and even products for her to wash herself. She had no choice but to put on the scratchy white lace and then sit on the chair and wait.

'Are you ready?' His voice was unsteady. He turned around.

'Lovely,' he said. 'Wait there while I get the other stuff you'll need.' He disappeared. The door was open but Gina didn't dare move, feeling all the bruises forming up and down her body. Eventually he came back in with a couple of plastic bags and placed them at her feet.

'You'll need these,' he said, pulling out fruit, bagels and bottles of water from one bag, and from another, a collection of make-up and a small compact mirror.

He handed her a bottle of water and gestured for her to drink. The cold liquid fell down her throat, easing the dryness. 'I'll leave you to it. I want you fully rested and ready for when I come back tonight.'

The make-up had gone on with shaking hands as she smoothed in foundation and brushed powder on her cheeks. She used the rest of the time to regain energy, sipping water and eating the fruit and bread slowly. Her bones ached every time she moved. The last thing she did was smash the mirror inside the compact and hide the parts in the lacy arms, tucked into the inner loose material so that they wouldn't cut her skin.

It had to be over soon.

She heard footsteps above, and in minutes he was downstairs. He was angry again, pacing, holding his phone up.

'Take the dress off,' he shouted, making her flinch. 'Now, I want you to beg for help.' He snatched at her arm. 'Do it now.'

The pieces of the mirror fell out of her sleeve and to his feet. He looked at the shards for a moment and then struck her across the face.

'Take it all off, plans have changed.' He was breathing heavily. 'Do what I said or your sister dies.'

After Gina had finished crying and pleading into his mobile phone as he stood and smiled, he blindfolded her, dragged her up the stairs, and bundled her back into the car.

CHAPTER FIFTY-THREE

Disappearing: 19.45 Sunday 31ˢᵗ August 2014

'This is all my fault.'

They both stood in the ice-cold basement. Charley was still holding the piece of paper she'd picked up off the floor. 'What do you mean?'

'Why she's disappeared,' he said. 'You think it's because of you, but it's because of me.'

'What did you do?' Charley asked slowly, edging towards the door. Anthony was pacing up and down, unsettling her. She'd never seen him like this before.

'Nothing,' he said. 'Well, I mean, I did nothing to stop her running out of here.'

'You had an argument?'

'I had a fight with Daniel,' he said. 'Gina went mad.'

'You were who she meant,' Charley replied, thinking of the words on the definition in her hand. 'What happened?'

'He was in your house.' He rubbed his forehead with his fingertips. 'He was having a go at Gina but he was in a proper mess.'

'What was he having a go at her over?'

'I couldn't really make sense of it.'

'Anthony, did Gina tell you what Daniel did?'

'No.'

'He killed someone,' she said. 'He didn't mean it, but he got away with it.'

Anthony stopped pacing and stared at her.

'Someone gave him a false alibi. The whole family are in on it.'

'Jesus.' He sat down on the sofa bed, with his head in his hands.

'Gina didn't believe that I was taking drugs again did she? Is that why I got those missed calls off your phone?' The guilt etched through her. If she'd answered, Gina might still have been here.

'I stuck up for you actually - made her realise that Daniel could have set it up,' he said. 'What does it matter now anyway, since you didn't tell me what a psycho Daniel is!'

'I didn't know all this then. You made out she was avoiding me because she still believed I was capable of something like that!'

'She wasn't answering the phone to me either,' Anthony insisted, his usually calm tone disappearing with each word. 'I saw her car was gone and thought she'd disappeared for some peace and quiet, away from all of us.'

'That's a load of shit!' Charley shouted, unable to help herself. 'Daniel had been in our house, threatened Gina, you'd had a fight and then you didn't even think it was weird when she went missing without a word. Why did you even let her go?'

'She wanted to be on her own.'

'Why didn't you go to the police?'

'And say what? That I argued with my not-even-girlfriend and she went off in her car and won't answer her phone and it's only been like a day!'

'You could have told me that she wasn't angry and didn't believe Daniel.'

'She said not to involve you, and for all I knew you actually *were* back on drugs again. To be honest, I was half trying to make her feel better by saying you weren't. You're not the must trustworthy person, are you?' He glared at her. Charley stepped back. His words were like a slap in the face.

'This isn't doing any good,' she said quietly. 'We need to find her, not argue about whose fault it is.

'I've been looking for her,' he said. 'I went to Daniel's dad's house, the offices in town, the warehouses, the Alderley Edge house…'

'Did you speak to anyone?'

'Only some weird bloke with an Everton tattoo at one of the warehouses,' he replied.

'Anthony, you have to come to the police with me,' she said. 'I know someone there. He's helping me with the case and you can tell him Daniel was in the house right before Gina went missing.'

'Ok.'

'I'll ring him so he can come here.'

'I think-'Anthony started and then looked at Charley.

'What?'

'Daniel was really drunk. That's why I got the better of him so easily. He wouldn't have been able to hurt anyone.'

'What are you saying?'

'That he wouldn't have been capable of anything.'

'You think someone else took her?

They didn't look at each other.

'Can we get out of this room?' She shivered.

'Anthony climbed the stairs ahead of her as she stopped to bring Mike's number up in her recent call list. Something caught her eye under the bed. She kicked it out and saw that it was Gina's purse.

'Why do you have her purse?' she called out. There was an almighty crash, which shook the basement ceiling and caused the bulb to dim momentarily.

Charley raced up the stairs, calling Anthony's name. In the kitchen, a bottle of whiskey was smashed on the floor, and the back door which led onto the garden was open. Charley walked carefully around the mess, calling Anthony over and over, and stepped outside. There was no one there.

301

She went back in, looking around her, and with shaking hands tried Mike's number. It went straight to voicemail. She had no option but to call the local police station. There was no way the standard emergency number would send someone out for this.

When the phone connected, she asked to speak to Mike, praying he would be available.

But it was Officer Thomson who came to the phone.

'It's Charlotte Ellison,' she told her. 'I need help and I can't get in touch with Mike - I mean Officer Field.'

There was a sigh down the end of the phone. 'Harassment of a police officer isn't something we take lightly, Miss Ellison.'

'He's helping me find my sister,' she managed to say.

'The one who turned up yesterday and doesn't want to talk to you?'

The phone left her hand and thudded to the floor. The shards of fear building in her stomach turned to ice. She had to get out of there. She picked up her phone and ran.

She got to her car and then she heard it. Low but unmistakable, Gina crying for help. A small downstairs window in their family home was open a crack, allowing the sound to travel from inside the dark house. There was no one else on the street, no sign of Anthony. Charley went into a blind panic. She fumbled in her pocket for her keys and then realised they were in Anthony's basement.

The side garden was overgrown. Gina had never really looked after it when she lived there, and some of the plants were tall enough to pull at Charley's legs, trying to hold her back. She climbed over the side gate, ignoring the splinters in her fingers.

She picked up a stone, heavy and thick, once used to form a sort of walkway entrance to the grass part of the garden, and smashed it through the small window that led to the downstairs toilet. She scrambled in the same way her sixteen-year-old self had that time, when her dad had replaced it with cheap glass and never known it had been her, off her face and with no key.

The light flicked on, illuminating the kitchen. Charley staggered back in horror when she saw Daniel on the floor, covered in blood, with Mike Field standing over him.

* * * * *

'I told him this wouldn't work,' he said, turning to face her with a twisted smile and holding up the phone. He pressed a button and Gina's anguished cries started again. 'Seems I was wrong.'

Charley tried to make a run for it, but he launched across the kitchen and fixed her in a vice-like grip, easily overpowering her. He dragged her back in and threw her down onto one of the kitchen chairs.

Daniel groaned from the floor.

'You can shut the fuck up.' Mike gave him a kick that caused his body to shudder. 'This is your own fault for not keeping your mouth shut, again.' He turned back to Charley. 'So, you're going to ask me why, aren't you?'

She quickly scanned the room for anything that could be used as a weapon. He moved closer towards her.

'I was seventeen,' he started, 'seventeen, and this little shit here was fifteen.' His face was right next to hers now, one of his tight back curls brushed against her cheek as he turned his head back to Daniel. 'I had to give a false alibi for him. I did it to save my dad, and I've spent my whole life making up for it since.' His fist banged down on the table, making Charley jump. 'My dad owed his dad money didn't he?'

There was silence as Mike seemed to get lost in his thoughts for a moment, staring down at Daniel. 'I can't have it fucked up by your bimbo of a sister or a little smackhead like you.' He paused. 'Aren't you going to say anything?'

'But your sister-'

'There was no sister. I needed you to trust me,' he said. 'Christ, I even tried to keep you away, but you're probably so

303

used to being full of all that shit that the stuff I put in your burger barely affected you.'

His face was brutal when it was angry; the lines took away the kindness. This was who he really was. Even with all her experience, she'd thought he was a good person, someone to trust. She had to keep him talking. 'Daniel's family won't let you get away with this.'

'I've done Bob a favour here,' he laughed. 'He knows when his boys need a lesson.' He looked down at Daniel again, with loathing in his eyes. 'Bob can be very violent, so you see why I had to give that alibi and help my dad.' He sighed. 'But I'm never free of this fucking family because he tells everyone who gets close to him what he did, and then I have to sort it out.'

'What do you mean?' she asked, thinking it might be best to keep him talking. Behind him, Daniel started to shift slightly and reached into his pocket.

'Sometimes they 'disappear'.'

Daniel was taking an object out of his pocket. It looked like keys. He bunched his hands around one.

'Disappear?'

'Well I don't like to do that,' he replied. 'Most of the time I'll turn up and give little warnings, like to that lad by your flats always sniffing around, or that one Jo who was talking too much about Daniel. She bloody loves her dog, will do anything to protect it. I turn up with my face covered for people like her. Then there was good old Megan, who managed to get away with only a minor warning. Thanks for leading me to her again by the way; the one who got away.'

Charley's insides clenched. 'What did you do to her?'

'She won't talk, put it that way,' he smirked, grabbing a bottle of liquid off the counter and a hankie out of his pocket.

'Please don't do this,'

'You know he could have stopped all this,' he said pointing at Daniel who had the key hidden between his fingers. 'I told him to get rid of you legally on the drugs charge. I could have assisted with that. But the idiot wouldn't do it, wouldn't even try to persuade Mark to press fake charges against you. Then we could have warned your sister off, but too many of you are involved now.'

There was a grunt from behind him as Daniel reached out with the keys and jabbed Mike in the leg, making him cry out. Charley managed to get to the kitchen door and into the hall.

She headed for the front door, running blind in the dark until she hit a soft but solid shape, and then she was falling, landing in a tangle of her own limbs. A face came into focus.

'Karen!' Charley collapsed with relief. Footsteps continued behind her. 'It's Daniel – he's hurt, and the police officer has Gina - we have to get help.'

Blinking through the light, she took Karen's outstretched hand and started to pull herself up. The shock pulsed through her as she felt a sharp, needle-like sensation in her arm. Blood was starting to appear from where Karen dug in her nails.

'What are you-' Charley started to speak but Karen pressed harder. The pain was overwhelming. Then she found herself being pushed back to the floor and a sharp tug on her hair as Karen dragged her back to the kitchen with the help of Mike Field until she was on the cold marble floor next to Daniel.

'Why?' she asked.

It was Mike who answered. 'Stop asking us questions. We aren't the kidnappers. Did you listen to anything?'

Her arm throbbed. 'Karen, look what he's done to Daniel. He's your family.'

'Danny's made his choice, *again*,' Karen replied, examining her nails. 'All we wanted was for him to settle down, nice wife and baby, giving us only one girl to worry about in his life, since he tells anyone he falls in 'love' with his whole bleeding past. If Gina had got knocked up, like I planned, then that would have kept her quiet for life, and we wouldn't have needed to do any of this. You'd hardly turn in the father of your child would yer?'

305

'Where's Gina?'

Karen stood up, her heels clicking as she walked across the kitchen. 'Thanks for leading us to Megan, by the way. I had no idea Jemma was such a sneaky cow.'

'Please tell me where Gina is. I won't go to the police. I won't tell anyone. I know Gina wouldn't either. Is she here too?'

'She's ready. That's all you need to know,' Mike replied. He tipped liquid from the bottle onto the hankie and moved towards her.

CHAPTER FIFTY-FOUR

Together: 20.45 Sunday 31ˢᵗ August 2014

A scream was trapped inside her head. Her surroundings were unfocussed, blurred. The air was raw with the smell of chemicals and car fumes. There was something grey directly in front of her and she couldn't lift her head to look beyond or around. A voice was becoming clearer and louder.

'I'm defending you all. You're my family. You can't blame a man for that.' Charley managed to look up. In a thin slit of a car mirror was a weathered face with stone grey eyes looking back at her.

'Awake are you? Nice to be together again girls?'

Doped and numb, with tight bindings on her wrists and ankles, Charley managed to move her head to the side, catching the edge of Daniel sitting in the front seat as she turned. To the side of her was Gina. Her eyes were closed. There was a dark bruise on her check and tight ropes around her wrist. . It didn't look like she was breathing. Her head was slumped to one side. Charley tried to call out but the words couldn't get past her mouth

Bob had started talking again as he casually spun the car around a corner. 'Had to change the plans to bring you back into it,' he sighed, as though this had been a great inconvenience. 'If you hadn't stuck your nose in then Gina could have been let off with a warning.'

She heard a groan and realised it was coming from Daniel.

'This is all your fucking fault!' Bob took his eyes off the road and turned his head towards his son. 'Can you believe he was going to warn you? Thank god for Fieldy, ey?' There was a low chuckle. 'His dad might be a complete waste of time, but that boy has never let me down.' He stopped the car and took off his seatbelt.

Charley felt a rush of fear through her body as he got out. All she could make out was darkness. All she could hear was the distant sound of cars as the door next to Gina opened.

On instinct, she tried to push and fight out of her bonds as Bob leaned over her sister.

'Still breathing. I thought I'd given her too much but her pulse is still strong.' He got back up and shut the door carefully. But he didn't go back to the driver's seat. Instead Charley could see him making his way towards her side of the car. The door opened.

His hand moved slowly towards Charley's face as he ripped the tape off her mouth. 'I need to ask you some questions,' he said, before slamming the door shut, and returning to the driver's seat.

Her breath came out in fast and furious bursts. The car started up again.

'I was thinking of making this look like a joint suicide at first. But who would believe that?' Bob called back at her. 'So what I'm going to do instead is a bit more along the lines of what people would find you capable of.'

Charley tried to reply but a coughing fit overtook her.

'Give me it, lad,' Bob said to Daniel, taking something out of his hand. He held it up, in-between the seats, so that Charley could see it. The light from the street lights bounced off the needle he held between his fingers. 'You see this is more like you. I've even dissolved it and all that. Good quality stuff too, considering Fieldy took it off that low-life you used to live with.

'So, here's the plan; Gina tries to sort you out by coming to pick you up. She's driving, you have a fight and you cause her to crash. They find the heroin in your system.'

'You won't get away with this,' said Charley, finding her strength.

He laughed again. 'It's all planned out sorry. I've already picked the tree you're going to drive into, very quiet street, CCTV on the blink. Don't worry, Fieldy has seen enough of these types of accidents to know the right speed and angle you need to achieve impact at.'

She twisted at the bonds on her hands. They started to loosen.

'We even have Anthony all ready to go,' he continued. 'Fieldy is bringing him to the garage so we can get him in the back. Shame he chose not to wear a seatbelt isn't it?'

Gina's steering lock was poking out from under the driver's seat. Charley kicked it with her tied feet and managed to get it out to directly below her.

The car jerked forward as it came to a sudden stop.

'I wish this gobshite here had picked someone like Melissa,' Bob said, 'someone who didn't ask questions and accepted what was given to her.'

'Yeah, great way to live that,' Daniel spoke for the first time, each word a rasp, 'living off handouts from your dad and brother.'

'He gets them for keeping silent about you, yer little fuck up.'

'I got the way I am because of you. Did you think we'd forget Mum's bruises, the shouting and screaming from her when you-'

Charley heard a thud as Daniel's head hit the passenger window.

'Shut up!' Bob went back to the road. 'I didn't think you'd still be whimpering on like this all these years later. Had to make you work for me so that you'd have a job you could stick at, then even signed it all over to you when I saw you could actually do it. Nothing wrong with you working to support me and your brother after all we've done for you.'

'And the rest.'

'There are people to pay off.'

'Why can't you pay these two off then?'

Charley stopped as she heard the attention focus back on her and Gina. The steering wheel lock was in the grasp of her right hand. The car slowed down. She raised the steering lock and brought it smashing down on Bob's head.

It wasn't enough. The car jerked to one side and bounced off the kerb as Bob grabbed the lock and threw it towards Daniel, tearing at Charley's hair and face. She cried out in pain. He dragged her head to the side of his seat, punching her with one hand while he controlled the car with the other. Charley felt her cheekbone crack with the weight of his repetitive blows.

The car skidded and stopped. There was a weight across her and a loud crack, followed by more thuds. Charley managed to duck her head under the back seat, where she could see Daniel throw a flurry of fists across the car seat until he got hold of the steering lock and the snap of bones reverberated around the car. There were police sirens in the distance.

'I rang the real police didn't I? Finally told them,' Daniel said, quietly. Bob was still. There was blood spilling from a wound in his head.

Charley crawled back to her sister. Gina's eyes were closed again. She wasn't moving.

CHAPTER FIFTY-FIVE

Zero ~ adjust to zero point

~ A zero pair has a positive and negative

~ It's ok to use negatives to help you start again.

5th September 2014

Thank you, Charley.

I kept saying it over and over in my head because there didn't seem like any point in saying it out loud. I wrapped my dressing gown around me as I walked back to my bed. I'd spent the first twenty-four hours after I woke up crying my eyes out when they told me the news, until my body couldn't take it anymore. When I went to see her, she looked so peaceful, the only thing giving away what had happened was the purple bruises and cuts on her cheek. The rest of her was covered up. When I cried at that moment, it hurt everywhere.

I haven't cried since, even when I went through everything with the police. They told me that Daniel had been arrested for manslaughter, as they reopened the case of the fifteen-year-old who was killed on his way home from school, whose family had been appealing for witnesses, information, anything, for years. His name was Andrew. His face was all over the news.

Daniel's family, Bob (or what was left of him - his skull was in pieces but somehow he'd survived), had been charged too. Matthew, that policeman, Ken and Karen were going to be done for accessory, and kidnapping. Karen managed to make a run for it. José helped the police to find her.

Walking past the TV screens in the waiting area, I saw that the story had even made it to the sports news.

Liverpool centre-forward José Bedolla fails drug test.
'Bedolla's contract with the club has been terminated, and he has been banned from playing for a year,' the presenter announced and then added, almost as an afterthought, 'Bedolla has co-operated with the police to uncover the whereabouts of his long-term partner Karen Henderson, who has now been arrested for kidnap and attempted murder.'

There was a light tap on my shoulder. It made me jump, despite the police guard we had on the door.

'Do you want a coffee?'

I gave Anthony a smile. 'Yeah, that would be great, thanks.'

We take it in turns to leave the room. There's always one of us. He walks slowly towards the exit, balancing on his crutches.

They found Anthony tied up in the warehouse where I'd had been kept. He was on one side of the room and Megan the other, both beaten pretty badly. Ken was sitting at his little desk on that building site, pretending not to have any knowledge. But they found the key to the room on him.

There have been other victims over the years to help hush up the family secret. Most of the time they've been paid off, moved to another place, at the worst attacked or threatened. This is the furthest the family has ever gone.

Megan's going to give evidence against them all. So am I, when I'm strong enough.

I rubbed at my wrists which are still red and raw. Aches ripple across my cheeks. I sat down at the side of the bed and start to write out my *Z* definition, our *zero* definition.

Everyone kept telling me she could hear me, so I might as well say it all out loud.

My phone rang. It was Dad. I walked out into the corridor to answer it.

'Jesus Christ, Gina! The kidnap story's all over the UK news.'

'Did you manage to get a flight?'

'We're still in the airport, trying. How's Charley?'

'She's the same.'

'We'll be there as fast as we can. After she gets better, Katherine and I can head down to London. We'll do it all in one trip -'

'What?'

'London. Katherine's daughter is getting on with her pregnancy and needs some help…' I tuned out as a skinny boy with a mop of brown hair, headed up the corridor. He ducked into a room and came out with a bunch of dishevelled-looking flowers, water dripping on the floor. His t-shirt rose up his body, exposing his stomach.

'Dad, what if Charley isn't ok?'

'Have the doctors said that?'

'I mean afterwards too, when she wakes up.' I kept back the 'if'. I stopped myself talking about all the support we might need, the road to recovery after the hospital.

'What do you mean?' he asked.

'You know what – do what you want, we'll be fine, as we always are. We don't need you. We never have done.' I turned the phone off. An unexpected wave of relief came over me.

'How is she?' Callum said.

'Go away.'

'I'm giving evidence against that police fella, y'know, the one who took my stash.'

'Is that all you care about?'

'No, I care about her.' His heavy-lidded eyes sunk towards the floor.

'You're bad for her, you know that.'

'We were bad for each other.' He sniffed and wiped a hand across his nose. 'I can't believe what they did to her. No matter what you think of me, I would never have done anything like that to her.'

We stood in silence. Callum peered around me and clocked the guard.

'Can I see her? Only for a minute.'

'She's finished with all that Callum, with people like you.'

'I know. I'm not here to try and get her back into my life. She was always too good for me.' He paused. 'I'm gonna try y'know.'

'Try what?'

'Go clean, sort meself out, like she did,' he replied. 'That bent copper took my last bags, then I saw on the telly that he used the stuff to overdose Charley.'

He kicked at the floor with his scuffed trainers. 'Please, can I see her for a minute?'

'Ok.' I don't know what made me relent, but as I watched him in the room with Charley, I could see how this was a full goodbye to her old life.

'You were always the person who stopped her going over the edge, even when she wouldn't let you be there. She wanted you to be proud of her,' he said as he sat by her side.

'I am.'

I always was. I would always have done anything for her.

In the car, while we waited for the police, I hugged her, tried to give my warmth to her, wanting to give her all my life. I told her nice things that I'd want to hear if I was scared. I told her she had to stay. It was a life-hug.

After Callum left, I took his place at the side of the bed. *You are safe now Charley, I promise you*. I kept telling her this.

I've started again before from a whole pile of negatives, we both have. But sometimes life doesn't let you simply reset. I wish I could say to Charley that it's ok to use negatives to start again, that she didn't have to go out and find more until they outweighed all the positives in her life, that Mum did love her. I have the letter to prove it, that I know Charley will be ready to read.

There were a lot of things I wished I'd said to Charley, sorry for a start. Sorry for dragging her into the whole thing, for not being able to protect her that moment when Bob stabbed the needle into her shoulder, which slowed her heart rate right down. They found her with her arms over me, protecting me. I'm sorry that I can't be strong enough not to let my heart break again.

A broken heart isn't a metaphor. It's everything breaking apart that you thought was real.

For the sake of Charley and Mum and everyone I've lost, I will try to weigh the negatives down. I'll do this on my own. I told Anthony that too. I know everyone likes a love story, but it isn't happening between us. I have to define myself first.

What I want to tell my sister the most is that our lives can be spilt into sections, that every time something bad happens you only need one positive to start again. She saved my life. That's Charley's positive and her definition is to start at zero as many times as she needs. Loss doesn't only mean death – it can mean letting go of bad things too.

I finished writing the definition and put the pen down. I picked up Mum's letter to Charley, which had remained unopened, jammed down the side of the wardrobe in her old room, and started to read.

Courageous ~ brave and fearless
~ my daughter, Charlotte
November 2006

My beautiful baby girl,

I'm writing this before I go into hospital. I feel really ill. I'll
do my best to recover, but I'm not sure I'll be able to. I love
you and always will. There is an intelligence in you that I
have always been in awe of. Please don't waste that spark you
have, and try not to over-think your actions and choices,
because if you make any mistakes, just start again. You were
such a perfectionist and I was always so worried that you
didn't see yourself as the clever, wonderful person you are.

The thought of death is frightening, overwhelming. It can
make you live in a constant state of fear. I was concerned for
you, even as a child, you sometimes found life overwhelming
already and I didn't want you to suffer. I hoped I could get
you out of this. I am sorry if I was sometimes harsh and didn't
tell you this in the right way. I have realised that you will
work through all this because *Courageous* is my
definition of what you are.

I loved being your mother because I loved seeing your smile
of delight when you learned something new. I loved seeing
your talents develop. I loved watching you grow up into
someone more certain of themselves. I could continue forever
praising you.

I hope you get more from this letter throughout your life.

I want to say that loss seems like a negative thing, but it can
be a positive.

I'm so proud that you're my daughter.

I hope this letter will help you through some difficult times.
My love for you and Gina will never die. Lots of love, Mum

The beeps of the hospital machine started to change their
pattern. They stopped and started again.

Charley opened her eyes.

Small Time: A Life in the Football Wilderness
by Justin Bryant

In 1988, 23-year-old American goalkeeper Justin Bryant thought a glorious career in professional football awaited him… Football, he learned, is 95% blood, sweat, and tears; but if you love it enough, the other 5% makes up for it.

The Hidden Whisper
by JJ Lumsden

pol-ter-geist (noun): 'Noisy spirit'; paranormal source of physical disturbances.

Paranormal researcher Dr. Luke Jackson reluctantly takes up an investigation and finds himself drawn into a series of unexplained events.

By real-life parapsychologist Dr JJ Lumsden.

Martians, Morlocks and Moon Landings: How British Science Fiction Conquered The World
by Jamie Austin

From Victorian literature through to the modern day - Martians, Morlocks and Moon Landings explores the genre's development through the imaginations of H G Wells, John Wyndham, George Orwell, Nigel Kneale, and many more.

Lightning Source UK Ltd.
Milton Keynes UK
UKOW04f2330251115

263547UK00001B/56/P